MURDER IN PARADISE

A body floating in the water was just a damned horrible thing.

I just went into automatic and did my job.

His right arm was bent at the elbow, the back of his hand over his mouth as if he were trying to stifle a scream or bite back pain. There was a small hole in his forehead.

This was clearly no drowning. He'd been dead before he went into the water. There were few places better than the ocean for dumping a body. Bad luck for whoever dumped him that he'd gotten caught in the coral.

I had a feeling that Allen Robsen was no longer missing.

Praise for *Swimming with the Dead*

"A likable, exuberant heroine, the fascinating world of scuba diving, and a fast-paced plot make *Swimming with the Dead* the kind of mystery that takes hold of you and doesn't let go until the last paragraph. A terrific debut for Kathy Brandt."
—Margaret Coel, *New York Times* bestselling author of *Killing Raven*

"An impressive debut sure to please the outdoor enthusiasts, *Swimming with the Dead* teems with captivating dive scenes, picture-perfect island settings, and a host of colorful characters. Dive in. The water's great. You won't regret taking the plunge!"
—Christine Goff, author of *A Nest in the Ashes*

"A very exciting new series. . . . There are many viable suspects who had reason to want the victim dead, so the reader is thoroughly entertained trying to figure out who the killer really is."
—*Midwest Book Review*

continued . . .

Kathy Brandt

Dark ~ Water Dive

AN UNDERWATER INVESTIGATION

A SIGNET BOOK

SIGNET
Published by New American Library, a division of
Penguin Group (USA) Inc., 375 Hudson Street,
New York, New York 10014, U.S.A.
Penguin Books Ltd, 80 Strand,
London WC2R 0RL, England
Penguin Books Australia Ltd, 250 Camberwell Road,
Camberwell, Victoria 3124, Australia
Penguin Books Canada Ltd, 10 Alcorn Avenue,
Toronto, Ontario, Canada M4V 3B2
Penguin Books (NZ), cnr Rosedale and Airborne Roads,
Albany, Auckland 1310, New Zealand

Penguin Books Ltd, Registered Offices:
80 Strand, London WC2R 0RL, England

First published by Signet, an imprint of New American Library,
a division of Penguin Group (USA) Inc.

First Printing, July 2004
10 9 8 7 6 5 4 3 2 1

For Ron

Chapter 1

Last night I'd stood on a rickety chair in the Blue Note, one hand over my heart, the other lifting a shot glass filled with tequila. I had taken an oath over the golden liquid.

"I, Hannah Sampson, recently retired homicide detective and team leader of the police scuba team, Denver PD, will never, ever again pull on a Goddamned dry suit and dive into icy black water with any of you guys."

The scuba team had thrown the going-away party of all going-away parties in my honor. I'd really rubbed it in, celebrating the fact that I would never again dive in water so thick with sediment and contamination that visibility was nonexistent. Never have to swallow the terror of imaginary monsters coming at me out of the muck.

I was thrilled to be leaving it behind. I was headed for sunnier climes, where the only diving I'd do was in crystal-clear, azure salt water. My flight was leaving at 3:12 P.M.

So why the hell, at nine o'clock that morning, did I find myself bouncing around in the back of the dive team van with White, my line tender, and Compton, my relief diver, pulling on the thermals, and getting into that watertight suit? So much for oaths. I was struggling into the right leg of the body-sized rubber glove when Crown, the van's driver, took one sharp corner too many. I landed on my ass, one leg still up on the bench and tangled in dive gear. Not the first time. Compton thought it was funny.

"Remember, Compton, this is the last time I'm doing this. Think about that the next time you're the one suiting up in this damned van."

I finished pulling on the dry suit while sitting safely on the floor. Once I was zipped in, not a drop of foreign water would contaminate my being, but that didn't mean I'd stay dry. By the time we got to the site, my entire body was clammy from the heat that had built up inside the suit. I'd actually be relieved to step into icy water.

The call had come in a half hour before. A fisherman, invisible in the willows, had seen two people out in a motorboat on Marston Reservoir. They'd been arguing. A shot; then someone went into the water. The other man had sped away.

After last night the entire dive team had one killer hangover. Damned if Stu Lopez, who was taking my place as dive team leader, didn't have the tequila flu. He and Mack, my partner in Homicide, had been matching each other shot for shot. Compton and I were the only two who were in any shape to dive. Crown, the driver and in charge of communication, was looking kind of green, but he'd made it in.

Last night none of us had imagined we'd be in demand today. There hadn't been a call for divers in weeks. The team had insisted on last night's debacle to send me off. Everyone was paying for it this morning, including me—the one who was retiring.

"Come on, Sampson," Compton said as he zipped up the back of my suit. "One more for old times' sake."

"Yeah, dammit, one more time. This is definitely the last."

The day was a monochrome gray, and icy. The sky was heavy with the promise of snow, a March storm that threatened to drop a foot of the white stuff. Out at the reservoir I couldn't tell where the water ended and the sky began. The place was deserted except for the guy standing on the water's edge in waders, holding a fishing pole, talking to a couple of street cops. We got out and joined them.

"Detectives Sampson and Compton," I said, then turned to the cops. "You guys get the call?"

"Yeah. Just about fifteen minutes ago. This is the guy who phoned in."

"Hardly ever anyone out here this time of the year," the fisherman said, turning our way. He was so typecast, I'd have placed him in one of those ads for Cabelas. He wore a pair of brown wool trousers that were tucked into the waders and a plaid wool shirt under a heavy vest covered with pockets. A couple of flies jutted from a red-and-black-checkered cap, like bugs stuck in flypaper. The built-in earmuffs were pulled tightly over his ears. He was an old guy, beard flecked in white, one side of his face bulging with a wad of chewing tobacco.

"Place is real quiet. Me, I like it that way," he said, turning and ejecting a stream of brown liquid into the water. "Name's Earl, Earl Cripps. Come out and stand in the water with my rod and think. Sometimes I actually catch something. Those guys probably thought they were the only ones out here. I was over there in the willows."

"Where did you see the man go into the water, Earl?" I asked. We needed to pinpoint the location as accurately as possible or it would take days to find the victim. On the remote chance that the guy was still alive, we intended to find him fast. By my calculations he'd probably been in the water about forty-five minutes. The water temperature meant it was possible that he could survive if we got him out.

I knew of victims who had been submerged up to sixty minutes, even longer, and completely recovered. Some say hypothermia, the drastic lowering of body temperature, reduces the body's need for oxygen. Blood circulation slows and is channeled to essential organs of heart, lungs, and brain. It's the same mechanism that occurs in whales and porpoises when they dive. Their physiology changes, breathing stops, and blood is shunted away from nonessential organs and directed to vital ones. Whatever the explanation, I wanted to find the guy fast.

While Crown and White got set up, Compton and I hurried Earl back along the shore to the place he'd stood when he saw the victim dumped into the water. From there, he'd have a better chance of identifying the location precisely, using landmarks as guides. As it turned out, Earl was a good witness. He remembered that when he'd seen the boat, he'd just waded out to a clear spot at the edge of the willows from which he'd cast his line.

"Fish always bitin' here. Boat was right out there," he said, pointing. "About halfway to the other side and about thirty feet from that stump sticking out of the water."

Earl followed us back to the van, rambling on about how he'd been in the war, was used to seeing this kind of thing. "You need any help, I'll be right here." He settled himself on a rock at the water's edge, took out his chewing tobacco, and gnawed on it as he watched us.

I pulled on my gloves and secured my hood. Compton helped me into my vest and tank. Then I snugged my AGA—a full face mask with regulator—in place. Also attached to my tank was a spare regulator, the depth gauge, and the submersible pressure gauge that measured my air supply. I was now encapsulated in watertight rubber. If there were no leaks, I would not be exposed to the cold and pollution in the water. Stuff like the brown goop that Earl periodically ejected into the lake.

My mask was equipped with a communication module, speaker and headphones, so that I could stay in touch with Crown on shore. I also carried two knives in case I got caught in debris. Lakes like these were filled with an assortment of junk—wire, tree limbs, fishing line, old ropes, car batteries, washing machines. I'd once swum right into a damned dumping ground for someone's trash, gotten my leg caught in the mesh of a lawn chair. It had taken me a good ten minutes to cut myself out.

As primary diver, I would be the first one in. Compton would stand at the water's edge, suited up, ready to relieve me or to assist if I had trouble. I was attached to a line and would start about thirty feet out, sweeping the area that Earl had identified. I'd do a standard arcing pattern. Since I would be diving almost blind, White would be guiding me from shore with the line. When he had determined that I'd completed a sweep on the arc, he would tug twice on the line and let out another twelve inches of rope. At that point, I would turn out until the line was again taut and sweep back the way I'd come in another, wider arc. We would continue in the pattern until I found the victim or my air got low, at which point Compton would take up the search where I'd left off.

I started in, walking backward, fins getting sucked into the muck. My equipment weighed me down and balance was almost impossible. I was nervous. Always was. I'd gotten into police diving because no one else was willing to fill the slot when one of the divers had drowned. And because of Jake. He'd been the team leader back then, and I'd felt relatively safe. The day he died, we'd spent the morning lying in bed, a square of sun reflecting on the covers. Then we went into the water and he didn't come out. After that I never felt safe again, diving or sleeping. That was four years ago. I took over as team leader and kept diving. What else was I supposed to do?

Now I swore to myself that this was the absolute last time I would ever do this kind of diving. Lopez owed me in a big way.

At about four feet, I pulled my fins out of the muck, turned, splashed into the brown liquid, and slipped under the surface. I was too nervous to notice the cold. As the water pushed in on me, my dive suit turned into a cold, clammy body glove pasted against my skin. Visibility was about a foot from the tip of my nose. I checked to make sure the tether was securely attached to my vest. Reassured that a meager line existed between me and life on shore, I swam deeper out into the lake, into the no-man's-land of opaque liquid that the dive team called goose crap. When the line was taut, I began my search, one hand grasping the rope, the other outstretched, sweeping back and forth in front of me.

I fell into a half-conscious rhythm of movement: Kick fins, sweep hand across bottom, kick fins, sweep hand. I kept from thinking too much about what my hand might encounter in the goop.

"Air check." It was Crown, the radio operator. His voice crackled through the line and into my receiver.

"Twenty-eight hundred," I responded. "Depth is forty feet." I knew that Crown was recording this information on his clipboard. This interaction served as much to keep the diver grounded in reality and the shore crew reassured that the diver was doing okay as to provide any data.

I could not see my hands reaching out as I swam into the gloom. An occasional tree limb protruding from the bottom brushed against my tank; sediment floated like spots in my vision. This was a place of complete isolation. In spite of the voice that periodically broke though the static on my radio, I felt utterly alone and confined by my suit, unable to move quickly or freely. More than likely I was the only person alive in this entire body of water. It was only sheer will and the fear that my team members would know I was scared shitless that kept me going in these times.

I stopped, breathed, and talked myself back from the brink. We all did it. Learned to bury the fear. I reminded myself that in about twenty minutes, I'd be out, breathing real air and sipping hot coffee.

I focused on simply moving forward and feeling ahead of me as I went. White gave me two tugs, indicating I had reached the end of the prescribed arc. I made the turn out and headed back, sweeping another arc deeper out into the lake. The bottom was rocky and strewn with litter. I ran into the inevitable shopping cart. In my years of diving, I'd come across enough to supply an entire store. God knows how or why they ended up in these places. Another ten feet and I

bumped up against a tire tangled in branches and fishing line. I stopped and shone my underwater light into
the sediment-filled water, trying to pick out anything in
the gloom.

"Okay, Hannah, what's your air?" Crown's voice
crackled through the receiver.

"One thousand," I said.

"Time to come out."

Shit. I'd hoped to make the recovery quickly. Get in,
find the victim, and get out. Not this time. I didn't argue
with Crown. As leader on this rescue, he had the authority. The diver never called the shots. Too often
judgment became impaired under the duress of the dive.
I'd insisted that every one of the team members follow
procedure. I was no exception.

I surfaced and gave the okay signal, then waited for
White, the line tender, to tie a knot in the line and take
a compass reading so that the next diver in could start
exactly where I had left off.

When I got to shore, Compton was suited up and
ready to go.

"Nothing out of the ordinary," I told him as he
snugged his AGA in place. "Same old black water and
muck."

He nodded and headed out.

I unsnapped my vest and leaned my tank against a
tree, pulled off my AGA, hood, and gloves, and walked
over to the staging area. Crown poured coffee from a
thermos, steam wafting into the frigid air.

Earl was still perched on a nearby rock. I went over
and sat next to him.

"You see anything out there?" he asked.

"Not much," I said, cradling the coffee in both hands,
warming fingers that were numb with the cold.

"You sure about the location?" With good witnesses, it wasn't unusual to locate the victim on the first sweep. But often that meant several witnesses who had seen the victim go under from different vantage points. That allowed the team to determine where their lines of sight intersected and establish the last-seen point more precisely. Today it was just one witness—Earl.

"Yeah, I'm sure," Earl said, defensive. "I'm used to paying attention. Kept me alive when I was in the damned jungles of Vietnam. See movement, better damned well keep track of where it's coming from. Maybe you swam right past that guy out there."

"Yeah." I stood and headed back over to shore. Compton would be getting low on air and about ready to come out. Usually there would have been a third diver to replace him. Not today.

"Damn, gonna be one of those days," Crown said, watching me suit up. "You sure you want to go back in? Maybe we should call it. Let the second team pick it up when they get out here."

"I'm fine. We'll find him and be out long before the other team gets here."

"What about your flight?" Crown asked.

"Plenty of time. Let's just get this done," I said.

Crown pulled a fresh tank out of the van, hefted it over his shoulder, and came back to where I stood. As I pulled on my hood and gloves, he hooked up the fresh tank and then helped me into the BC. He noticed me shiver. I'd gotten cold sitting on shore. I dreaded stepping back into the water.

"You sure you're okay?" Crown asked. "Don't need another body out there, for chrissake."

"I'm sure," I said. "I'll find him on this sweep."

"I know you, Hannah—never know when to quit.

But you're the one always harping on the procedures. Any doubts about diving, you don't dive," Crown warned.

"I have no doubts, Crown. I'm fine," I assured him. I wanted to resolve this thing and do it now, successfully complete the job. Especially this one, which would be, as I had promised, my last for the team.

"Seems like we shoulda snagged him by now," White said as I stepped back into the water and pulled on my fins. "Think we should start in a few feet closer to shore and sweep the area again."

"Okay," I said. "How about I move six feet in and start the sweep there?"

"Yeah, sounds good," White said. "I'll make the adjustment on the line."

Compton gave me a thumbs-up as he came out and I headed back in. I plunged beneath the surface, trying hard to ignore the cold that seemed to be pumping through my bloodstream. This time the arcs were tighter and shallower. White gave two tugs. I turned out and started the arc back. The bottom in this area was strewn with boulders, and I had to move slowly. I could easily miss the body if it were wedged under a rocky outcropping.

"Air check." Crown again.

"Jeez, I just started. It's two thousand, for chrissake."

"Don't be cranky, Hannah." I knew Crown was worried. He wanted to make sure I was doing okay. Not losing reason on my second dive in dark, frigid water.

I kept moving, encountering one boulder after another, running my hand along the rough surface, searching blindly, expecting at any moment to encounter the soft texture of flesh. I knew I'd about reached my limit in both air supply and endurance. I was having more and more difficulty keeping my fins moving and my arm out. Every muscle was tightening, and my right calf was beginning to spasm and on the verge of a major cramp.

I was swimming over yet another boulder when I saw it: the characteristic greenish-white glow. I knew what it was—light reflecting on skin. I knew the guy was dead. His eyes, open and empty, glared at me through the viscous liquid, as if blaming me for his fate. Blood still seeped from the hole in his chest, tingeing the water pink. I gave the line three sharp tugs, indicating that I had found the body. Again White would tie off the line and take a compass reading, pinpointing the location. I tied the line around a nearby rock and radioed Crown.

"Victim is dead. I've tied off the line. Will do a preliminary search of the area."

"What's your air?"

I checked my gauge. "Twelve hundred psi."

"Okay, two minutes; then you're out," Crown commanded.

Three feet from the body was a handgun. The killer probably believed that neither the body nor the gun would ever be found. But even if Earl hadn't seen the whole thing, the body would have eventually surfaced when gases accumulated. Sometimes it was just a matter of days. It all depended on the condition of the victim, such as body mass and the last meal, and on water temperature and depth.

I left the scene untouched and swam back to shore. By the time I got there the second dive team had arrived, along with several cops and an ambulance crew. Earl was in the middle of it all, telling his story to whomever would listen.

Crown was filling in the second team, and a fresh

diver was already suited up. He headed into the water with the underwater camera to begin documenting the scene. Once he finished, a team would recover the victim and any evidence. It would all be done by the book, carefully recorded, evidence painstakingly preserved so that it could be used if the case came to trial. I was more than willing to leave it in my colleagues' capable hands. My job was done. And I had a plane to catch.

By the time I got back to my apartment, Mack was there, sitting on the stoop with Sadie, my golden retriever.

"Jesus, Sampson, where the hell you been? You've got less than an hour to make your plane."

"On a dive," I said, "thanks to your drinking contest with Lopez. He would have been upchucking in his regulator."

Next to Sadie, Mack was probably the best friend I'd ever had. He was my partner in Homicide. The only time we didn't work together was when I went out on a dive recovery. In landlocked Denver, that involved maybe one call every couple of months. There was no way Mack would have ever strapped an air tank on his back.

Mack helped me load one overstuffed suitcase and Sadie into his car and we headed for the airport.

"I'm telling you, Sampson," Mack said, one hand on the wheel, one in a bag of chips, as he drove out to DIA, "this move to the islands is not going to cut it. Ain't no such thing as paradise, and a damn good thing. You'll be bored stiff."

"I want out of this rat race, Mack. I'm sick of the phone ringing at two in the morning, of seeing kids bleeding on the sidewalk or sitting in alleys shooting up. Life's too short."

"Evil is just the other side of the coin," he said. "Can't have good without the bad. Kind of an essential part of the whole."

Mack was a damned philosopher. But I knew his point of view kept him going. He'd been in the department for twenty-eight years, seen it all and accepted it. Not me. I needed out. We argued about it all the time. He'd been angry when I said I was quitting, but he hadn't been surprised.

"You're kidding yourself if you think you can escape," he said. "You only escape when you're dead. Besides, you love the chase. You'll be happy in that back-to-simplicity dream of yours for about a week and then you'll be climbing the walls."

He dropped me off at Departures. "I give you a month, Sampson. Then you'll be back here after your old job."

"Wrong," I said. "You and Sue need to come down for a visit." I could just see Mack lounging on the beach in Bermuda shorts. I gave him a hug, which he returned in his quick, awkward manner. I knew he'd miss me. I left him standing at the curb, hands in the pockets of his Rockies jacket, shaking his head.

Chapter 2

Mack had been right about my need to escape. But I wasn't just running away. I was running to something—looking for some joy. Of course, I'd never say anything like that to Mack, but I was tired of being so caught up in the job that I'd never taken the time to actually live. I was still angry about Jake's death. I blamed myself, and I'd started to lose focus.

That's how I'd ended up lying on a sidewalk with a bullet in my shoulder a year ago. Next to me a kid lay bleeding. Mack had taken him down. The boy was all of fifteen. That brush with death and senselessness had completed the shift. I didn't want to wake up at fifty-five or sixty and realize that I'd never lived any life that was meaningful—that I'd missed the moments of my life, the now. I'd started meditating, reading books about Buddhism, stuff by Joseph Campbell.

I figured that the British Virgin Islands was the perfect place to run to. Unlike the U.S. Virgins, the BVI is relatively undeveloped. The population tops out at about sixteen thousand residents. You won't find any high-rise hotels littering the beaches. Mostly small resorts and operations run by locals—little hideaways nestled in the trees. The biggest draw is the sailing. Somewhere around 400,000 sailors come to the islands every year to navigate these pristine waters. The diving is unlike any I'd ever done in Denver, the water warm, clear, and rich with life.

I'd been down two months earlier, in January, on a case. The Denver police commissioner's son had died diving in one of the wrecks. John Dunn, the police chief on Tortola, had determined the death accidental. I'd found out otherwise. Dunn was a good sport about it, though. Didn't hold a grudge. Had actually offered me a job. Said he needed a detective who was trained in underwater investigation and thought an American woman would be a good addition to his team. With all the tourists in the islands, mostly sailors, he could use someone whom they might relate to more easily. I wasn't sure whether this was an insult or a compliment, and I didn't bother to tell him that tact was not my strong suit.

I'd sold all my furniture, given the TV and microwave to my sister. In a last symbolic gesture, I'd flattened my cell phone in the trash compactor. All I'd brought with me was my Smith & Wesson, a few clothes, my dive gear, and Sadie. Sadie was a gift from my overprotective father, who thought she'd make a good watchdog. But she's just not the type.

I worried about her now below in the plane's luggage compartment. The vet had given her a tranquilizer. She was probably in better shape than I was at the moment. I hate flying. Right now I was in a window seat, next to a guy who weighed about 350 pounds. I'd been sitting with my elbows crunched into my ribs for hours. At least Sadie had the luxury of her own cage.

By the time we landed at the airport in San Juan, I

felt like a pretzel. I got off and stretched. With two hours to kill before the puddle jumper to Tortola, I took a long, fast walk through the terminal, trying to get my heart rate up, my blood flowing, and loosen the growing knot of tension that was building in my stomach. The farther I got from Denver, the more I questioned whether my decision to leave Mack and the dive team wasn't one big mistake.

The airport was crowded with people speaking rapid-fire Spanish. Long lines snaked in a maze of confusion, hundreds held hostage as security personnel searched an endless stream of baggage before allowing it to be tagged for flight. I narrowly avoided trampling a toddler who had managed to escape his mother's grip while she struggled with another kid and a pile of luggage. I decided to seek refuge back at the gate.

Down on the concourse, I stopped at a snack bar and spent $10.62 for a cold hot dog and a diet Pepsi, then found a quiet corner at the gate and pulled out the books I'd been collecting about the Caribbean. I'd read through all of them at least once—a couple of histories of the islands, complex accounts of exploitation, colonization, settlement, the killing off of entire races, the evolution of political institutions, social forms, and economics, stories of slavery and piracy.

I also had a complete series on the identification of sea creatures. What was it about the human need to name things? Somehow a name made things real, allowed one to categorize. I wanted to know what I saw when I encountered it a hundred feet below the ocean's surface, especially if it was something that might bite, sting, or consume me whole.

But at the moment all I wanted was distraction from the tension that had turned to fire in the pit of my stomach. I opened one of the guides to the section on jelly-fish, as varied and strange as their names: moon, cannonball, cassiopea. I'd narrowly missed swimming right into the translucent float of a Portuguese Man-of-War, one of the most toxic of jellyfish, when I'd dived in the islands just two months ago. It had looked like a pink-ish plastic bag until I'd gotten close enough to see the cluster of tentacles from its float.

By the time the flight was called, I'd moved on to the section about tunicates. I zipped the books back into my carry-on and boarded the flight.

Forty minutes later the small plane landed smoothly on Beef Island and taxied to the terminal. The attendant opened the door, and I breathed in the Caribbean—moist, ocean filled, tinged with blossoms. I felt the tension in my body ease a bit with the scented recollection of the place.

But everything about the airport had been transformed since I'd left just a couple of months ago. The ramshackle terminal, where chickens had scampered underfoot and goats had grazed, was gone. Now the Terrence B. Lettsome International Airport stood in its place, a small but modern gray block, surrounded by concrete walks and parking lots. It was remarkable only in its sterility; not a goat or chicken in sight, a little piece of island paradise destroyed. I'm sure that wasn't the perspective of the officials who had pushed for a new airport. They would have argued that it brought the islands into the twenty-first century, providing a modern facility for the increased traffic to the region.

At least they had not built jetways. I walked across the tarmac with a herd of forty others, some locals but the majority I guessed to be sailors. They wore boat shoes, T-shirts with sailboats, caps with sailing logos,

huge-brimmed canvas hats, their faces pale and tense,
shorts neatly creased. An identical group was boarding
a flight nearby, faces tanned, smiles tinged with regret,
shorts wrinkled, T-shirts dirty, hats stained.

The sun glared off the hot cement. A breeze rustled
through palm leaves, and I could hear the surf breaking
off the rocks beyond the runway. It was a glorious
March day.

Still I worried. When Dunn had offered me the job, it
had seemed like a real opportunity. I'd jumped at the
chance to escape all the urban violence and find a sim-
pler way to live, away from the frenzied existence I'd so
easily gotten caught up in. Besides, the diving I would
do for the police force was completely unlike the black-
water diving I'd been doing. Here the water was another
world, an amazingly serene and orderly place. And, of
course, there was O'Brien.

But Denver had been home and Mack someone I'd
depended on. He'd always been there to watch my back.
I thought about what he'd said: *Ain't no such thing as
paradise.* I knew he was right, that I was looking for
something that didn't exist. But I'd been sure things
would be better here. Now doubt was creeping in. I
would miss the connections of home. Here I was a
foreigner.

Damned if the sign at immigrations didn't reinforce
my foreign status. I was directed to the one labeled
"Nonbelongers," and informed that those who were
born in the BVI or whose parents were born here could
be in the "Belongers" line. Like the sign said, I did not
belong. Maybe I'd romanticized the whole place, made
it more than it was because I'd needed to. Before I could
change my mind, though, the stern-faced official
stamped my passport and waved me through.

I could hear Sadie barking as the luggage carousel started to turn and her crate came into view.

"Sweet Sadie. It's okay, girl." She whined and wagged her tail, ecstatic to realize that I had not deserted her.

When I hefted the cage from the conveyer belt and released her, she almost knocked me over. I knelt, wrapped my arms around her, whispered in her ear, waiting for her to calm. She stuck by my side as I made my way through customs. Her majesty's royal customs agent hardly gave my luggage or the stack of papers I'd collected to get Sadie into the country a second look.

"Welcome to our beautiful islands!" he said, a wide grin filling his face.

Inside the terminal, I noticed that the woman who once sold postcards, plastic place mats, and native dolls from her concession stand in the old terminal had pulled up stakes, probably unable to afford the higher rent.

When I'd waited for my flight home a couple months ago, I'd spoken to the shop owner's mother, an eccentric old woman who hung out in the waiting area while her daughter worked the store. She'd been close to a hundred, her skin raisined. She was decked out in a turquoise dress with gold buttons and a matching straw hat. I'd heard her entire family history, the story of generations making a life on a tiny island, harvesting salt from the salt pond for the queen. I wondered where she was now, whether she'd found another place and others who would listen to her stories.

Sadie pulled on her leash as we headed out the doors into the sunlight. I spied Peter O'Brien right away, leaning against a SeaSail van talking with a local black man in a flowered shirt. O'Brien wore tan shorts and boat shoes, no socks. He looked up, saw me, and smiled, that open, boyish smile.

"Hannah. I'm so glad you're back." He wrapped tan, lean arms around me and pulled me in. Okay, maybe things would be okay.

I'd met O'Brien during my investigation in January. He'd been a suspect. I'd fallen for him long before I'd ruled him out as a murderer.

O'Brien owns SeaSail, one of the largest sailboat charter companies in the BVI. He'd come to the BVI with his parents when he was a kid. They'd started the company with one small boat. Now SeaSail is worth a bundle.

O'Brien is more at ease at the helm of a sailboat than anywhere else. He always looks like he's just come off the sea, hair windblown, dark, and wild, white smile wrinkles embedded in his tan.

We loaded my luggage and Sadie into the van and headed toward Road Town. O'Brien had found a place for me to live—a thirty-seven-foot Island Packet, out-fitted as a live-aboard. I'd been skeptical. I'd never con-sidered living on a damned boat. I was accustomed to having something more solid under my feet. This sounded small and rocky. The people who owned her had returned to California after living on her for a year. Evidently a year had been about eleven months too long. They were back in their six-thousand-square-foot house on the coast and sailing their twenty-six-foot Cape Dory on weekends. My rent would pay for their docking and storage fees and a little more. It was docked just minutes east of Road Town, the only real city in the BVI and the capital.

"You'll love it," O'Brien said as he gunned the van and passed a slow-moving truck. O'Brien drove like every other islander—fast, honking at livestock in the road, waving at friends, and swerving around the tardy.

"The Pickerings are wonderful. The marina is their dream. It's small, only about twenty boats, all long-term boat owners who store their boats with them. Some live-aboards. The place was really run-down but they've worked hard to fix it up. Bought it when they were married, with a small loan from their parents. Tilda runs the little store, stocks groceries and marine supplies. Calvin tends the boats.

"This is it." O'Brien pulled into a dirt lot, scattering chickens and ruffling the feathers of one stubborn-looking rooster.

The cove was protected on three sides by land lined with coconut palms and sea grapes. It opened to the sea, the water turquoise glass that lapped up to the white sand. A couple of piers jutted from the beach into the bay, each lined with boats, one of which would be mine.

Two children ran to greet us. "Peta, Peta," they called in unison. O'Brien grabbed the youngest, a petite girl of about three, and swung her up into his arms.

"Do it again! Again!" She giggled as O'Brien swung her skyward. He knelt and hugged the other child, who stood back a bit, older and quieter. Her hair was braided in tight cornrows fixed on the end with colorful beads.

"Rebecca, Daisy, this is the lady I told you about, Hannah."

The little one, Daisy, reached her tiny arms up to me. When I picked her up, she hugged me hard around the neck. Jeez, she already had me. Rebecca held back, standing behind O'Brien, an arm around his leg.

"Hello, Rebecca," I said. She smiled and buried her face in the hem of O'Brien's shorts.

About then Sadie, at the end of her patience, barked

from the van, upset that she was being ignored. When I opened the door she ran to Rebecca and gave her a wet slurp on the cheek. That was it. Shy Rebecca had found a friend.

"Hey, dar, Peter." A man and woman emerged from the marina office, a freshly painted wooden structure in tones of violet, lime, and yellow.

"Tilda, Calvin, this is Hannah Sampson."

"Good day to ya, Hannah. Welcome to Pickerings Landing," Calvin said, his island accent strong. He offered his hand, which felt rough and callused in mine. He was a handsome man of about thirty, dressed in oil-stained khakis and a T-shirt, his skin the color of an eggplant. His wife, Tilda, was a bit younger, slim, an exotic beauty.

"We've been expecting you," Tilda said, taking my hand. Like Calvin's, her palm was hardened by work. "Boat is all ready. She's on dock A."

We followed Tilda out to the end of the pier.

"We put the live-aboards out here where there's more breeze, quieter, nice view of the open water."

Sea Bird was etched in script on the side of the boat.

O'Brien could hardly wait to show me around. He'd been thrilled when he'd found the *Sea Bird*. But then, O'Brien could think of few things better than a damned boat.

"These boats have a Full Foil Keel, really strong, and great windward performance," O'Brien said. "The hull design makes them fast, maneuverable, and comfortable when under way."

Typical O'Brien. I was more concerned about living on the thing than I was about how much it heeled over under sail. I had no intention of taking her out until I could tell a reef line from a jib sheet.

O'Brien stepped on board and offered me a hand. With some coaxing, Sadie finally jumped onto the boat. She'd been a mountain dog her whole life. The idea of leaping onto a structure surrounded by a bunch of water was counter to every dog instinct in her being.

The boat felt like home the minute I stepped below. It was cozy, warmly lit, reflecting deep hues of fabric and wood. Nestled at the base of the stairs across from the desk was the galley, with a four-burner range and an oven, a tiny refrigerator and a freezer. Bookshelves lined the walls of the salon, with richly colored tapestries.

On one side of the salon was an L-shaped settee. The seat cushions around the teak dining table had been re-covered with sturdy fabric in reds, blues, and tans. On the other side another small teak table was nestled between two overstuffed chairs. A lamp hung from the wall above. The perfect place to read, though Sadie was already claiming one of the chairs as hers.

The aft sleeping quarters had been converted into a little office and storage area. The forward quarters with head were beyond the wall divider in the bow, the bed coming to a point to fit the shape. Along the walls were more built-in shelves. A small triangular table filled a space next to the bed.

Unbelievable aromas permeated the boat. Something was simmering on the stove.

"A bit of welcome-to-the-islands supper," Tilda said. "Enjoy. We be leaving you to settle in. If you need anything, we live on the second floor of the marina. The bathhouse is just there on the first floor, the green door right past the store."

O'Brien and I went up top with them and watched as

they strolled back down the dock, the girls skipping ahead of them.

"Nice people," I said.

"Yes, this is a good place for you," O'Brien said, wrapping his arm around me. "God, I'm glad you're back, Hannah. I've missed you." He leaned down and kissed me. "Tilda made enough for both of us, and I brought a bottle of cabernet. Hope you don't mind my company."

"Come here, O'Brien." I pulled him into me. "I missed you too."

We ate on deck as the sun sank behind the western hills. O'Brien didn't leave after dinner. I was happy to have him in my bed that night. I lay awake long after he drifted off, listening to the night sounds, gentle waves lapping the beach, the cry of a distant bird. A fish splashed out of the water, darting from the hunter that prowled beneath the surface.

Chapter 3

O'Brien was gone when I next opened my eyes. I made coffee and went up on deck. It was a gorgeous Sunday morning, quiet, a hibiscus breeze cooling the morning sun. Sadie was standing on the deck with her Frisbee between her teeth, wagging her tail and whining.

"Jeez, Sadie, can't I even finish my coffee?" She nuzzled my arm, forcing coffee over the rim of my cup. "Okay, okay, let's go."

I refilled the cup and we headed down the dock to the sand. Rebecca and Daisy were romping on the beach in their Sunday best, matching taffeta dresses with lace collars and hems. Around their waists, impeccably tied bows flapped as they ran.

"Hannah, Hannah," Daisy yelled, running toward me through the sand. "Don't I look pretty?" She twirled, her skirt encircling her in a pink blur.

"You're gorgeous! You both look beautiful."

Rebecca stood quietly, hands behind her back until Sadie nudged her belly.

"Sadie." She giggled and wrapped her tiny arms around the dog's neck. Sadie nuzzled her nose under Rebecca's chin and licked.

"Mornin', Hannah. How was your first night on the boat?" Calvin and Tilda walked toward the girls hand in hand. They were also dressed for church, he in a dark suit, white shirt, and blue tie, Tilda in a tan linen suit that reached midcalf, with matching heels and a straw hat.

"Fine. I love the boat. But I think I'm about to lose my dog," I said, smiling at Rebecca.

"I'm afraid you could be right. Becca loves animals. I hope you don't mind her playing with Sadie," Tilda said.

"Not at all. We all need every friend we can get. Becca, you can play with Sadie whenever you want, as long as it's all right with your parents. Okay?"

"Thank you, Hannah." Again that shy smile.

"Come on, girls. We don't want to be late for church," Tilda said. "Store's open if you need supplies, Hannah. Just write down what you get in the ledger on the counter. You can pay later."

"Thanks, Tilda." Christ, the honor system. I hadn't been in an environment this trusting since the third grade in Sister Evanelina's music class. She'd let me borrow a viola for an entire year. Most of that time it had gathered dust under my bed.

Calvin lifted Daisy into the car, Becca scrambled in behind, and they headed off to church. I felt a twinge of regret as I watched them pull onto the road and drive away. I envied the Pickerings. They were happy. Tilda and Calvin were committed to each other and in love. They were a good team, working together to make a living and raise their two girls.

They'd developed this little enclave—the marina and store and their home. Who could want anything more? It was something I'd never have. I knew myself well enough to realize I'd get antsy, bored with the day-to-day routine. At thirty-seven I'd given up any idea of children of my own.

I sat in the warm sand, digging my toes in, pushing the regret away, and let Sadie run on the beach. This was all new to Sadie. Her turf had been the park near the Denver Zoo, chasing the Frisbee through a foot of fresh January powder or the newly mowed grass of July. She was a quick study, though. One mouthful of sand and she knew this stuff wasn't snow. She didn't hesitate at the water's edge. Nothing like a golden. Again and again she raced into the surf and swam out to capture the Frisbee.

When she tired I left her under a tree licking sand from between her paws and went into the store. Inside it was dark and cool. I wandered down one aisle and up another, gathering boxes and cans with familiar labels—Kellogg's, Nestlé, Folgers, and tea cookies and biscuits, delicacies made in some faraway English bakery. A rainbow of vegetables rested in vibrant rows along the back wall—lettuce, tomatoes, cucumber, cantaloupe, mangos, bananas, and guavas. I found eggs, a loaf of fresh bread, dog food, and a Sunday paper, wrote it all down in the ledger, and headed back to the boat, Sadie at my heels.

It took me a half hour to find and turn on the propane for the stove, then another fifteen minutes to figure out that the gas switch on the electrical panel had to be on before I could light the damn thing. Everything was more complicated on this darned boat. Finally, a decadent breakfast in hand, I took it up on deck and settled in the shade of the bimini.

"Sweet Sadie," I said, scratching soft, downy ears. Tired and full, she lay at my feet, a wet, sloppy tongue periodically slurping against my ankle.

When I finally opened the newspaper, the headline shouted at me, *Crime Wave Hits Tranquil BVI!* Damn, I was not ready to let reality ruin my morning. I ignored the entire front page, turning instead to the sailing news inside. Always good for a picture of a boat, sail filled, tipping in the wind, accompanied by the results of the latest sailing regatta.

Eventually I forced myself back to the front page. After all, I was starting work on the police force the next morning. I needed to be informed. *Police Commissioner Avery Wright is appealing for public support as the Royal Virgin Islands police force fights an upsurge in crime in the territory.* The crime wave consisted of a dozen or so burglaries in the last three months. Evidently the latest occurred last night near Cappoon's Bay on the west end, when two armed intruders broke into the home of William and Dorothy Elbert, robbing them of $200 in jewelry. During a tussle, Mr. Elbert was shot in the foot.

The commissioner, the paper said, *has announced that all vacation leave for police officers has been canceled, and those already on leave have been ordered back immediately. He urges anyone with any information about these robberies to contact the police. The governor is talking about increasing funds to the police force to "nip this in the bud."*

I wasn't looking forward to my first day on the job. Those guys being pulled in from vacation were going to be upset. But I was not going to let it ruin my day. I spent the rest of the morning stuffing clothes in drawers and trying to figure out the intricacies of the boat. Finally I gave it up, went back on deck, and stretched out on the bow, relaxing with the rocking of waves that splashed against the boat. The newspaper I'd been scanning for used cars covered my face.

"Ahoy on *Sea Bird*!" I bolted up, newspaper flying. I grabbed the pages before they ended up polluting the sea.

"Hello," I said, groggy and confused. Oh, yeah, boat, in the BVI, new job. It was all coming back. I wondered how long I'd been asleep.

"I'm sorry I startled you," the woman said. "Thought I should introduce myself, and besides, you're starting to turn the color of watermelon flesh."

A black woman stood on the end of the dock, amused. She was small-boned, about five-three, hair short and stylishly cut, a pair of tinted granny glasses perched on her nose. She wore shorts and a beige T-shirt with a logo, a turtle encircled by lettering, *Society of Conservation*. "A tree hugger" was what Mack would call her.

"I'm Elyse Henry. Live on the *Caribbe*," she said, pointing to a wide-bodied motorboat tied to the other side of the dock. It looked like its top speed was about five miles per hour, even with the two one-hundred-horsepower engines on the back. "Welcome to Pickerings Landing."

"Hi, Hannah Sampson," I said. "Come on aboard."

"This is a lovely boat," she said.

"Thanks, guess it's home."

"Hey, if you ever want to go out for a sail, give me a holler. I grew up in these islands, been sailing since I was five."

She noticed the automobile ads I had circled in the paper. Damned if ten minutes later I didn't find myself riding with Elyse up Paraquita Bay Road into the hills. Turned out her good friend had a car to sell. Just what I needed. I hated these kinds of things—friends of friends with something for sale. It always spelled trouble. And what could you do when the car turned out to be a lemon? Everybody ended up mad at everybody else.

Elyse didn't get it, though. I had her pegged for one of those people who were always in the middle of things, trying to help people out, solve their problems. And she couldn't take a hint. She heard "no" as "convince me." Which she obviously had, since I was riding with her to go look at the damned car.

On the way I heard Elyse's life story. Energy eked from every pore as she spoke. The woman was a dynamo. She'd grown up on Tortola and had lived here all her life except for the six years she'd spent at university in London. Now she was the one-woman office for the Society of Conservation, a London-based environmental nonprofit. She was paid to "keep an eye on things," as she put it. I was sure she was good at it. She was the perfect type to have her nose in everything.

"At one time or another, I've been assisted by the U.S. Coast Guard, the BVI Police, the Department of Conservation and Fisheries. Whomever I could enlist for help. Don't be surprised if I call on you someday."

That was what I was afraid of. Evidently her job was to light fires, blow whistles. At the moment she was ranting about sharks.

We turned onto a gravel drive and headed up a winding road through trees and bushes thick with blossoms. At the end, a house was nestled in the trees facing out to the sea. It was perfectly kept, the gardens weeded, the grounds manicured. A woman who'd been working in one of the flower beds stood when she saw us pull up. She stretched, her arms on her lower back, then waved and smiled. A few snow white strands escaped a wide-brimmed hat. She had to be at least eighty.

"Elyse! What brings you up this way?"

"Hello, Mary." Elyse gave the woman a warm hug. "This is Hannah Sampson, my new neighbor."

"Good to meet you, Hannah." The woman's speech was heavily accented British. "Come in, come in. I'll put the teakettle on."

Mary had brought England to the islands with her. The living room was dark and filled with antiques, table lamps with hand-painted glass shades, Queen Anne chairs with intricately embroidered cushions, and delicate china figurines placed on an old marble-topped washstand. The kitchen was a relief of light. It was painted white with yellow and blue accents, a vase of yellow tulips on the table.

She led us out to a shady back patio. While Mary and Elyse went back into the kitchen, I relaxed. Suddenly a dark, fuzzy creature with a long tail and pointed ears scurried across the yard and into one of the flower beds. A snake dangled from between its teeth.

I could hear the two women rattling dishes and talking. Soon Elyse emerged carrying a tray, Mary behind her.

"A mongoose," she said when I described the animal to Mary. "They were brought in to control the rats back when they infested the sugarcane plantations. Now the mongoose have overrun the islands."

She placed a delicate blue china cup before me. I was afraid to pick it up, sure it would shatter with the mere touch. Jeez, the last time I'd attended a tea party I'd been about eight. My sister had set out her new tea set on a blanket under a huge elm and invited me to join her. This was almost as nice—china instead of plastic, and real tea.

"Hannah needs a car," Elyse said. "I thought right

away about the Rambler. You've been thinking about selling it. No sense letting it rot in your garage."

"Well, let's go look at it after we have our tea. Let me talk to you a bit, Elyse. It's been almost a month."

"Oh, Mary, I'm fine." She turned to me. "Mary watches over me like a mother hen. But I have to let her. She saved my life. Now she feels responsible." Elyse gave Mary a look of mixed humor and affection. Mary glanced my way, unsure.

"Would you like to talk alone? I'd be happy with a stroll through your garden. It's absolutely fantastic."

"No, Hannah. You might as well know the real Elyse Henry," Elyse said. "We will be neighbors, after all, and I'm not ashamed of who I am."

Jeez, I had been dragged up here to buy a car and now I was to be privy to some sort of intrigue between Elyse and an eighty-year-old woman.

"Mary is my psychiatrist as well as my friend. She retired a few years back, but she couldn't get rid of me."

"Psychiatrist?"

"Elyse has bipolar disorder. The older term is manic depression. Do you know about such an illness?"

"Very little." I told them about one of the girls in the dorm during my sophomore year in college. She was extremely bright and aced most of her classes, but quiet. Then she started acting completely out of character. Friends whispered about her increasingly bizarre behavior for several weeks before it became obvious she needed help. The police picked her up walking down the street at three in the morning in ten-degree weather wearing a tank top and shorts without shoes, socks, or a coat.

"I'd guess she was having her first manic episode," Mary said. "Onset often occurs in the early twenties and can be associated with stress like being in college, away from home, pressured by grades. In a case like that, the manic episode is usually followed by profound, debilitating depression. About one percent of the population has bipolar disorder. It's thought to have a genetic link. We still don't know exactly what chemical differences exist in the brain. You hear a lot about neurotransmitters, intracellular second messengers, neuropeptides.

"Fortunately, we know a lot more than we did fifteen or twenty years ago. Back then the treatment was to institutionalize. In the nineties we started learning about medications—mood stabilizers, antipsychotics, antidepressants—that work to restore balance. But it's still trial and error to find the right medicinal therapy for each patient. Every individual responds differently to these drugs."

"I remember how scared that girl was when she came back to school the following semester," I said, "and how embarrassed she was to face her friends. She just didn't know how people would react."

Mary just shook her head, frustration and anger fixing her mouth in a hard line. "That's the trouble," she said. "There is so much stigma attached to brain disorders. I just don't understand how people can see an imbalance in the brain as being any different from, say, diabetes. It's the historical/religious part, I guess—people once suspected that demons and devils lurked in those with this disease."

"Mary gets kind of worked up about it," Elyse apologized.

I smiled at her to let her know it was okay.

"Some of the most celebrated and talented people in history have been manic-depressive," Mary said. "Winston Churchill, for example, Abraham Lincoln, Vincent van Gogh, Ernest Hemingway, Virginia Woolf. Some even call it the CEO disease, because so many high-level Wall Street types suffer from it.

"One of the problems with bipolar disorder is that the person who has it can't tell when she is getting sick, when her behavior is changing or her reality slipping. With time, people can learn to look for cues—maybe feeling more agitated or sleeping less. Often they depend on someone close to them to watch for the signals, such as hyperactivity and pressured speech. Even if someone is taking her medication faithfully, body chemistry can shift."

Mary was clearly passionate about the subject.

"Every person I have ever treated goes off their medication. They start feeling better, don't like the side effects of the meds, are drawn to the high of mania. This is the most difficult aspect of the disease. When a person is manic, she feels fine, especially in the initial stages—elated, infallible, grandiose."

I would have never guessed that any of what Mary was telling me applied to Elyse.

"That was me," Elyse said. "I was in school too, in London, far from home, on a scholarship, a black Caribbean woman competing with students whose educations were far superior to mine.

"At first I just felt more effective, able to accomplish more, more outgoing. Then I became euphoric; my senses were enhanced. I felt a spiritual communion. Sunsets were unbelievably spectacular. Instead of a symphony, I heard each instrument, individual notes."

"I was brilliant, felt invincible. I could talk profoundly with anyone about anything. One of the hardest things for me to accept was that none of it was real. Or isn't once I'm not manic anymore. With each episode, the symptoms became more problematic. I'd get anxious, short-tempered, critical of others. Then the depression would hit."

Elyse stopped, took a sip of tea, and smiled at Mary. "Thank God for Mary."

"Elyse is a strong woman. She's done well, learned to cope with this disorder, but not just cope—to succeed. She has amazing insight. So back to the original question, Elyse. How are you?"

Mary refilled each teacup and patiently waited for Ellyse to formulate a reply.

"You see right through me, Mary. I did have another reason for visiting today. I'm kind of on edge. Having some trouble sleeping. I've been upset with some problems with the local fishermen. It's the same old conflict—their livelihood versus the damage to the environment. I'm probably just reacting to the pressure of the job, but I do feel out of balance."

"I want you to have your blood levels checked tomorrow." Mary jotted the order on a prescription pad that she pulled out of her pocket. I had to laugh. Either she carried it with her at all times or she had anticipated the need when she saw Elyse.

Several cups of tea later, we finally got around to the car. We walked out to the garage, where a 1964 Rambler was parked beside a brand-new red Miata.

"Thought it would be fun to have something a little sportier," Mary said. "Always wanted a red convertible."

The Rambler was a black box with a white convertible top. I had never seen another like it and was sure that any of its ilk were now all buried in car cemeteries. These were not the kind of cars one savored, restoring to original beauty. But it looked to be in perfect condition, the upholstery was like new, and it had only twenty thousand miles on it. I guess it's hard to put a lot of miles on a car on an island that is only eight miles long. The car was ideal.

Mary insisted I drive it home. We would meet in Road Town later in the week, when my funds were transferred to the bank here.

I followed Elyse back. Good thing. Otherwise I'd have been driving on the right, which in the islands was the wrong side of the road.

I loved the Rambler. It performed perfectly. I'd put the top down before we left and delighted in the warm breeze blowing through my hair. The quiet tune I'd been humming turned to all-out song. I sang only when I was sure no one could hear me—like in a convertible with the wind carrying the notes off into the empty road behind me.

God, I felt good. I had a wonderful place to live, had met two women who I was pretty sure would turn into close friends, and I was driving a 1964 Rambler convertible down a winding road in paradise. Damned if I could just let it be, though. Again Mack's warnings to the wise echoed in the back of my head: *I'm telling you, Sampson . . . ain't no such thing as paradise.*

Chapter 4

The next morning, when I climbed into the Rambler, it was scented with blossoms that had blown in through an open window during the night. The floor was littered with bougainvillea. I swept them off the driver's seat and let the rest be.

Calvin waved from the roof. He had a nail between his teeth and was lifting his hammer toward the sky as I pulled out and turned west onto Blackburn Highway. Hardly a highway in my book. It was a narrow two-lane road littered with potholes and bumps. Roadside snack shacks met the pavement, and goats ambled along the edge. But highway it was.

Sometimes the road took me along the shore, then curved through communities of homes, shops, and businesses mixed up in a jumble of wood, concrete, and stucco. Driving on this road was like maneuvering on a speedway where everyone drove on the wrong side. Cars darted past me, and others sped up on my tail, then shot around, honking. I tried to keep up and still be ready to swerve around the inevitable car that would be stopped right around a bend in the road, its driver shooting the breeze with a friend. Finally I made it into Road

Town, veered into the police department parking lot, and breathed, trying to regain my composure.

The department was located in a one-level concrete building, gray and ugly. The inside was even bleaker than out—a bunch of little cubicles divided by dusty movable partitions. The place was deserted. So much for all officers on duty. Maybe they were all out already. Finally I scared up Dunn's secretary.

"Hello, you must be Detective Sampson. I be Jean," she said.

She was young, maybe twenty, skin the shade of moist brown earth, dark eyes set in an open, friendly face. She was heavy around the hips, and her ample breasts were hardly contained under a flowered island blouse that puckered at the buttons. Her hair was pulled back and bound in intricate braids that reached to her waist, strands of copper, brown, and black spun in a beautifully complex weave.

"Please call me Hannah," I said. "You must have just started." I knew this because Dunn and I had arrested his previous secretary in January. One nasty lady, but that's another story.

"Been here just one month," she said. "Chief said that Deputy Snyder should be showin' you around. Jimmy!" she called into the back room.

Jimmy appeared from around the corner. He couldn't have been much over eighteen, skin the color of walnuts, with a disarming smile. Good thing, because I'd guess that was the only way Snyder would ever disarm anyone. He was skinny, all legs and arms. Maybe the rest of his body would grow into his limbs someday. I had the feeling he was low man on the totem pole around here. That he was called a deputy at all was a tribute to Dunn's knack for finesse.

"Deputy Snyder," he said importantly, emphasizing the *Deputy* part. "You can be callin' me Jimmy."

"Hannah Sampson," I said, taking his outstretched hand.

Snyder showed me to my cubicle: metal desk, an ergonomically incorrect chair, a phone, file cabinet. Not even a computer. But wasn't that just what I had been running from? Besides, I'd try to spend as little time as possible here.

"Let me know if you be needin' anything," he said as he left, that smile filling his face.

I sat down and tried to figure out what the heck I should be doing. I supposed I could have brought some personal stuff to enliven the space. A photo of Sadie, my parents, maybe. The picture of Jake. Back in my apartment in Denver I'd kept Jake buried at the bottom of a drawer, to be retrieved only when I was feeling sorry for myself—that usually occurred on a dark night alone when I'd decided to inhale several strong scotches. When I packed, I'd left most of my stuff behind, stored in my parents' basement. I considered it progress.

The plaques and awards I'd won over the years—marksmanship, arrest records, scuba recovery recognition—had never meant much. The only one I'd ever hung was a plaque from a couple of the other detectives that said, "To Dead-end Sam. We told her it couldn't be done, and it couldn't." It had been a joke. I'd followed one lead after another in a case that went nowhere. Then one day a guy turned up dead in an abandoned warehouse and that was it. Not one of the hundred-some hours that I'd put in had made an iota of difference, but I'd been too damned stubborn to give up.

On my desk, an ID with my name on it and a badge held down a neat stack of papers. Forms, clearly meant

for me. I hate forms, and damned if these didn't actually
have carbon paper between them. I hadn't seen carbon
paper since I'd been in grade school. Maybe I'd get to
them later.

I opened the desk drawer. Someone had stocked it
with a few pens and pencils, a legal pad. I pulled a pencil and the paper out and started to doodle. Maybe Mack
had been right. What the hell was I doing here anyway?
I'd fallen in love with the islands when I'd been down
in January. Nothing like the tropics when it's twenty degrees and snowing at home. But could I really find a
place here among these people? I could see Snyder over
by the coffee machine shooting the breeze with Jean. I
headed over.

"Like some coffee?" Jean asked.

"Yeah, I'll get it," I said. My small effort to redefine
the role of the secretary. I always got my own coffee,
but then, I was a woman. Christ. I poured a cup and
added cream.

"Good brew." The stuff at the Denver PD tasted like
dirt and was thick enough to chew most of the time.

Out one of the only windows in the entire office I
could see boats, sails flapping in the wind, and a big
cruise ship tied up at the dock. A bunch of tourists were
going ashore and being accosted by local vendors who
set up booths right on the dock.

"I can't believe those big cruise ships would come in
here," I said.

"They won't stay," Jean said. "Dem tourists spend a
couple of hours in Road Town or on one of da beaches
on the other side of the island and then they go back to
da luxury of those staterooms. The BVI ain't the kind of
place for the kinda tourists on dose cruise ships. Too
small. One ship practically doubles the entire popula-

tion. Road Town ain't no 'in' spot. Ship will take them to another port."

"Where do they go?" I asked her.

"That one be goin' over to Charlotte Amalie on St. Thomas. Dem cruise ships dump thousands of visitors over there every week. They flood da streets and duty-free stores. Go back to da ship loaded down with jewelry, cameras, perfume, liquor. Here, all dey be findin is T-shirts, handmade dolls, a postcard or two."

"Sounds like you're happy they don't stay."

"Mos' folks around here, we be likin' our island da way it is. Don't need no crowds in the streets all da time. By the way, Chief jus' got in. He wants you to go ahead in to see him," she said.

Good. I hoped he'd get me out with the others, running down information about the robberies.

His door was open, but he was on the phone when I knocked. He waved me in with an angry, frustrated look and pointed to the red vinyl chair on the other side of his desk. Dunn had the only real office. Same metal desk, but a huge window that looked out toward the harbor.

I waited for him to get off the phone. His conversation seemed pretty one-sided. He was mostly listening. From the look on Dunn's face I'd bet it was the police commissioner. He was probably giving Dunn all kinds of shit about the robberies. Some things are the same no matter where you are. I'd guess that the commissioner was being pressured by the governor, who was worried about reelection and the effects an increase in crime could have on tourism. The commissioner in turn was pressuring Dunn.

"Commissioner," he said by way of explanation when he hung up the phone.

"Yeah," I said, "I figured."

"Can't just let me do my job. I been at it for twenty years. Think he'd give me some credit for knowing how to handle this," he said, shaking his head. "You settled in?"

"Yeah, not much to settle. I'm ready to get to work."

"Good, got a call this morning from one of the sailors anchored over in Cane Garden Bay. Says her husband is missing. Didn't come back to the boat last night. Told her we'd send someone over. That would be you."

"Christ, Chief. He's probably nursing a hangover with one of the ladies from the Doubloon. Be back before I even get over there. Let me help on these burglaries."

"Detective Sampson, I make the assignments in the office," Dunn said, turning on his official in-charge demeanor.

He was good at it. Dunn was a huge black man, six-four, about 225, a paunch developing above his belt, his close-cropped hair flecked with gray. He was a proud and stately islander, impeccable and clearly in charge. I'd never seen him in anything but a suit.

People didn't mess with Dunn. Our initial animosity when I'd come down to investigate a murder had developed into respect, and then a friendship of sorts. He knew when he asked me to stay on that he'd have to put up with my stubborn nature. Obviously he could. Right now he was poised for a skirmish, back straight, arms crossed over his chest. Splotches of perspiration spread across his shirt. His coat was hung neatly in the corner.

"The couple are Americans. You should be able to relate to them, and I don't want the tourists thinking that we take their troubles lightly. Especially with all the heat from the commissioner about these robberies. Can't afford any complaints. So go over there and see what she has to say. Name is Patricia Robsen; boat is *Wind Runner*, a thirty-two-foot SeaSail. Take Snyder with you."

"Snyder?"

"Don't argue with me, Detective Sampson," he said. "Just go."

Chapter 5

Cane Garden Bay is one of those places right off a postcard. Horseshoe shaped, white sandy beach, palms swaying in the breeze. Something that smelled a lot like lobster mingled with the scent of fresh-baked bread. A couple of kids were arguing over the tire swing hanging from a palm tree on the beach in front of Stanley's Restaurant.

Five or six other restaurants dotted the shore. Kayaks and windsurfers were pulled up on the beach. A couple of tiny stores were nestled along the street among local homes. Callwoods rum distillery was down the road, still producing white and gold rum from the cane grown in the hills. I'd read about the place. Slaves brought in from Africa had worked the plantations harvesting the cane.

In fact, the histories of the Caribbean tell a sordid and bloody tale. When Columbus landed in the islands in 1492, the Caribbean was home to as many as six million Carib and Arawak. Twenty years later almost all were dead, killed by diseases to which they had no resistance, and by colonists who wanted their land. Today only a couple of small villages of Carib can be found in the islands, on Dominica and St. Vincent. The Arawak people no longer exist anywhere on earth.

With the development of sugarcane and cotton plantations in the mid-1600's came slavery. Some estimate that more that 220,000 slaves were brought to the Virgin Islands to work in the fields. By 1848 it had ended and the slaves were freed. Today most of the inhabitants of the Virgin Islands are of African heritage, descendants of those slaves. They are the political and professional leaders in the islands. Places like the plantation that once produced cane above Cane Garden Bay are one of the few reminders of the past.

It had taken us less than a half hour to motor over to the bay in the police cruiser, the *Wahoo*, a twenty-foot Boston Whaler with two 150-horsepower Yamaha engines. Snyder took advantage of every one of the horses. I'd need a chiropractor to adjust the vertebrae I was sure had been jarred out of alignment when he'd hit a couple of swells hard, head-on. No finessing or reading the water for this guy. It was gung ho all the way. Next time I'd make sure to take the wheel.

Fifteen or twenty boats were anchored in the harbor. We spotted the *Wind Runner* easily. She was flying an American flag and was the only thirty-two-footer with the yellow-and-blue SeaSail logo on its bow. One of Peter O'Brien's boats.

I got the bumpers out of the locker and tied them to the side cleats just in time to keep Snyder from banging up the side of the boat. He came roaring in, oblivious to the boats he left pitching in his wake. He turned and throttled back at the last minute, sliding up to the *Wind Runner* and sending a spray of water over her rail. The guy was just a maniac.

"Jesus, Snyder, maybe you should slow down a bit."

"I can be doin' dat," he said, shrugging his shoulders, hanging his head.

I'd actually hurt his feelings. I had a sensitive eighteen-year-old speed demon on my hands. Apparently he considered his boating technique one to be admired. This must be the island equivalent of the kid laying rubber down the middle of Main Street, girlfriend looking on.

Snyder cut the engine and we tied our lines to the *Wind Runner*'s cleats.

"Ahoy, on *Wind Runner*," Snyder called.

"Hello," a woman called as she stepped up from below deck.

"Police," I said. "Responding to a call from Patricia Robsen?"

"Yes, I'm Trish Robsen. I'm so glad you're here. Please come aboard."

Snyder was already over the rail and standing in the cockpit while I was still trying to figure out how to keep from looking like a complete klutz getting from the motorboat up into the sailboat. He picked up on my dilemma and offered me a hand.

"I can handle it," I said.

I was really getting kind of crabby. Pissed, actually, at Dunn, for hooking me up with this kid. I stepped on the side of the motorboat, grabbed the metal railing, and pulled myself up and in.

Trish Robsen was attractive, maybe forty-five, and about ten pounds overweight. She reminded me of my sister—always on a diet, trying to recover the prekids figure—pregnancy, childbirth, and the subsequent temptations of cupboards full of Twinkies. It made me mad. She cooked, drove kids to piano lessons and soccer, worked at a law office, never had a minute of her own, and was still supposed to look like Christy Brinkley.

Trish wore shorts over her swimming suit and sported one of those transparent visors that said *Wet and Wild* across the bill. Somehow I didn't think it was an accurate description of Trish Robsen.

She insisted on bringing us lemonade and cookies. I went below to help her. It was a compact little boat, one cabin, one head, and the salon with galley. Everything was neatly stowed and immaculate. No dirty dishes in the sink, no wet towels piled on the seats.

"Nice boat," I said, trying to fill the silence.

"All I've been doing since dawn is cleaning," she said. "Trying to keep my mind off of Allen."

We brought glasses, a pitcher of lemonade, and cookies up top. Snyder, who looked like he'd dozed off in the cockpit, immediately perked up. He had finished his first cookie before Trish had even poured the lemonade. Cookies and lemonade didn't do it for me. A lot like drinking beer and eating chocolate cake. Yuck.

I have to admit, though, it was nice—more than nice—sitting on a boat in this glassy harbor, sun shimmering off the water, gulls circling, sipping lemonade. I'd have to rub it in when I talked to Mack. The last time I'd interviewed a victim, it had been in a run-down 7-Eleven near Coors Field in Denver.

Trish was trying hard not to appear to be an overreacting spouse, but she had twisted her napkin into a tight knot and wasn't touching her lemonade.

"Why don't you tell me what's going on, Mrs. Robsen," I said, leaving an opening for her to vent. She obviously needed to get down to business and talk.

"Please call me Trish," she said. "Allen never came back to the boat last night. I'm really worried. I've imagined everything from shark attack to heart attack. He never stays out without calling to let me know where he is. Then it's only getting in late, working on a project, heavy game of poker with the guys. In the entire twenty-five years of our marriage, I could count the number of times that's happened on one hand," she said, holding up five fingers to emphasize her point.

I was about to mention that it might be a little hard to call her on the boat unless he had access to a radio and she left the boat radio on all night, but she was a step ahead of me.

"We have a boat phone," she said. "Calls are expensive, but I just can't handle being out of touch so completely with our kids and grandkids. If there's an emergency, I want them to be able to get ahold of us."

"When did you last see your husband?" I pulled out my pen and notebook. Snyder, in the process of inhaling his fourth cookie, was way too busy to write.

"Last night about ten-thirty, eleven o'clock. We were over on the *Calypso*." She pointed to a beautiful two-masted yacht across the bay.

"What were you doing over there?"

"An impromptu get-together. We'd been dining at the Pelican on shore," she said.

"I be knowin' da place. Best reggae music on da island," Snyder said. "You heard dat song, 'Dancin' on da Reef'? Owner of da Pelican done wrote dat song." Snyder actually started singing the song and strumming an imaginary guitar. Jesus. I couldn't believe that Dunn had paired me with this ditzy kid.

"Snyder, let's let Mrs. Robsen tell us what happened, okay?" I said, trying to keep from yelling at him.

"I can be doin' dat." Damned if I hadn't hurt his feelings again.

"We went in with the Manettis. They're on the forty-foot SeaSail," Trish said, gesturing to the boat anchored about seventy feet off the bow. "We'd heard great things about the reggae musician there. He is fantastic. He sang 'Dancing on the Reef,'" she said, smiling at Snyder. Typical mother, I thought. Trying to make the kid feel better.

"We got to talking with some of the other boaters in the restaurant. Sharing adventures, the best anchorages, good places to eat. One of the other sailors, Guy Pembrook, over on the *Calypso*, mentioned that he is selling his boat. Of course, Allen's ears perked up. He's boat-crazy. The Pembrooks invited us all over to the *Calypso* for nightcaps. Guy Pembrook and Allen got involved in talking about boats. He wanted to see every nook and cranny of the *Calypso*, not that we could ever afford a boat like that. I think one of the other fellows was seriously interested.

"I hitched a ride back to our boat with the Manettis so that Allen could come back in our dinghy. He never came home."

"Maybe he's still over on da *Calypso*," Snyder said as he chomped on yet another cookie. "Dat look like one nice place to lay your head."

"He's not. I took a morning swim over there. Elizabeth Pembrook said Allen had left about one-thirty. She said some of them were going back to shore to continue the party, but I searched the dock with the binoculars. Our dinghy is not tied up there."

"Who was at the party?" I asked.

"Allen and I, the Manettis, and two couples from Texas on another boat. I'm not sure which one. Is it important?"

"I'll need to talk to them. Maybe they know where

your husband went. Maybe he's on their boat, or maybe they all crashed under a palm tree on the beach," I said.

"I hope you're right," she said. She didn't believe it, though.

"Tell me about this trip. How long you've been down here, where you've been."

"This was an anniversary gift to each other—our twenty-fifth. A month sailing in the Virgin Islands. We've been down here three weeks. Sailed around St. John and down to St. Croix the first ten days. Now we're sailing around the BVI. We've been anchored in Cane Garden Bay for the past five nights. Going out for day sails and relaxing on the boat and on the beach.

"We've done a lot of sailing at home in Vermont. This was the dream trip. Allen is in computers; he's worked hard, done well. Our kids are all grown—three, a boy and two girls. We wanted to take some time for ourselves. Now this."

"He probably went to shore and decided to stay put for the night. Anyone he might have stayed with?" I asked.

"No, of course not," she said. But she'd hesitated.

"I'll talk to the Pembrooks, do some checking on shore," I said. "What does your husband look like?"

"He's five-eleven, about a hundred and eighty pounds. He's in good shape, watches the calories. Grayish-green eyes, brown hair, starting to gray at the temples. Has the most wonderful smile," she said, her voice softening.

"Do you remember what he was wearing last night?"

"Tan shorts and tennis shoes, a T-shirt, new. It's one of those with a chart of the islands on the front of it. He bought it in the market over in Road Town."

She went below and found a photo, she and Allen standing on a sun-drenched beach holding hands.

"Thanks. I'll get this back to you. Try not to worry. He'll probably be back before dark."

I'd bet that Allen had found some willing woman to spend the night with. After twenty-five years and three kids, it might be hard for Trish Robsen to admit betrayal.

Chapter 6

The *Calypso* was a completely restored fifty-foot wooden schooner that had received meticulous care. Two wooden masts, the one in back taller than the one in front, jutted into the air. A wooden bowsprit, netting draped off it, pointed out in front. Brass fittings sparkled in the sun, polished to a rich hue. The boat had to be in the $2 million category, probably more. It would be beautiful under sail. Now the sails were nestled under sail covers. Radar was attached to the aft mast. Ropes crisscrossed and draped gracefully through antique pulleys and around brass winches. A wind generator did lazy circles in the breeze.

A woman was sunning on deck. When she heard our boat approaching, she stood up, naked and seemingly unconcerned. She took her time pulling on a suit. I wondered why she bothered. It didn't cover much. Strings held up little patches of material in vital places. Two tiny fluorescent pink triangles served only to decorate ample breasts; two more made up the bottom—one in front, one in back. But I guess she could get away with it. She was about twenty-seven, beautiful and knew it.

I had insisted on taking the wheel. Good thing. Snyder's eighteen-year-old hormones were out of control. He would never have been able to conduct the maneuver at which he'd been so adept back at the Robsens' boat. At the moment he was trying to nonchalantly cover the bulge in his pants. I motored to the back of the boat, and Snyder managed to throw her the line, which she tied to a cleat. We stepped onto the back transom and then let the motorboat drift back.

"I'm Detective Sampson, Tortola Police Department. This is Deputy Snyder," I said.

"Hi, Elizabeth Pembrook. Is there a problem, Officer?" she asked, directing an amused smile Snyder's way.

"Trish Robsen called us about her husband."

"Oh, that," she said. "Yes, she was over here looking for him this morning. I told her he wasn't here. Can't believe she called the police. Hubby's probably sleeping it off somewhere. Don't know how we can help you."

Just then a man staggered topside from below deck. He looked like he had just gotten up: dark hair, a few flecks of gray at the temples, chin with a three-day stubble. He had a coffee cup in one hand, a cigarette in the other. Definitely hungover. He was shirtless, wearing a red spandex Speedo that outlined more than I wanted to see. He had a body that he clearly worked to maintain. He was about five-ten, deeply tanned, and his hair had been styled by a pro. He gave the impression of a man who had grown up with money, didn't even think about it or know that there was any other way to live.

"Guy, this is Detective . . . Samuels, is it?" she asked, doubtful.

"Sampson," I replied, "and Deputy Snyder."

"Hi, Guy Pembrook," he said, holding out his hand. "Afraid I just got up. Kind of a late night."

"They're looking for one of the guys who was here last night. Didn't go back to his boat. What was his name?" she asked, turning toward me.

"Robsen, Allen Robsen." I was beginning to think that Mrs. Pembrook had either done a few too many drugs or was plain dumb. Or maybe she was just good at playing the role.

"Do you know what time he left?" I asked.

"Musta been about one-thirty, give or take," Guy said.

"Do you know where he was going?"

"Seemed like he planned to head into shore," he said. "Meeting a couple of the others."

"Who was at the party?"

"Started out with the Robsens and the Manettis over on the *Celebration*. And the two couples from the *Dallas*. The Manettis and Trish Robsen left early. Took the other two women back to the *Dallas*."

"Only woman who hung in there was Ursala," Elizabeth said.

"Ursala?"

"Ursala and Frank Downing came over later," Guy said. "Live up on the hill in the big white house. We got into the Wild Turkey. Me, Robsen, the two guys from the *Dallas*, Ursala, and Frank."

"Yeah, Ursala was really putting the moves on Robsen," Elizabeth said. "Right in front of her husband, too. Frank didn't seem to care that much, though."

"Why would he," Guy asked her, "when he had you to flirt with?"

She gave him a look that said "get a life," but she didn't say anything. Odd couple, I thought. Not what I would call really connected, the way some married people are. I had the feeling that Elizabeth would never consider calling the police if Guy were out all night. Probably happened all the time.

"What time did everyone else leave?" I asked.

"Must have been around one, one-thirty, right before Robsen. They were all going to shore for a nightcap. Guess Robsen went. Last time I saw him he was motoring his dinghy toward the docks. He's probably shacked up with Ursala somewhere. She seems to be good at getting what she wants," Guy said.

"Do you know her well?" I asked.

"Met her the day we came into Cane Garden Bay. That'd be about a week ago. She tends to hit happy hour at one of the bars on the beach every day. I've watched her in action. She can really turn on the charm."

"How long will you be here?" I asked. I didn't want them sailing off into the sunset if I needed to talk to them again.

"Probably another week, maybe two. We've put the boat up for sale. Have a couple of interested buyers," Guy said.

"Really, why are you selling her? She's a beauty."

"Yeah, she is. Be hard to give her up. But it's time we headed back to the States. We bought her for this cruise, planning to sell her at the end. Been down here almost a year now," he said.

"Wow, nice vacation. Where have you sailed?" The Pembrooks had to have a bundle. Buying a boat like this. Taking off for a year. Now I was curious.

"Been sailing up the Caribbean from Venezuela, though the Windwards and Leewards. Really a working vacation. I'm a writer. Been working on a kind of nature lover's guide to the Caribbean. We spend as long as we need in a location, mapping out trails, photographing and gathering information on the animals and plants on each island. Time to go back and put it together. Publisher is clamoring for the finished manuscript. Last one I did was *The Nature Lover's Guide to the Hawaiian Islands*."

"Sounds like nice work if you can get it," I said.

"Damned straight. I can write all the travel off as expenses."

"Thanks for your time, Mr. Pembrook. I'll look forward to reading your book."

"No problem," he said.

He helped me into the boat, brushing against my breast. Snyder climbed in after me, I fired up the engine, and Pembrook threw Snyder the line.

"Those be unusual folks," Snyder said.

"What do you mean?" I was surprised that Snyder had noticed anything but Elizabeth's cleavage.

"Dat man doesn't seem like he be sitting around with a pen in his hand all da time."

I had to give Snyder credit: I'd been thinking the same thing. The Pembrooks looked highly successful. But I would have never pegged Guy Pembrook as a published author. And a nature writer at that. He didn't strike me as someone with that kind of discipline. He looked more like a rich playboy.

We swung by the Manettis' boat. No one aboard. I made a note to check back with them, but I figured Robsen would show up before then. The *Dallas* was easy to locate. It was the only boat in the harbor with a Texas flag the size of a small sail flying off the back.

Jack Rodriguez, skipper and owner, did most of the talking. Allen Robsen had not slept it off on their boat. Rodriguez and his sailing buddy Bill Andrews had stayed on the *Calypso* about an hour after their wives had returned to the *Dallas*. Rodriguez said he was seriously considering buying the *Calypso*. From the looks of it, I'd say he could probably afford it. A diamond the size of a quarter sparkled from his wife's finger, complemented by matching necklace and earrings. Yachting jewels, no doubt. God knows what she wore to a Dallas soiree.

"Got kind of lit drinking those damn Turkey shooters. Should have known better," Rodriguez was saying. "Paying for it today, but what the hell, we're on vacation, right?"

"What time did you leave?"

"Damned if I know. Time wasn't too important. Bill and me headed back to shore, though. Figured on a nightcap over at the Beach Bar. The band was still playing and it was swinging in there."

"The boys staggered back to the boat about three A.M.," Rodriguez's wife said. I could see she was pissed. "Next time we'll be dragging their asses home with us. Whole day is shot. We'd planned to sail to St. Thomas today. Julie and I are tired of these damned isolated island paradises. The shops in St. Thomas are supposed to be unbelievable."

Christ, I thought, come all the way to the islands to shop? I'd never been able to relate to the compulsion. I'd rather go to the dentist than be surrounded by the crowds in St. Thomas engaged in purchasing frenzies. I'd read about the place. Three or four cruise ships and dozens of jumbo jets deposit thousands of tourists on St. Thomas. Traffic snarls the roads, resorts dominate the beaches, and the crime rate is high. To their credit, the citizens of St. Thomas are beginning to speak out against crime, corruption, and further development. But there was no contest with this pristine anchorage. I could see that Bill and Jack were thinking the same thing.

"Did Allen Robsen go in to shore with you?" I asked.

"No, he was still on the *Calypso*. Pembrook was showing him around. They were going below deck when we left. Robsen said he'd probably just head back to his boat."

"Guy Pembrook said he thought he had gone in to shore."

"Huh. Well, maybe he changed his mind."

"What about Ursala and Frank Downing?" I asked.

"Frank came into the bar not long after we got there. Said Ursala had gone home. He had one drink and left. Seemed kind of pissed off. Probably at Ursala. She was really putting the moves on Robsen all evening."

"Did you see Ursala again that night?"

"No, she never came into the bar, and we headed back to our boat after the place shut down."

"If you happen to run into Robsen, tell him he needs to call his wife. She's worried," I said.

We headed to shore, tied up at the dock, and checked around. No one could tell us much. "Dem tourists, day all looks alike" was the general reply.

The Beach Bar was quiet when Snyder and I walked in. A man and woman at a corner table were hunched over a late breakfast. Empty Bloody Mary glasses littered their table. It didn't look like the drinks were helping. The woman was ashen and kept rubbing her temple, while her companion pushed food around his plate with his fork.

A woman worked behind the bar washing glasses. We pulled up bar stools and Snyder got real official.

"I am Deputy Snyder. This is Detective Sampson. Tortola Police."

She wasn't impressed. She said she'd worked last night. She didn't tell us anything that we didn't already know. The two guys from the *Dallas* had been there until closing.

"So were dem folks in the corner. Jeez, they were lit. Can't believe they made it outta bed at all today."

"Was this man in here last night?" I asked, showing her the picture of Robsen that Trish had given me.

"Naw, never seen him before."

I asked to use her phone. One last place to look. I figured Robsen would find his way home by himself anyway.

She pointed the way. I thumbed through the phone book and found the Downings' number. After three rings, a woman answered.

"Downing residence," she said.

She told me that the Downings were not at home. They'd both been gone when she'd gotten there. And no, no one else was there either.

I'd done what I could. Robsen hadn't even been missing for twenty-four hours. I was sure he'd come stumbling back to his boat, contrite, before dark.

Hell, he could have headed over to Road Town or anywhere else on the island. More than likely he had shacked up in some quiet bungalow for the night.

I felt sorry for Trish Robsen, but marital infidelity was not a crime.

Chapter 7

When Snyder and I got back to the office, the deputies assigned to the recent spate of robberies had their heads together in the far corner.

Snyder did the introductions. "Detectives Mahler, Stark, and Worthington."

The only one who bothered to get up and offer his hand was Mahler. He was the oldest of the three. Lighter skinned, more Latin influence. He was a compact man, thick, hairy arms, no neck, wavy jet-black hair. He was about my height, five-seven, but carrying fifty or sixty more pounds. He had to weigh in at 175 at least, mostly muscle with a little padding.

"How is the investigation going?" I asked them.

"It's goin'." Stark's voice resonated from somewhere deep. He was the biggest of the three, and his head reflected light like highly polished bronze. What he lacked on his head was made up for on his chin, the beard a mass of Brillo. A pair of sunglasses perched precariously on his shiny head. He wore a black tank top, one small gold chain out of proportion around his thick neck, a pair of tan Dockers, and sandals.

He was the only one of the three who didn't wear a

wedding band. He looked like a well-placed drug dealer, not a cop. I suppose that was the intent. The guy had an icy presence that put me on edge. He was openly hostile, yet distant and uninterested—an attitude I was amazed could be pulled off simultaneously by one person. Stark was a natural.

"Any leads?" I asked.

"Couple." The guy obviously wasn't interested in sharing. He was crushing a cigarette into an ashtray, twisting it until it was a pile of tobacco, and smirking at me.

"Be glad to help if I can. Worked that beat for years in Denver." I should have quit while I was still only slightly behind.

"We don't be needin' any help. Think we some stupid black folk from the sticks? Can't handle a case like you hotshots in the U.S.?" This was Worthington. He was the antithesis of Stark, a swarthy guy with tightly cropped hair, plaid short-sleeved shirt, brown polyester pants, and wing-tipped shoes. He couldn't maintain the cool hostility that Stark had perfected. Worthington was ready for combat.

"Jeez, no, I—"

"Just be stayin' out of our way," Worthington said. The two of them walked out without another word.

"Don't worry about them," Mahler said. "They'll come around. They're not used to having outsiders in the department." He seemed to be speaking from experience.

"What about you?"

"I'm a down-islander, born in St. Kitts. That makes me a nonbelonger, but I've lived here since I was a child. Takes some time to be accepted in the islands."

I guess I couldn't blame Stark and Worthington. What place did a white American woman have in their office? I hoped Dunn knew what he'd been doing when he'd asked me to join the department. He'd said it would take time for them to accept me but assured me that they would. Now I wasn't so sure.

"I didn't like you when I met you either," Dunn said a little later when I mentioned my concern. He was sitting at his desk, buried in paper.

"Well, thanks a lot," I said.

"You were an American nosing around in island affairs. But you're determined and smart. They will learn to respect you, maybe even like you," he said. "Now, anything on that missing tourist?"

"Nothing yet."

I planned to call Trish later, in the afternoon. I was sure that Robsen would turn up by then. I could see it now. He'd be in big trouble. He and Trish would not be talking to each other. What a way to ruin a twenty-fifth-anniversary vacation. I wondered how people got past such things. Would she forgive him? Would they cut things short and go home?

I decided to fill the time poring over the notices that Snyder had collected to get me up to speed on recent events in the islands. On the top of the stack was a notice about modern-day pirating, for chrissake. Someone, probably Snyder, had drawn a skull and crossbones in the margin.

As I read the report, I learned that boaters in the southern Caribbean disappear regularly, maybe one every year or two. Officials believe these people are lost at sea, perhaps in a storm or some other mishap that wrecks the boat. Most are not reported missing for weeks, until family or friends begin to worry when they are overdue at home or work.

Sailors in small craft out in the open sea sometimes ram a whale or smash into a huge piece of debris and sink. But officials in the southern islands get suspicious when no signs of wreckage ever appear, not even a life preserver or boat cushions.

With no better explanation, conjecture turns to piracy. It wasn't unheard-of for someone to commandeer a boat, take on the identity of the owners, run up their charge cards, and live high for a few months, then abandon the boat in some crowded port.

The report included a list of missing vessels, the boat name, owner name, description. Seven in all during the past five years. Law enforcement was asked to keep an eye out for these boats, but warned that they would likely be drastically changed—painted and renamed. Maybe gone entirely, lying at the bottom of the sea. I got the feeling no one spent much time looking. It would be like searching for the needle in a haystack with the thousands of coves and inlets in the islands.

Other police issues included domestic violence, reports of public nuisance, drunkenness, prostitution, and, of course, drugs. There were several sheets of statistics. Evidently drug use in the Caribbean is below international averages. About 3.7 percent of the population uses illicit drugs annually. Makes sense. I mean, who would need to alter their reality in paradise? I knew this was simplistic, and that people here suffered just as they did on the streets of L.A. or New York, but damn, I hoped I'd never again have to bust ten-year-olds selling on their own private street corner or arrest kids shooting up in alleys.

But while the Caribbean didn't have an active drug abuse problem, law enforcement did have other issues to deal with. Heroin, cocaine, and marijuana have been transported through the Caribbean for decades, coming from Latin America and destined for markets in Europe and North America. Huge quantities come from Colombia where drug syndicates refine 80 percent of the world's cocaine. After the September 11 terrorist attack on the United States, illegal trafficking through the Caribbean increased some 25 percent because DEA officers were pulled out of drug interdiction and pressed into antiterrorism patrols. Drug traffickers took good advantage of the opportunity.

Drugs are moved in boats and airplanes, in baggage, in postal and express parcels, taped around people's bodies, or sewn in clothing. Snyder's stack of reports detailed many instances of drug arrests. One woman was caught in the airport in St. Thomas with four bundles of cocaine wrapped in aluminum foil and taped around her waist. The foil set off the metal detectors. Last month off the coast of Puerto Rico, three thousand pounds of cocaine were found on a boat, hidden in fishing buoys. Another report detailed the interception of 2.75 tons of cocaine on a speedboat headed for a rendevous with a cohort on an ocean liner bound for the United States. No wonder programs like *Miami Vice* could run for so many years. The material was endless, the techniques creative.

I thumbed to the reports about the break-ins on Tortola. Most had occurred on the northeast end of the island. The one at Capoone's Bay, one in Belmont, two at Apple Bay, several in the hills above Cane Garden Bay—at Arundel, Shannon, Mayaba. Though the robberies were all in the same general location, the character of the crimes was markedly different. Or maybe the perpetrators were getting smarter, more assured, and more violent.

All but one of the earlier break-ins occurred when the

residents were away. The stuff taken in those heists ranged from TVs and VCRs to Game Boys and computers. One victim had lost his high-tech stereo system and every CD he owned, some five hundred.

Recently some of the incidents had occurred when residents were home, around dinnertime. They targeted the wealthiest on the island. The thieves actually rang the bell and when the door opened they pushed their way in, armed, nylon stockings pulled over their faces. They'd locked their victims in bathrooms or garages and taken jewelry and money. They'd been selective, only the good stuff. Surely the detectives had seen the pattern. I was marking the locations, dates, and MOs on a map when Dunn came in.

"Come on, Sampson. Some snorkelers found a body out at Sandy Cay. Snyder's loading the scuba tanks on the boat."

Dunn's insistence that he needed an experienced dive investigator on the force was about to be put to the test. Before I'd been brought in, one of the local rescue divers would have been called in to bring the body up, without any consideration of the crime scene. Any evidence that might have existed would not have been identified. I guess hiring me was progress. A few years ago Dunn would have never even considered such a move. But paradise had changed since then.

Forty-five minutes later we dropped anchor at Sandy Cay, a tiny lump of land with a few palm trees, fringed with a white beach and surrounded by turquoise water. It is just off of Jost Van Dyke, an island about five miles northwest of Tortola. Five or six sailboats were anchored on the southwest side. As we got closer, we could see a bunch of people standing on the beach; no one was in the water.

We anchored next to a huge catamaran in about fifteen feet of water, loaded my dive gear into the dinghy, and motored to shore. Snyder expertly maneuvered it onto the beach and we got out without even getting our feet wet. Good thing. Dunn was wearing his black dress shoes, his tie, and a jacket. That was Dunn. He was incongruous, stepping out of the dinghy and onto the sand. Everyone else on the beach was in bikinis and swim trunks. But Dunn was not the kind of man one laughed at. He had a presence. Made everyone else feel inappropriately attired.

The tourists on the beach were all talking at once, one couple in French, everyone else in English. A couple of people were a bit hysterical, and one woman was trying to soothe a little girl of about seven and keep her ten-year-old boy out of the water at the same time.

"Okay, okay. How about one person do the talking here," Dunn said, looking at a man in green swim trunks who appeared to be calmer and more reasonable than some of the others.

"Kid came swimming in yelling that there was a dead man out in the water," he said, pointing to the boy still trying to wrestle out of his mother's grip. "Couple of us swam out. It's a body, all right. Over on the reef, caught in the coral, maybe twenty-five feet down."

"Anybody disturb anything out there?" I asked.

"No, we took a look. Saw the kid was right and swam back to shore. I took my dinghy over to my boat and radioed in."

"What about you, kid? You touch anything out there?" I asked. The kid was a brat, alternately whining about going swimming and bragging about how he found the guy.

"No way," he said. "I've seen those detective shows.

Never s'posed to touch the evidence. Can I go with you when you get him?" The fact that this was a dead man didn't seem to bother him at all. Typical ten-year-old. Too many video games.

"'Fraid not. Just do what your mom says and stay out of the water," I said, maybe a tad too harshly.

Dunn shot me a look that said "watch yourself, Sampson." I ignored it.

I donned my wet suit and attached the buoyancy control vest, or "BC," to the tank. Once in the water, I would release air from the BC vest so that I could descend. On the bottom I would regulate the air in the vest so that I could hover just above the bottom. Next I hooked my regulator with alternate to the tank and the vest. The alternate is an extra regulator that allows another diver to share air if he or she has equipment failure.

Snyder helped me into the vest. I opened the air valve and breathed through the mouthpiece. I'd done this so many times that I didn't even think about it, but the mechanics of preparation always calmed me. I'd done hundreds of dives. Before every one, I developed a tiny knot in the pit of my stomach. You'd think by now I'd be used to it. But breathing underwater, whether at twenty-five feet or a hundred, was one of the most unnatural things that humans did. This was for animals with gills, for chrissake. And I never knew what I might encounter. I have never lost sight of the dangers. The divers who do are the ones who die.

I lumbered out and sat in the sand in about three feet of water, pulled on my fins, spit in my mask and rinsed it out to keep it from fogging, snugged it in place, rolled over, and swam out. With a couple of kicks, I was twenty feet from shore, descending as I went. Yellowtail snappers and sergeant majors followed me out.

Diving in crystal-clear water feels a lot like flying, soaring above the ocean floor. Here the bottom started out sandy. I scared up a flounder that had been camouflaged in the sand. I could see the trails made by several huge conchs that were making their way to God knows where. Soon the sandy bottom gave way to turtle grass, the occasional sea cucumber or starfish hidden in the stems.

Another few yards and I was at the coral reef. An orange, yellow, purple, and green tapestry of sponges and algae mingled with the coral. Purple sea fans, with striped snails attached to their lacework, swayed in the water. A couple of angelfish swimming through an outstretched golden elkhorn coral were chased away by a damselfish.

I swam around a towering pillar coral and over an octopus hidden in an old conch. Scattered around it were scores of broken shells, the remains of his most recent meal.

The spell of the underworld was hypnotizing. I'd almost forgotten why I was down there. Until I swam right into the face of the dead man.

I pushed away, trying to put some distance between me and the corpse in the water next to me. Suddenly this was a lonely place to be—the only human in an expanse of ocean with death alongside. Dunn and the others standing on a sun-drenched beach right now seemed a world away—out of touch, sight, hearing. A body floating in the water was just a damned horrible thing.

After a moment, my panic subsided. I shifted into automatic and did my job, carefully observing everything around me, gathering preliminary impressions without disturbing the scene.

The guy was wearing shorts and a T-shirt that had a

chart of the BVI on it, with a long-sleeved plaid shirt, unbuttoned, over it. The T-shirt was pulled up on one side, revealing the chest, gashed by coral. The wounds were being nibbled on by fish. His right arm was bent at the elbow, the back of his hand over his mouth as if he were trying to stifle a scream or bite back pain. His left arm was outstretched, swaying in the current. On his finger a gold wedding band reflected rippled light. He wore tennis shoes without socks. One foot was wedged between two coral heads, the ankle worn to the bone. A rope with the dinghy anchor attached was wrapped around his other ankle, but it had not been heavy enough to hold him in the place he'd been dumped. Instead, he'd drifted with the current into the reef.

There was a small hole in his forehead. This was clearly no drowning. He'd been dead when he went into the water. The small anchor had not been enough weight to send the body to the bottom. It looked like it had washed into the reef with the current. It might have just as easily missed this little cay. Once past Jost Van Dyke it was open ocean all the way to Florida. He'd have simply disappeared. There were few places better than the ocean for dumping a body. Bad luck for whoever dumped him that he'd gotten caught in the coral.

I had a feeling that Allen Robsen was no longer missing.

Chapter 8

I left the body where it was and swam back to shore. I needed my underwater camera, an evidence bag, and a body bag. I would photograph the scene, then search the surrounding area for anything that might provide a clue. I'd once found a shotgun lying about ten feet from a victim. Amazing how stupid people can be. Traced the gun easily to the owner and that was that. Guess he thought we'd never find either the body or the gun.

I figured we probably wouldn't be that lucky this time. But there was no telling what might turn up. I'd want the boat right up top. Not cool to bring a body to shore, especially among a bunch of people on vacation. The kid would be disappointed.

Dunn helped me out of my BC and tank as I gave him the rundown.

"It looks like Allen Robsen," I said. "From Trish Robsen's description, I'd say it's him out there."

"Okay," Dunn said. "Let's get the body up."

We motored the dinghy back out to the police boat. I grabbed the camera and a net bag, attached a fresh tank to my BC, and rolled backward off the boat into the water. Dunn had radioed the coroner. He would be out, bringing another diver to help me retrieve the body.

The victim was visible from the surface in the crystal water. I started down, releasing air from my BC as I descended. When I was about ten feet from the body, I began photographing the scene, moving in closer with the wide-angle lens to place the body in context. Then I photographed the body from every angle and took close-ups of the wounds. No telling what kind of damage might occur once the body was bagged and hauled into the boat and then to the coroner's. I wanted accurate documentation.

I noted the depth, thirty-three feet, and water temperature, eighty-two degrees. I'd get coordinates from the GPS on the boat.

That done, I began to slowly check out the surrounding area. The sea floor dropped off gently to the deep ocean floor. I could see some big fish swimming out there, a barracuda, an amberjack, a couple of permits.

I moved in for a closer look at the immediate area, shining my light in crevices and under coral ledges. I scared an eel that quickly retreated into his hole. A trumpet fish, long and skinny, hovered vertically nearby, camouflaged among branching soft coral waiting for lunch to swim by. The reef was alive with fish, blue tangs, French angels, parrot fish, squirrelfish, and spotted drums.

I didn't really expect to find much among the sea life. I was pretty sure that the body had drifted in. Anything that was dumped with it could wash up anywhere or more than likely sink into oblivion.

I worked in circles, moving farther and farther out from the body. At first I thought the brown spot in the sand was a rock, but as I moved closer I could see that the shape was too regular. It was a wallet. Must have washed out of the victim's pocket. Unless, of course, it had fallen off a boat or some swimmer had jumped in, forgetting to remove it from his pocket.

I picked it up and opened it. A driver's license with a photo of a smiling Allen Robsen. I placed the wallet in my evidence bag, finished the sweep, and headed back to examine the body.

I had little doubt that the small circular wound in the head was a bullet hole. There was a deep gash in the knee. Maybe it had occurred when the victim had fallen after being shot, or maybe when he'd been tumbled overboard off a boat. Arms and legs were scraped. I'd seen enough of this sort of injury to know they were travel abrasions from the body being washed over the coral beds until it had caught. These lacerations are markedly different from defensive wounds that are usually deep cuts or blunt trauma injuries. Travel abrasions are like scuff marks from the skin being worn away. The coroner would look for pieces of sand or coral in these wounds as further confirmation of the source of injury.

All the wounds were in the process of being enlarged by hungry saltwater shrimp. A few sea lice were gathered around the nose and mouth. Based on the extent of feeding, I'd guess Robsen had been in the water no more than twelve hours. That meant he'd been killed shortly after leaving the *Calypso*. I'd retrieved bodies that had no flesh remaining after twelve hours, but that was when there was an abundance of crustaceans present in the water, which was not the case here.

Postmortem rigidity was consistent with the position of Robsen's body in the water, his torso twisted with the current. He'd been dumped in the water within an hour or two of death, before rigor mortis had a chance to set in.

I was just completing the visual examination when another diver approached. It was Edmund Carr. I'd met him during my investigation in January. He was a banker and an expert diver who volunteered for the island rescue team. I'd learned to trust Carr. He gave me the thumbs-up.

I had given Carr a few pointers in underwater investigation and evidence collection. Until then, as a rescue diver, he'd go down, find the victim, and bring him up. That was it. Now he understood the importance of careful observation and preservation of the crime scene. He let me take the lead, hovering nearby to assist.

First I gently moved Robsen's right arm from his face so that I could look at his watch. If we waited until he was brought to the surface, jarring, a change in water pressure, or any number of other factors might alter the evidence. It was a cheap digital with a canvas band that you could buy in any discount store. On the rim it indicated it was waterproof to twenty feet. It was flooded with salt water and had stopped at 2:17. Probably about a minute after the body had hit the water and sunk.

Although I was sure that Robsen was dead when he went in the water, I followed routine. I checked carefully around his head, looking for vomit or bloody foam, signs of drowning. Robsen's jaw was open slightly. I shone my light inside, checking for inhaled bottom debris or vegetation. I could see bits of sea grass and algae around his teeth that I was sure had been washed in by the current. His jaw resisted when I pushed it closed to preserve the contents of his mouth for closer examination.

Carr and I enclosed Robsen's head and hands in

plastic bags and secured them with a Velcro strap; then Carr carefully pulled the victim's foot out from between the coral. He'd be as concerned about damaging the coral as he would about tearing flesh. Carr, like most of the local divers, had a tremendous respect for the fragile reef. It took decades for coral to develop, and the big ones here were centuries old.

We had to force the arms alongside the body in order to get it into the body bag. God, I hated this. The left arm, well established in its outstretched rigor, resisted. I could feel the weird stubbornness of the death posture shift subtly right before the limb gave way.

We placed the body into a yellow canvas bag that had mesh vents to allow the water to drain out. Underwater, the average adult male weighs between nine and sixteen pounds. Robsen was no exception. Carr and I swam easily to the surface, with the body between us. Dunn and Snyder were waiting to pull it into the boat. They hefted the bag in, careful not to bang it against the side.

Carr and I climbed in after.

"Good to see you, Hannah," Carr said. It was the first time since we'd seen each other below the surface that we'd actually been able to speak. All our communication had been through hand signals.

"Thanks for your help down there, Ed," I said as we struggled out of our dive gear.

"You know who the guy is?"

"Yeah, wife reported him missing this morning."

"Amazing how the sea sometimes gives up its dead so quickly," he said. "Other times she holds on forever."

I knew that Carr had lost a couple friends years ago. Evidently they'd gone out on a dive and never returned. The boat was found floating bottom up, but no sign was ever found of either of the divers.

The coroner unzipped the body bag as I knelt on the other side. A few sea creatures scattered as he gently pulled the plastic bag off of Robsen's head. I asked him to examine the eyes before the dry air altered their appearance. Again, standard procedure. If the eyes were open after death and exposed to air, a film would form on the cornea. If closed after death or if the victim was immediately submerged in water, the eyes would retain a glistening appearance.

Normally I would have examined them myself, but I didn't want to alienate a man I'd want to work with me. As he carefully pulled the eyelids open, I leaned in for a closer look. I could see a horizontal line between the clear and cloudy areas on Robsen's cornea. Just one more indication he'd died on land. Again, nothing too surprising. Not too many people could survive a bullet to the brain. The small round hole was even more apparent above water. He replaced the plastic bag around the head, zipped up the body bag, and stood.

"I've seen enough," he said. "Let's get him in for a closer look."

"Snyder, you go back with the coroner," Dunn said, starting up the *Wahoo*. "Come on, Detective Sampson. Let's go talk to Mrs. Robsen."

This was the absolute worst part of the job. I'd hoped to go back to Road Town with the body, but Dunn was right: I needed to accompany him to break the news to Trish Robsen.

As we approached it was clear she'd heard us coming. She was standing on the stern of *Wind Runner* ready to grab our lines.

"Did you find Allen?" she asked, a mixture of hope and dread in her voice.

"I'm afraid we did," I said.

She knew right away. She crumpled onto the cockpit bench, leaned over, head in hands, and rocked, whimpering quietly.

I went over and sat next to her. Put an arm around her. Let her cry it out. There wasn't anything to say. Never was. As soon as she got past the shock, she'd start asking questions. For some it took hours, for others minutes. I'd learned to just be there and wait it out.

Dunn went below and brought up a glass of water and a towel and sat down on the other side. He'd done this before too. Finally she took the towel from him, wiped her face, and then sipped the water.

"What happened? Where did you find him? How could this be? We were on vacation! I knew something was wrong when he didn't come back."

"Some snorkelers found him in the water over near Jost Van Dyke," Dunn said.

"In the water? You mean he drowned? Allen was an excellent swimmer. He wouldn't drown." She said it like people had choices in these things.

"It appears he was shot, Mrs. Robsen," Dunn said. "We can't be sure until the coroner examines him, but that's pretty much what it looks like."

"Shot! No one would shoot Allen. That's just not possible. How can you be sure it's him?" Time for hope to spring. More like denial. Almost always happened.

"We found his wallet, and the description matches yours as well as the picture on his driver's license. I'm afraid you'll have to come in to identify the body."

"All right," she said, standing, "let's go."

"You don't have to do it now," Dunn said. "Maybe you want to take it slow."

"No, now. I want to see Allen. Oh, God," she cried, sinking back on the bench. "Just give me a minute."

"Take all the time you want," I said. I understood why she wanted to go. She needed to connect with her husband, know it was real. See him. It wasn't something you could put off.

She went below quickly, came back up with a skirt on and carrying a pair of sandals. She glanced around the boat. Habit. Making sure everything was secure, then realized she didn't care. Dunn helped her into the police boat and we headed over to Road Town in silence.

When we got to the coroner's office, I went in first to make sure the body was presentable. Robsen was laid out on a cold metal table, even grayer and more ghostlike than he'd looked in the water. His lower body was damaged by sea life and coral, but his face was untouched except for the small hole in his forehead above the left eye. The bullet had not exited the back. It had to be a small caliber, probably a twenty-two. It would have hit the back of his skull and ricocheted around inside, slashing at brain tissue until it lost momentum. As I studied the face, a couple of sea lice crawled out of his mouth.

I told the coroner the wife was here. Asked him to get the body set up for viewing. He brushed the errant sea life off the face, stuffed cotton way up into the nose and mouth to keep anything else from escaping, and threw a sheet over the body.

I was sorry Trish had to see her husband the way he looked. She was a strong woman but this wasn't going to be easy for her. Dunn and I stood next to her as the coroner pulled the sheet off of his face.

She grasped the edge of the gurney to keep herself up. Disbelief and pain crossed her face. She didn't know what to do. I could see that she wanted to touch him. Finally she did, placing one hand on his chest and the other on his head, bending over him.

"Allen," she said, "what happened?" She looked at me for an answer.

All I could do was shake my head.

"I'm so sorry, Trish."

Dunn took her arm and led her out to a chair, where she hunched over, rambling on about Allen, the trip, how could this happen, she must be having a nightmare, they should have never come down here. "God," she said, "I wish we were home. Allen mowing the lawn or something. Me inside fixing lunch. How can I make it without him? We've been together practically our entire lives."

Her pain hung in the air, so thick I could practically touch it. I couldn't imagine how it would feel to lose a life mate. I'd never been lucky enough to find one. I'd been with Jake only two years when he'd died.

Finally she sat up, wiped her eyes, and tried to regain some control. "I've got to call home," she said. "What will I tell the children?" I could see she needed to connect with her family, the people she loved. Not be so alone. At the same time, she clearly dreaded it.

I helped her find a phone and get the international operator. I was about to leave her alone when she grabbed my arm and shook her head. She wanted me to stay with her.

She called her son. She didn't shed a tear as she spoke. I could tell her son was crying on the other end. She was comforting him. Telling him it would be okay. Typical parent, sucking it up even for her adult son. He planned to get the first flight down. I was glad she wouldn't be alone. She refused Dunn's offer to arrange a hotel for the night. She wanted to stay on her boat.

I brought her back over to Cane Garden Bay and got her settled on the *Wind Runner*. Although she insisted she was fine, I worried about leaving her alone. I could see the Manettis lounging in the cockpit of the *Celebration* and decided to stop.

"Anything wrong, Officer?" Manetti grabbed my line when I tossed it to him. Don Manetti was hairy chested, with a belly that hung over his shorts. A cigar hung out of the side of his mouth. At three-thirty, it was already cocktail time on the *Celebration*, looked like martinis.

I didn't bother to step aboard. I was anxious to get back to talk with the coroner and didn't want to play Twenty Questions with the Manettis.

"We found Trish Robsen's husband. He's dead."

"Dead?" Melissa Manetti was stunned. "My God, we never dreamed. We saw Trish earlier. She said he hadn't come home last night, but dead . . . What happened?"

"We're investigating. I'd like to come by and talk with you tomorrow morning, if that's okay." I asked them to look in on her and headed back to Road Town.

There was nothing else I could do except find out who killed her husband.

Chapter 9

I went straight back to the coroner's office. I figured I knew as much about forensic medicine as he did. In other words, nothing. He surprised me, though. He had already opened the chest and stomach cavity and was examining the stomach.

"Looks like the contents are only partially digested, well preserved in alcohol too. He died about four or five hours after his last meal. By the condition of the body, I'd say he was in the water twelve hours, maybe less."

I agreed. I'd brought enough victims out of the water to be familiar with the appearance, and his analysis matched my underwater observations. The photos had already been developed and were spread out on a nearby table.

"Pretty obvious what killed him. Bullet to the brain. Died right away. Probably never knew what hit him, though I guess he'd have seen it coming. It's a contact wound—gun was directly against the forehead. You can see the star pattern, kind of a circular pattern with radiating breaks."

"Did you get the bullet?"

"Yeah," he said, pulling the cylindrical object from a

tray. "It's a twenty-two-caliber. Amazing what a small hole it makes going in. Did a lot of rattling around in his head, though. Pretty typical—a twenty-two lacks velocity to penetrate the skull a second time; does lots of damage ricocheting inside instead."

"Any other injuries?" I asked. I wondered if Allen Robsen had fought for his life.

"Just postmortem, torn-up ankle from where his foot was wedged in the coral. Gash in the knee, abrasions, all occurred after death, mostly travel abrasions, as you guessed. Sharp pieces of coral and bits of sand embedded in the wounds."

"Did you find anything under his fingernails?" I asked.

"Nothing. No hair, no skin. Like I said, he probably had just seconds to react. Nothing indicates there was any struggle at all."

He motioned toward the dinghy anchor and line that now lay on a nearby table. "We'll have that anchor analyzed for prints."

Good luck, I thought. The chances of finding a print on that anchor were slim to none. Though in rare cases we'd been able to lift prints from firearms submerged for weeks, the chances of lifting suitable prints is slim, even with a fingerprint expert at the recovery site. In the case of this anchor? Christ, it was so severely pitted and corroded that I was sure there'd be no prints.

"What about his clothes? Anything there?"

"Haven't had a chance to look. Be my guest," he said, pointing to a pile on a nearby chair.

There wasn't much. A pair of khaki shorts, the white T-shirt with the chart of the BVI, a plaid overshirt. He probably put it on when it got cool in the evening. I pulled on a pair of latex gloves and checked the pockets in his shorts. Nothing but one of those utility gadget things with every tool known to man in one handy little device—needle-nose pliers, knife, file.

In the shirt pocket I found a scrap of soggy paper, glossy, beige. It had typing on it and a photograph but nothing distinguishable. The salt water had done its work. It was about four by four inches and looked like something torn out of a magazine. Could have been something that caught Robsen's interest the night he died or days before. Hell, it might have been in there when he'd packed the shirt for the trip.

His wallet was there too. I found his driver's license, charge cards, and $87. Clearly robbery had not been a motive. In a side pocket protected by one of those plastic folders were photos: a family shot of him and Trish with three grown kids, two girls and a boy; an old picture of the couple, arms around each other, dressed in formal attire, celebrating something.

I placed the wallet, its contents, and the torn slip of paper on the counter to dry out, and asked the coroner's assistant to take care of them. I'd seen enough. I headed back to the office. Stark, Mahler, and Worthington were there, hunched over a map of Tortola, doing the same thing I'd been doing earlier, marking the location of the break-ins.

"You guys are working late." I was trying to be sociable.

"Yeah," Stark mumbled.

"Finding a pattern?" I asked.

"Maybe." I was beginning to think that Stark was incapable of a sentence composed of more than one word.

Worthington just glared.

"Could be we're looking at more than one set of perpetrators, or else they've changed their approach. Last couple of times they've been armed, threatening residents instead of breaking in when folks are gone," Mahler said.

"Hear you got a murder on your hands." Worthington was gloating. "You need any help you just let us know. Between the three of us, we probably got forty years of experience." He was rubbing it in, my remark about having worked robbery.

I considered an acerbic comeback but refrained. At some point I would have to find a way to make a truce with these guys.

"I might just do that," I said, and left them to their mapping.

I booted up one of the two computers in the office. They were set up in a corner gathering dust. The BVI police shared information with the United States because of the proximity to the U.S. Virgins. St. John was within spitting distance, and a good portion of the tourism and offshore banking activity involved the United States.

I started with the Robsens. I didn't expect to find anything, so I wasn't surprised when I didn't. It seemed that the Robsens led the squeaky-clean life that Trish had indicated. Nothing on the Manettis either. Jack Rodriguez had two DUIs in the past couple of years—both dropped. All it takes is enough money and a good lawyer, I thought wryly. Rodriguez had both. Nothing on Guy Pembrook either. Not even jaywalking. Nothing in any of their backgrounds spelled murder.

It was apparent that Robsen had been killed the night of the party on the *Calypso* sometime after Trish had gone home and everyone had gone back to shore. The last time that the Pembrooks had seen him he'd been motoring to shore, but the Texans said he never showed up at the bar while they were there. Where had he gone after he'd left the *Calypso*? Had he met up with a woman or run into someone on shore?

If the coroner was right and he'd been killed four or five hours after eating, that would put it at somewhere around one or two in the morning. He'd left the *Calypso* at one-thirty. If he'd been in the water for somewhere around twelve hours, he'd been dumped shortly after being shot. The rigor mortis that had set in while he was in the water confirmed this.

If I could depend on the watch, he had been killed sometime between one-thirty and two-fifteen; then his body was loaded into a boat and driven out into open water. The postmortem gash to his knee could have occurred when his body was being loaded into a dinghy or motorboat, or when it was pushed overboard. Fiberglass dinghies have metal oarlocks on the gunwales where the oars attach. The wound could have come from one—it matched in size.

If Robsen's body hadn't drifted into Sandy Cay, it would probably have washed out to open water. What had happened to his dinghy? I wondered.

Who would want to kill a forty-five-year-old guy who was sailing in the islands with his wife? He didn't really know anyone. Had he seen something? Gotten involved with someone? Enough. I shut the computer down and called Mack in Denver.

"Hi, Sampson. You ready to come home yet?"

"Jeez, Mack. I just got here." Then I told him about the case.

"Your first day on the job and you've got a murder on your hands. So much for escaping the crime-ridden city."

I asked him to do some checking for me on Robsen,

Rodriguez, Manetti, and Pembrook. Mack had access to information that I couldn't get to in the islands. He'd call his friendly hacker, talk to couple of contacts and local law-enforcement types.

"No problem, Sampson." I knew Mack would have entire life stories on all four of them by tomorrow.

Stark was the only one still around when I left. He was studying the map, tapping a pencil on his desk, deep in contemplation.

"Night, Stark."

"Night," he said. I was surprised he'd responded. It was progress, anyway.

Sadie was stretched out at the end of the dock when I got home. O'Brien was sitting beside her, scratching her ear, his feet dangling in the water. I'd forgotten I'd invited him to dinner.

Sadie yelped and ran to meet me. O'Brien was a bit slower on the uptake.

"Hannah, don't look so sheepish. I saw John Dunn today. He said you were already up to your ears in a case. I had Marta put together something," he said, holding up a bag from which irresistible smells emanated. Marta was O'Brien's cook, more like a chef. She could make even conch fritters seem like a delicacy.

"Poached flounder," O'Brien said. God, not only was this man drop-dead gorgeous, but thoughtful as well.

We ate out on the deck, watching the sun set into the water while I told him about Allen and Trish Robsen.

"I don't like it when these things happen in the islands," he said. "How can a man sailing with his wife down here end up murdered? And the Robsens were chartering one of my boats. I don't understand it."

"What kind of information do you get when someone wants to charter one of your boats?"

"We ask them to fill out a sailing résumé, which includes questions about what kind of sailing the potential charterer has done, where, on what size boats, and who they have chartered with."

"I guess you'd have information on the Robsens, then."

"Sure. We can stop by the office tomorrow and Louis will pull the files."

It was a place to start, anyway. Maybe I'd find one small item in the file that would lead me to another small item and then another until I had a complete picture of the murder, an explanation of why a forty-five-year-old man with three kids on vacation in the Caribbean had ended up in the sea with a bullet in his head.

O'Brien and I were below doing dishes when a voice called from up top, "Hannah, you home?"

"Elyse, come on down." A pair of bare feet appeared on the steps, blue shorts, then the rest. Fatigue and something else, despair maybe, were written all over her face.

"What's wrong, Elyse?"

"Bad day. Hi, Peter." She smiled at O'Brien.

"You guys know each other?"

"Sure. Elyse's determination to save every animal in the sea has spilled over on me more than once."

"You okay, Elyse? You staying on your meds?" O'Brien asked.

"Jeez, every time I'm a little down or up, it's the first thing someone asks. Yes, for chrissake, I'm okay. And yes, I'm on my meds. I'm always on my meds. I had my blood levels checked today. Mary tweaked things a little."

"I'm sorry, Elyse," Peter said.

"Sorry, I didn't mean to snap at you. I know you're just concerned."

"So what's going on?" I asked.

"I was diving over on the *Rhone*, checking the condition of the reef life. While I was there I came across a shark lying on the bottom, bleeding. Its fins had been removed but it was still alive. It was awful. I just left it down there."

"Why the hell would anyone cut the fins off a shark?" I asked.

"For soup," both O'Brien and Elyse responded, amazed I wouldn't know this.

"Soup?"

"Soup. It is considered a delicacy in some some East Asian cities. Sells for a hundred dollars a bowl," O'Brien explained. "The wholesale price in some regions can run up to two hundred dollars a pound for shark fins, as opposed to about fifty cents a pound for shark meat. The profit is enormous. Recently I read of one ship that sold forty tons of fins for export to China for some nine million dollars."

"Okay, I agree that maiming any animal is bad business, but I don't understand why you're so upset, Elyse. What's the problem with fishing for a few sharks?" I asked.

"A few? It's turning into a massacre. Estimates are that one hundred million sharks are killed every year, most of them just for the fins. One hundred million! Many species face extinction.

"Fortunately marine scientists have recognized that the shark population is in real danger. The U.S. has passed laws like the Shark Finning Prohibition Act that make it illegal for U.S. fishing boats or any boat in U.S.

waters to possess fins without the rest of the carcass," Elyse said.

"Jeez, Elyse, you mean besides manatees, turtles, whales, and God knows what else, now we've got to worry about the damned sharks?"

"Absolutely. Can you imagine our oceans without sharks? They are predators just like the cheetahs in the Serengeti. The ocean is a natural wilderness and sharks are a part of it. Without them the whole ocean ecology would change. As top predators they maintain the important balance in the number of other ocean animals. They eliminate diseased or genetically defective individuals and stabilize populations. God knows what the effects of eliminating them would be."

"I've got a good example," O'Brien said. "A shark fishery in Tasmania. It went out of business after only two years of overfishing for sharks. Then the spiny lobster industry also collapsed. The lobster were decimated by octopus, whose populations exploded when their predators, the sharks, were decimated."

"Every part of nature is connected," Elyse said. "We should know that by now. Many marine scientists argue that sharks should not be fished at all. Their populations are way too fragile to withstand any exploitation. They don't reproduce that fast. Sand tiger sharks mature at twelve and then produce twins every other year. The dusky shark doesn't breed until it is twenty to twenty-five and then it has small litters only every three years."

"So what do you intend to do about this injured shark?" O'Brien asked.

"I've got to go back down. I can't just leave it there dying on the bottom. It was awful. The poor thing was trying hopelessly to swim, struggling to make its way to a place of safety. It had been horribly maimed for a bowl of Chinese soup!"

"It's probably dead by now," O'Brien said. "Or soon will be. Let nature take its course."

"It's not nature; it's greedy men. The thing could languish for days. Besides, what about all the divers that dive the *Rhone*? It could be dangerous if they decide to go in for a close look."

"Jeez, Elyse."

"Come on, Peter. I could use some help. Besides, I bet Hannah hasn't dived out at the site."

"Why not?" I said. I could see Elyse was going with or without us.

"Okay, what about air?" O'Brien asked.

"I've got four full tanks on the *Caribbe*," Elyse said.

O'Brien sighed. "I guess we're doing this, then. I'll bring a couple more air tanks. Let's take the *Caribbe* and get out there early. How's six tomorrow morning?"

"Six it is," Elyse said.

Damned if I wasn't disappointed when I realized O'Brien wasn't staying. He needed to get his gear and be back early in the morning. I followed him up onto deck.

"Night, Hannah."

"Night, O'Brien." I wrapped my arms around his waist and pulled him into me. He bent down, brushed his lips against my face, and quickly jumped to the dock.

"Jeez, Hannah, that man is crazy about you." Elyse was sitting in the salon, feet tucked under her, sipping tea.

"Come on, Elyse." I didn't really want to hear it.

"Hell, I saw the way he looks at you. Can't believe someone's finally managed to capture O'Brien's heart."

"What do you mean?"

"He's been available for a very long time. Never seems to be with one woman for more than a few weeks."

"I'm not really looking for a relationship. I've got enough on my hands as it is."

"Well, you'd be nuts not to give O'Brien a chance. He is one of the best people I know."

"How long have you known O'Brien?" Christ, I felt a twinge of jealousy. I abhor jealous people. Elyse picked up on it right away.

"Oh, it's not like that. Peter and I are friends. He was several years ahead of me in school. I was a scrawny, ugly kid. One of the nasty little boys in my third-grade class used to lie in wait for me after school, call me terrible names. One day I was running away and ran right into Peter. He was probably eleven then. He bent down, saw my tears and then the kid that was following me. He grabbed the boy by the collar and hauled him down the sidewalk and around the corner. To this day I don't know what Peter said or did, but that boy never called me a name again."

"Well, you certainly aren't a scrawny kid anymore, Elyse."

"Thanks, Hannah. It's amazing how those labels impact you, though. Peter's always been there for me. He's seen me at my worst. When I got sick the first time, the dean insisted that I return home for a semester. I was in bad shape. Still manic. O'Brien helped my parents and Mary ease me back to reality."

"Reality? What the heck is that?"

"Good question," Elyse said, and laughed. "Good question."

Chapter 10

At six the next morning, Elyse and I were sipping coffee on the *Caribbe* when O'Brien arrived. He was lugging an air tank in each hand and had his BC and regulator thrown over one shoulder. He'd already discarded his shirt and shoes. He looked like he'd been up for hours. We loaded the gear and got ready to cast off. Sadie was sitting on the dock with a "you aren't leaving me here alone all day again" gaze. Rebecca was in school until three o'clock.

"Let's take her along," Elyse said.

"Okay," I said to Sadie. "You can come, but you're going to have to sit in the boat and behave. You'll probably get seasick."

She yelped and jumped onto Elyse's boat, overjoyed to be going along no matter where. Such devotion.

O'Brien released the lines and jumped on board as Elyse threw the engine into gear, pulled the *Caribbe* away from the dock, and headed out into the Sir Francis Drake Channel. Once outside the protection of the cove, the water was choppy, a moderate wind whipping it into whitecapped peaks. The farther we got from shore, the happier Sadie seemed. She'd found a place sitting in the front between O'Brien and Elyse, wind blowing in her face and plastering her ears back. Elyse steered straight across the channel heading to Salt Island, the site of the *Rhone*. A few small boats, brilliant in the morning sun, dotted the sea, fishermen out early checking their fish pots.

The dive site was deserted except for a couple of seagulls soaring overhead and some pelicans floating lazily near shore. Every once in a while one rose, flapping its huge wings and soaring high into the sky. Then it would do a wide arc, tuck its wings in, and dive into the water. When it surfaced, it tipped its head back and swallowed the prey that filled its pouch.

When we arrived at the rocky point at Salt Island Elyse maneuvered the boat up to one of several moorings that had been installed over the wreck. O'Brien stood on the bow with the boat hook. He easily captured the yellow line that drifted in the water near the mooring ball and wrapped it around the cleat. Then Elyse cut the engine.

"In another hour or so most of the moorings will be filled," Elyse said. "The dive companies like to get out early while the water is still relatively calm. This site has a lot of surge, and can be rolly."

I'd noticed. The boat rocked from one side to the other, nothing like Colorado lakes. Pots and pans in the cupboards below clanked loudly against one another. Sadie, who had been struggling to maintain her balance, finally gave up and found a soft spot on some life jackets in the corner and lay down. O'Brien pulled out the dive flag, red with a diagonal white stripe through the center, to indicate that we were diving.

O'Brien looked at me and grinned. He'd been trying to get me out to the *Rhone* since we'd met. It's reputed to be one of the best wreck dives in the Caribbean. A movie, *The Deep*, had brought fame to the site. I'm pretty sure I saw it. Something about treasure diving.

"The ship, a three-hundred-and-ten-foot steamer, was built in England in 1865 and was considered one of the most advanced designs of her time. She had more than three hundred cabins," O'Brien explained. "She left Southampton under the command of Capt. Robert F. Wooley, and a month later she anchored off Great Harbour, Peter Island, in the BVI to take on cargo and supplies for the return trip."

"What happened?" I asked.

"As the story goes, a beautiful calm morning suddenly turned into a nightmare. The barometer dropped, the sky darkened, and hurricane-force winds struck. With the engines full-out, the ship rode out the storm. When a lull came Wooley decided to head out to safer open water to weather the second half of the storm. She was just passing through the channel between Salt and Peter islands, almost to open sea, when the winds struck with a vengeance, forcing her onto the rocks at Salt Island. She heeled over, broke in two, and sank quickly. Only one passenger and a handful of crew survived.

"Now she's preserved on the sandy bottom. One piece, the bow, is in seventy to eighty feet of water. The stern, with rudder and propeller nearby, sit in fifteen to thirty, ruined on Black Point Rock one hundred fifty years ago."

"Sounds like a fantastic dive," I said.

"So where did you see the shark, Elyse?" O'Brien asked.

"It was inside the wreck, hidden in the recesses of the bow section along the starboard side."

We pulled on our wet suits, attached regulators to

BCs and tanks, checked our gauges, and prepared to roll off the back of the boat into the water. Sadie was curled up in the shade under the bimini, barely lifting her head to acknowledge we were leaving.

We descended along the mooring line to the sandy bottom, followed by a school of yellowtail snapper. A 360-degree scan and I didn't see any wreck. O'Brien pointed the way. In a matter of minutes I could make out dark shapes that looked liked the columns of the Parthenon. As we got closer, the dark mass grew into pillars of color, alive with sponges, coral, and algae—orange, red, yellow, green. French angels and butterfly fish, grunts, parrot fish, black durgon swarmed around the brilliant columns.

At the bow I could see an opening that led into the interior of the ship. O'Brien pointed, indicating that this was the place to swim through. I had read the dive profile in the guide the night before. It said *Penetration of the wreck should be performed only by properly trained and equipped wreck divers.* Of course, I had the training and O'Brien and Elyse had probably logged months of underwater time. But I remember the last time I'd swum into a wreck. I'd gotten trapped inside with a guy who had a knife that he'd intended to use—on me.

I followed O'Brien, who was already through the opening. Elyse was right behind me. The wreck was narrow in sections, and our tanks banged on the top of the enclosure, sending watery reverberations through the hull. Blue light permeated the inside of the ship, leaching color from the dark interior. Forms were eerie silhouettes of corroded iron. Bony joists held the shape of the ship, like the inside of a rib cage. Dark fish swam past, mere shadowy outlines. A barracuda hovered in the recesses, following our movements.

I could imagine the terror of the people who died in the wreck almost 150 years ago, trapped in this steel tomb. There were no signs of the tragedy, though—just the empty water-filled cavern that marked their grave.

We searched the entire interior, but found no shark, injured or otherwise. As we headed out the other side, we flushed a hawksbill turtle from its resting place. He glided away from us, flippers gracefully moving him through the water, like a bird in slow motion. We could see him outlined by the light ahead before he disappeared in the open water.

We were about to follow him out when a light flashed across the interior from behind me. More divers had come in. I turned to see one in trouble and panicking. He was completely out of control, twisting in the water, pulling at his hose, which had gotten caught on a jagged piece of the ship. Then the diver began grabbing at his partner, his movements even more panicky than before. I suddenly realized what had happened: The hose was cut but still caught. Now he was trapped in the hull without air. His partner was also close to panic.

I swam to the diver but stayed out of his reach. I didn't want him tearing my regulator out of my mouth or disabling my equipment. I moved quickly behind him, grabbed his tank valve assembly, pulled his useless regulator out of his mouth, and stuffed my alternate in. He kept twisting, fighting me, trying to escape, but he couldn't reach me. I simply held on to his tank and waited for him to calm down. O'Brien hovered a few feet in front of him, making eye contact, trying to get the guy to focus. Finally, with each breath he got quieter. I signaled to him that I was going to untangle his useless regulator, and then we would swim to the surface. His frightened dive partner, a woman, watched.

Once I got the hose untangled, the five of us made our way out of the hull, Elyse with the woman, O'Brien and I with the other diver. Once out of the wreck, the guy would have headed to the surface as fast as he could—with me along for the ride since he was still sharing my air—if O'Brien hadn't pulled him down. We weren't sure how long they'd been down, but after diving at seventy feet for over forty minutes, the ascent needed to be slow and we needed to do a safety stop for a couple of minutes at fifteen feet. If this guy ever knew the procedure, he had forgotten it in his panic.

As we hung there at fifteen feet, I noticed the collection bag he had tied on his wrist—a couple of starfish, a conch, a purple fan coral. Right now they were beautiful, still alive, but when they died they'd turn gray and brittle. I wondered whether this guy was worth saving. I grabbed the bag and opened it, releasing its contents back into the sea. The coral would die, but the other creatures would drift back to the bottom.

We surfaced and swam over to his boat, a rented motorboat, and climbed aboard.

"Thanks, man," he said, then realized for the first time that his rescuer was a woman. He immediately got blustery and defensive, trying to figure out how to put the right spin on things.

"Jeez, Carla here got scared when we went in the ship. Had to turn around and help her. Got stuck on that damn piece of metal. She didn't know what to do."

Right, I thought. "How long you been diving?" I asked.

"Hey, I done plenty, but Carla here is pretty new at it."

Carla was glaring at him. "Come on, Bruce, you've

made what, about five dives? I told you I didn't want to go inside that wreck."

"Do you have dive cards?" I asked. I knew that none of the dive shops would rent equipment or air tanks without checking to make sure that the divers were trained and certified. But the shops didn't gauge how much experience the diver had. The dive training emphasized safety and the importance of diving responsibly and at locations that matched experience. The *Rhone* was considered an advanced open-water dive site, or intermediate when accompanied by a dive master.

"Sure," he said, pulling them out of Carla's purse.

"Yeah, looks like you've been certified about three months. Do you know it's illegal to do any collecting out here? This is a national park. And two novices swimming into that wreck alone. Talk about stupid. You know, if we hadn't been there, you'd be trapped down there and dead right now. God knows whether Carla here would have been able to get out. I don't want to see you diving in these waters again without a dive master along. Believe me, I'll be watching for you."

"The hell you will," he said, moving toward me. I would have put him in one of my famous judo holds if O'Brien hadn't stepped in.

"You'd better back off," he said. "Unless you want to end up in jail. She's a cop."

We left the two of them glaring at each other in their boat and swam back to the *Caribbe* to get fresh tanks. This time we headed to the stern section. We found the shark tucked up against the propeller. It was barely alive, half-hidden under the ship. It was a nurse shark, maybe six feet long, cut up and still seeping blood. It lay on its side, floundering, trying to right itself and swim, not understanding why it couldn't do what it had always been able to do.

Elyse pulled out her dive knife, tucked the blade under its head, and drove it in. She knew what she was doing. It was fast. The shark swung its tail once, shuddered, and was still.

We rigged a hoist—a sling with air bags on each end—and wrestled the dead shark into it. Elyse inflated the bags with air from her alternate regulator and the fish slowly rose to the surface. She would examine it more closely out of the water. We'd pick it up from the boat after we surfaced.

With tanks still half-full, Elyse signaled that she wanted to check the area. Damned if we didn't find two more nurse sharks, fins amputated. Both were already dead. They were young and small, maybe three feet long. They lay on their sides, swaying in the current, discarded corpses. We left them there and swam back to the boat.

"Dammit!" Elyse climbed onto the transom and threw her gear into the boat. O'Brien fired up the engine and I released the line from the mooring. While Elyse sat with her face in the towel, working for composure, O'Brien maneuvered the boat over to the floats.

We wrestled the shark, some 250 pounds of it, into the back of the boat. Sadie, who been ecstatic when we'd returned, now sat in a corner and whined. Elyse went right to work examining the body. Every one of its fins had been sliced off.

"This fish was tangled in a drift net," she said. "You can see the pattern of slices on her belly, and she's got a piece of netting caught in her mouth. The other two small ones would have been captured the same way. Whoever massacred them was probably somewhere out there in open water. No telling how many more were taken, not to mention the other creatures that would have happened along, barracuda, tuna, probably a sea turtle or two—a green or hawksbill. And it looks like this shark was about to give birth." Elyse had cut the fish open and pointed to the embryo that nestled in the shark's uterus. O'Brien and I looked, and shook our heads. There was nothing to say.

Elyse was uncharacteristically quiet on the way back. "You okay?" I asked.

"I'm fine. Be even better when I catch up with the people responsible for the carnage."

"Don't do anything stupid," I said. "And call me if you need help."

She dropped O'Brien and me off at SeaSail and motored back to Pickerings Landing with Sadie. I wanted to have a look at the SeaSail files on the Robsens and the Manettis before I headed over to Cane Garden Bay to see Trish.

O'Brien owned one of the biggest and most successful charter companies on the island. He'd gained a reputation for service and quality. His boats were kept in immaculate condition, and his employees bent over backward to accommodate the customer. His parents had started the company with one beautiful wooden boat, the *Catherine*, a fifty-foot wooden schooner that still floated majestically in the harbor. Now SeaSail had some two hundred boats and was known worldwide.

We found Louis, O'Brien's base manager, in the back office, buried in paperwork. He'd been with SeaSail since the beginning, and treated O'Brien like a son. He was a wiry black man of sixty-five, engine oil permanently embedded in his hands.

"Hey, dar, Ms. Hannah. You be back to our islands to stay dis time, I hope." He gave me a gentle hug.

"Louis, Hannah would like to look at the files for a couple of our charterers. Would you pull them for her? I'll be over on dock C. Want to check on that new catamaran that just came in."

Louis rumbled around in the back for a minute, returning with the files and coffee. "Take yourself a seat at dat desk. You be needin' anything else you let me know."

"Thank you, Louis." The coffee was hot and strong.

I started with the Robsens' file. Allen Robsen had made arrangements for the boat eight months ago, putting down a deposit and then making the two scheduled payments for the charter. Their sailing résumé included a four-day sailing course in San Diego on a forty-two-foot Catalina, a three-day charter in Mexico, and a lot of day sailing in Vermont on a little twenty-footer that they kept at a marina. It all fit with what Trish had told me.

It looked like the Manettis had done absolutely no planning for their charter. They had come to the office, filled out the forms, and arranged to take the boat the next day. I asked Louis about it.

"Not the usual way folks do it, but it happens. They come to the islands to vacation, plan to stay in a hotel. Then they see all the boats, hear about nothing but the great sailing, and decide to charter."

"Do you check their sailing résumés?"

"We don't have time to check everyone. Kind of spot-check and look at the ones that don't seem legit. With a drop-in like this, we might take them out to check their skills before we let them take the boat."

The Manettis' résumé indicated limited sailing experience off the coast of Florida, around the keys.

"Did anyone go out with the Manettis?"

"Let me take a look." Louis checked through the file. "No. They just got a briefing and a tour of the boat to acquaint them with the equipment. It's hard to get into too much trouble in these waters as long as charterers stay away from the shallows. We've marked anything even remotely tricky off-limits on the charts."

Nothing in the files told me anything useful, except that other boats might want to stay clear of the Manettis if the couple decided to put their sails up.

Chapter 11

I had intended to head over to Cane Garden Bay alone, but Dunn again insisted that I take Snyder. I wasn't sure whether he didn't trust me with the *Wahoo* or if he just didn't want Snyder hanging around the office. Either way, I was stuck with the kid.

Trish Robsen was sitting on the deck of *Wind Runner* sipping coffee when we pulled up. The Manettis were with her. Melissa Manetti brought us each a cup. I was already buzzing from the caffeine that Louis had poured. This was even stronger.

"Her son will be in around three o'clock today," Melissa said. "Plans to stay on the boat with Trish until things are resolved."

"Good." I said. "I spoke with the owner of SeaSail. He asked me to tell you to stay on the boat as long as you need to, no charge, and he sends his condolences." Snyder shot me a knowing look. Evidently my sex life was island news.

I didn't mention to Trish that she would have to stay around. She was a suspect.

"I'd like to talk to Trish for a few minutes and then come by your boat," I said to Melissa. This was a subtle hint for them to leave. It was never a good idea to talk to people with others around. Tended to skew their story or keep them from saying everything they might.

"Sure," Don Manetti said, taking the hint. "We'll be on our boat."

Although all the coffee was making me a little jittery, it didn't seem to be having much of an effect on Trish Robsen. She seemed dazed, not really present.

"I'm sorry to put you through this, but can you tell me about the night Allen disappeared?" I asked. "I know it's hard, but it's best to talk before things get vague."

Snyder actually pulled out a pad of paper and a pen. I resisted doing the same. I didn't want to hurt his feelings again. I just hoped he got it all down.

"I don't mind, but I don't know what more I can tell you. We were on the *Calypso*, like I said. I came home early with the Manettis. Allen stayed over there. I went to bed. Woke up around two. He wasn't in yet but I figured he was still over there swapping sailing stories. Allen never got enough of it. When he wasn't back when I woke up at six o'clock, I took a morning swim over to the Pembrooks. Our dinghy wasn't there. When I woke up Elizabeth, she said everyone had left by one-thirty."

Snyder was writing furiously, every word.

"What about the other people there that night?"

"We didn't really know anyone but the Manettis. They all seemed nice enough, but I'm afraid I can't tell you much about them. I think that the people over on the *Dallas* keep their boat here and come down several times a year.

"The Manettis are charterers like us. We met them a

couple of days ago when they anchored nearby. Had them over to our boat for dinner and did some sightseeing on shore together. After weeks on board with just your spouse, you get kind of anxious for some other company."

"Did Allen have any enemies? A colleague? Maybe a competitor? Did he owe anyone money? Gamble? Anything at all that could lead to trouble?" I asked.

"No. Nothing like that. Allen is an honest businessman. People respect him. We live in a small town. He belongs to the chamber of commerce, the Kiwanis. He's in computers. It's all pretty mundane. We're just normal people, raised kids, belong to a bowling league, play penny-ante poker with friends on Saturday nights. This is crazy." I was sorry I had to ask all these questions, but it had to be done.

I noticed that Trish was speaking about Allen as if he were still alive.

"You said you've been down here for several weeks. Have you run into any trouble?"

Trish sat for a while, thinking aloud about what they had been doing in the islands—snorkeling around St. John, several days on St. Croix, touring the BVI.

"Allen did have a run-in with a man from one of the charter companies," she said.

"What happened?" I asked.

"We were anchored in Manchioneel Bay over at Cooper Island last week. We'd been at the Baths and come into the bay too late to pick up a mooring. They were all occupied. We'd dropped the anchor in about forty feet of water and were confident it was holding.

"We had just finished dinner when another boat bumped up against us. We couldn't figure out what had happened at first. It was dark, but we had the anchor light on, a light on below deck, one in the cockpit. We should have been clearly visible. The other boat was completely dark, and we finally realized that no one was on board.

"Allen thought that the boat's anchor had let loose and that it had drifted into us. We knew that anchoring in the bay was tricky. There's a lot of turtle grass, and sometimes the anchor won't dig into it. It will just lie on top. Then the wind picks up and the anchor starts to drag.

"Anyway, Allen lashed the boat alongside ours to keep it from drifting into shore and grounding. Then we radioed to the restaurant on shore and told them what was going on. We gave them the name of the boat and they said they'd check for the owner. Pretty soon a dinghy came racing out. It seemed that the boat was part of a flotilla organized by one of the charter companies. The man in the dinghy was in charge. He had anchored all the boats, about six, because none of the charterers on any of the boats were skilled enough to set an anchor. He had taken his dinghy from one boat to the next dropping anchors."

"Did you get this guy's name?"

"It was Davies. I don't know what his first name is. Anyway, this guy thought he could do no wrong. He told Allen that an anchor he set would never let loose. He accused us of anchoring too close to him and was sure that our boat had swung into his. Allen got really angry. He told Davies he should have let the boat ground.

"That's when he took a swing at Allen. He missed him, though. The woman he was with interceded and apologized. She knew that the boat had come off its anchor. That the captain had been careless. But no sailor, especially a professional, likes to admit his anchor didn't hold. Anyway, we reported the incident to the charter company. We could understand an anchor letting loose, but we felt that no one that volatile should be in charge of a flotilla of boats."

"Do you know what the results were?"

"No, Allen made the one call and let it drop."

"Do you remember the name of the charter company?"

"Yes. It was Blue Water Charters out of Soper's Hole."

If this Davies had lost his job because of Robsen, he might be angry enough to go after him.

"I'll be talking to the folks at Blue Water Charters. Anything else you can think of?" I was sure that there was something that Trish still wasn't saying. "What about over on St. John or when you were in St. Croix?" I prodded, trying to jar something loose.

"No, nothing, really. We only spent a couple days on St. John. Didn't meet anyone to speak of. Then we took a day to sail to St. Croix. We spent several days touring the island, did a little shopping; then we came back here."

"Did you have any trouble at all in St. Croix?"

"You know, on the way back, about twenty miles out from Tortola, we encountered the strangest boat."

"Tell me about it."

"Well, it was this fishing boat. Maybe ninety feet long. Allen thought they might be having problems, because the boat was sitting so low in the water, just drifting out there. When we got close enough to see the name, Allen radioed to ask if they were taking on water, whether they needed help.

"The man on the radio told Allen that they were fine,

just loaded down with fish. We could see several big
bundles stacked on board and a couple of guys struggling to push a pretty good-size shark overboard. We
tacked away from them and went on our way."

"What was the name of the boat?"

"The *Emerald Queen* out of St. Thomas. We didn't
see it again. We never gave it another thought. I don't
think it means anything."

"Well, what does? Why would someone put a bullet
into your husband?" I was getting frustrated now.

"I just don't know!" she said.

"Something got your husband killed, Trish. What
aren't you telling me?"

"What do you mean?"

"I've been a cop for a long time. I know when someone's holding back."

"There was a woman," she finally admitted.

"A woman?"

"It was nothing. I'm embarrassed about it, that's all.
I didn't want you to think Allen was unfaithful. I certainly don't want the children to hear about it. She
meant nothing. Allen was a good husband and father."

"You'd better tell me."

"Well, as I said, after a couple weeks the boat was
getting kind of small. Allen and I had a fight. It was
silly. I can't even remember what it was about. Allen
left angry. Went to a bar and had several drinks. A
woman hit on him. He told me the whole thing. He'd
gotten pretty drunk. And he was mad at me. She invited
him up to her villa and he actually went. Stupid, he'd
admitted."

"What happened?"

"Allen said she really started putting the moves on him.
About the time she started undressing, he came to his

senses and got out of there. Came home contrite. We figured that was the end of it. He was embarrassed about the whole thing. But Allen ran into her a couple of times. She kept after him, even when I was with him."

"What's this woman's name?"

"Ursala. Ursala Downing."

No surprise there. Same woman that Elizabeth Pembrook and the people on the *Dallas* had said was after Allen Robsen that night on the *Calypso*. Maybe he had met her after he'd left the *Calypso*.

"Anything else you should be telling me?" I asked.

"No, there's nothing. Listen, Allen and I were happy. He never cheated on me. It's hard to admit he'd gotten involved that way, but he was really sorry that it had happened. And that woman. I don't know. She's not normal."

"What do you mean?"

"Well, the way she was pursuing him. Why Allen? Oh, he is a wonderful person, nice-looking, fantastic sense of humor . . ." She trailed off, tears building. "I don't know. Do you think she could be involved?" she asked, incredulous.

"Probably not," I said. I didn't want her going around accusing anyone, but I'd be talking with Ursala. "Do you know where he met her?"

"The Watering Hole. That little bar right on the beach with the red roof."

We left Trish sitting on deck staring out at the sea.

Chapter 12

D on Manetti was climbing up the swim ladder when
we pulled alongside the *Celebration*. I could have
used a swim myself. It wasn't even noon and the sun
was already bouncing white-hot off the deck of the
Wahoo. The water in the bay was crystal-clear and
turquoise. I could see a stingray moving slowly across
the sandy bottom, a dark, flat triangle with a tail.

Melissa had been sunning on deck. As we stepped
aboard, she stood and pulled a robe on.

"What can you tell me about that night?" I asked as
the four of us settled in the cockpit. Again Snyder was
poised, pen in hand.

"Jeez, not much." I could hear the defensiveness
creep into Don Manetti's voice. I was used to it.

"We had dinner with Allen and Trish on shore at the
Pelican. Started talking to other boaters. The Pembrooks invited us over to their boat for drinks."

"What time was that?"

"Musta been, what, about ten o'clock?" he said, turning to Melissa for confirmation.

"Yes," she said. "We only stayed about an hour. Had
one drink."

"Who else was there?"

"The folks from the *Dallas*, the Pembrooks, the Robsens. Allen wanted to stay. He was into a heavy discussion with Pembrook about sailing and he was entranced by the *Calypso*. We dropped Trish off at her boat."

"Did you come down here to sail?" I wondered if the Manettis had anything to hide. If I'd catch them in a lie. I didn't.

"We were leaving our options open. It was a spur-of-the-moment decision to come down here. We got a good deal on airfares. The first couple days we stayed in a hotel over on Frenchman's Cay, then decided to rent a boat."

"Have you done much sailing?"

"Enough to stay out of trouble. We live in Miami. A good place to escape from."

"What do you do?"

"Real estate, commercial. We own our own company."

"What's the name of your company?" Snyder asked.

"Miami Realty, Inc."

I watched Snyder write it down. Good.

"What can you tell us about the Robsens?"

"They seemed like a nice couple, but we didn't know them that well."

"Think Allen Robsen had any enemies?"

"Can't imagine. I mean, how do you develop enemies on vacation in the Caribbean?" Don asked.

I wondered the same thing.

"You have any trouble with Robsen?"

"Jeez, no. We're just down here on vacation. Al was a nice guy. The two of us went out one day while the wives were in town. He was a very experienced sailor. Gave me a few pointers."

"Did Robsen seem worried or upset about anything?"

"Naw, he was a guy on vacation. Enjoying himself."

"What about the marriage? You think the Robsens were happy?"

"It sure seemed like they were. As much as most of us, maybe more. They seemed real tight," Don said.

"Well, Trish did tell me about the trouble with that woman," Melissa interjected. It was the first time she'd spoken in a while.

"What? What woman?" Don said, incredulous. "You never mentioned it."

"She and Al had a fight. He got drunk and met a woman in a bar. He told Trish he managed to back out with his pants still on, which I actually believe— Al didn't seem like a player. Trish said he was really upset about the whole thing. Didn't know how it had gotten out of hand. But she was really angry at him."

"Did you hear or see anything after you came back to your boat that night?"

"No. We went straight to bed. I crashed."

"What about you, Mrs. Manetti?"

"Nothing, really. The music on shore. Maybe a boat motoring in the harbor. Most nights someone's out late. Nothing unusual."

"How long you folks stayin' in our islands?" Snyder asked.

"A few more days, maybe a week."

"If you remember anything else, please call the department," I said. Snyder handed them the number.

"Will do," Manetti said.

We climbed into the *Wahoo* and Manetti threw me the line. Snyder took the wheel before I had a chance to.

I shot him a warning look. He smiled, that damn disarming smile, and gunned it.

"Snyder!"

"Jus' foolin'! I be slowin' down."

He backed off the throttle and we made a circuit of the harbor. No one could tell us much. Most said they were usually asleep by nine o'clock. So much for the party life of the sailor.

There was one cruiser anchored off a bit from the other boats, a forty-foot single-masted sloop rigged for long stretches at sea—wind generator, radar. The bimini was sun bleached and worn. It was obviously wash day; laundry hung on the lifelines along both sides of the boat.

"Ahoy on the *Barnacle*," I called. A fitting name for the boat. She was crusted, overgrown with the sea. Her owner matched her appearance. He stepped up from below, bearded and wearing stained shorts and a shirt that no washing would ever remedy. He was followed by his mate, a heavy woman in a tube top and nylon shorts, clearly unconcerned about the flab that hung in rolls from arms, belly, thighs. Both smiled widely.

Snyder pulled alongside. I refused their invitation to come aboard, holding on to the rail of the *Barnacle* instead so we could talk. They'd been in the harbor for a week, would leave tomorrow to head south. The BVI, they said, was too crowded for them, too many charterers, too many moorings. They had been cruising for twelve years. They had just spent six months in St. Martin getting their engine repaired.

They were from California, had a couple of grown kids, had returned to the States only twice in all that time, once for their son's wedding, another just for a visit. I couldn't imagine living this sort of life, sailing around the Caribbean from one port to another, sometimes a week in a harbor, sometimes months, then on to another.

"We always start heading south come hurricane season because the storms don't hit down there. Usually stay around Grenada, Trinidad through November, then come back up north," he said. "We're about to start heading that way. This is as far north as we're going this year."

I wondered about their ties to others, especially their family. Maybe they weren't important to them, but it must hurt those they left behind, especially their kids. I could never desert my parents, sister, Mack for years at a time. That's what it would seem like—desertion. Seemed selfish. But hell, maybe I had done the same thing by moving down here. I made a mental note to invite my family down in the next couple months.

Preliminaries complete and my guilt assuaged, I finally got around to asking them about Sunday night. All they could tell us was that they had been aware of the get-together on the *Calypso* but had not seen or heard anything unusual.

Snyder and I motored out to the farthest boat, anchored out in about forty feet of water. No one aboard. We could see a dinghy pulled up on shore across the way. Two children were playing in the trees along the water's edge, chasing goats. Their parents walked hand in hand picking up shells.

"We'd best be warnin' them about dem trees," Snyder said, turning the boat toward shore. The kids were playing under a stand of manchineel trees. One was perched on tiptoe trying to pull one of the green apples off a branch just out of reach. He kept jumping, trying to grab the limb.

When Snyder had the boat close enough to shore, I leapt out into about three feet of water and waded to shore. The couple looked up and waved.

"Hey, you kids, come out of those trees right now!" I hollered, jogging toward them. They turned and looked at me, bewildered.

"They aren't hurting anything," the father yelled from down the beach.

"Come on, you guys," I said, putting an arm around each kid. I ushered them down to the shore and prodded them into the water.

"What's the problem?" the father said, steaming up to us, angry.

"Those trees are poisonous," I explained.

"Poison?" Alarm bells were going off in their mother's head. "Did you kids touch the trees?"

"Nope," the older one said. Typical. I remembered when I was a kid—the theory was never admit to anything.

Snyder had gotten the *Wahoo* anchored and was walking up the beach with the first-aid kit. "This is Deputy Snyder and I'm Detective Sampson, Tortola Police."

That got the kids' attention. "Are we arrested?" the younger one asked. "I promise we didn't hurt the trees."

"No, you not be arrested," Snyder said. "Those be manchineel trees. They can hurt you. Let me be takin' a look at your skin," he said, after he and the kids' mother had washed them down in seawater.

"Dem trees got a sap dat burn your skin and eyes real good. Need to be stayin' away from those trees. Good thing you didn't get a hold of the fruit. It be makin' you real sick."

Snyder didn't mention that it could be deadly. The kids had been lucky. One of them had a small blister on the back of his hand. That was it. While Snyder applied salve to the boy's hand, I questioned the parents about Sunday night.

They remembered that night because of the party on the *Calypso*. Nothing too loud. They'd gone to bed about eleven. During the night the youngest child had awakened suddenly with a nightmare, and woke up his parents and brother. Once they'd gotten the boys back to sleep, the father had gone up top to check the anchor. The *Calypso* was quiet and dark by that point.

"Did you hear or see anything at all on shore?"

"Sure, the bar was still open, lights shining out on the water, music playing."

"Anything unusual?"

"Nothing that isn't happening most nights in this harbor, as far as I can tell."

"Nothing on the *Calypso*?"

"Naw, like I said, it was real quiet, dark, maybe just a dim light below deck."

"If you think of anything at all would you give me a call?" I said, handing him the number.

"You know, there was one thing," he said, rubbing his chin. "There was a small boat heading out of the harbor. Couldn't see it very well. It was already pretty far out. Looked like it was pulling something. Struck me as a little strange, someone heading out to the channel so late."

"What time do you think it was?"

"Musta been around two."

We walked back down the beach with them, the kids skipping through the waves as we went.

"Hey, thanks for rescuing the kids," the father said, shaking our hands. "Never dreamed they were in any danger in those trees. I guess sometimes the most innocent things can be deadly."

Chapter 13

Snyder and I headed over to Blue Water Charters in Soper's Hole, a protected harbor on the west end of Tortola, just south of Cane Garden Bay. The customs office was located in the harbor, a port of entry for vessels entering or leaving the BVI. The ferry was pulling up at the dock, just in from the U.S. Virgin Islands. The line handler jumped to shore as the captain reversed engines and nudged her expertly up to the docks. About twenty people, a few tourists and several locals, stepped off. This was the business side of the harbor, not quite as well kept, buildings functional and in need of a coat of paint.

Across the way was the marina, where a couple of docks, filled with sailboats, jutted out into the water. The waterfront was picturesque, decorated with yellow, blue, pink, green, and purple buildings freshly painted, palm trees scattered among them. Clothing stores, a couple of restaurants, a dive shop. Behind, a hillside of deep green.

Snyder pulled along the dock and I tied the *Wahoo* up to a cleat. Blue Water Charters was at the end of the pier, a whitewashed stucco with blue awnings. It was hot on shore, no breeze, and the dock sizzled underfoot. By the time we reached the end, sweat ran down my face and stung my eyes. Snyder was in the same condition, swiping at his brow with a red bandanna he pulled out of his back pocket.

We stepped into the office, which was only slightly cooler, a ceiling fan throwing circles of air on wet skin.

"Hey, dar, Celia," Snyder said to an attractive black woman behind the counter.

"Hey, Jimmy."

"How you doin' dis fine day? You looking lovely today." Damned if Snyder wasn't flirting.

"I be doin' fine, and how about yourself?"

"Can't complain," he said. "You be going to dat music festival over by Long Bay on Saturday?"

"Snyder!" I didn't bother to keep the irritation out of my voice.

"Sorry, this is Detective Sampson. We be investigatin' a case." Snyder was still at it, impressing the young woman.

"Hello, Detective. I be hearin' the chief hired an American woman. Nice to meet you."

Snyder jumped back in, taking charge. "We're wantin' to talk to one of your boat captains had a flotilla over at Cooper. Let's see . . ." He pulled his notepad out with a flourish and thumbed through it. I thought about giving her the details myself, but what the hell.

"Woulda been sometime last week," he said.

Celia pulled out a ledger and ran her finger down the page. "Here it is. That would have been Davies, Clement Davies."

"That's the man. He around?" Snyder asked.

"Nah. He got himself fired on Friday. He was not what you'd be callin' good with da customers. Kind of impatient, cocky. Boss said he took a swing at some guy. Da man called and complained."

"Probably Robsen," Snyder said, turning to me.

"You know where we can find Davies?" I asked.

"He lives just down da road. Shacks up there with his girlfriend. Go out round back to da street, down about a block. It's a yellow house with a metal roof. Can't miss it. All kindsa junk outside."

"Thanks, Celia. Hey, you be wantin' a ride to dat festival? I sure would like to take you." Snyder actually took her hand.

"Sure, Jimmy. Dat be great."

"I can come 'round about six."

"Okay." Celia smiled.

"Come on, Deputy Snyder." I played up the *Deputy* part. Hell, I was glad he had scored.

Snyder sang under his breath all the way to Davies's house. Marley. "I wanna love you and treat you right . . . share my single bed. I wanna . . ."

Chickens were pecking at garbage out in the yard. The place was a mess, strewn with rusting car parts, an old boat motor, and torn fishing nets. We went up the front steps and knocked. Nothing.

Snyder walked around the back while I stood on the porch. I began to wonder what the hell he was up to when he opened the front door.

"Snyder. That's called breaking and entering."

"I didn't do no breaking. Door was open. I just came in."

The place was deserted. It looked as though Davies had taken off. He hadn't bothered with anything but personal items. Dresser and closet were empty except for hangers and a couple pairs of worn shoes. All that re-

mained in the bathroom was a bar of soap and an empty
bottle of shampoo.

In the living room, a lamp lay in pieces on the floor.
Nearby a clay flowerpot was shattered, dirt and a dying
ivy littering the floor. There was a square in the dust on
a bookshelf where a stereo had once sat. Probably the
only other item Davies took. I found nothing to indicate
where Davies might have gone.

By the time I'd finished checking the place, Snyder
was outside talking to a neighbor, an old woman in a
blue flowered dress and a yellow scarf wrapped around
her head, leaning on a cane. They were engaged in
heavy patois, not a word of which I could understand,
though I knew there was some English in it somewhere.
She was gesturing and pointing at the house and shaking her head. Snyder was nodding and seemed to be
asking her to elaborate. They went on like that for at
least ten minutes. I sat on the steps and waited.

I was thinking that maybe Dunn's pairing me with
Snyder wasn't such a bad idea. Snyder was an islander.
He'd had no trouble finding out about Clement Davies
from Celia, and it was clear that the old woman was
telling him everything he wanted to know and more. I
didn't think I would have gotten the same cooperation.
Hell, I probably wouldn't have been able to communicate with the old lady.

Finally the woman smiled, nodded my way, and hob-
bled back to her house, swiping at a squawking chicken
in her path with her cane. Snyder sauntered back over
and sat down next to me.

"Well, you want to fill me in, Snyder, or you gonna
keep me in the dark?"

Snyder grinned and proceeded. Seems Clement
Davies came home Friday night smelling like the rum

distillery and ready for a fight. Went in and started tearing the house apart, throwing stuff out the window, breaking up the furniture. When his girlfriend got home, he started on her. He had her on the floor in a choke hold when the old lady showed up and started beating him with her cane. The girlfriend got out fast. Davies knew enough to stay away from that old woman.

"Yeah, smart man. Does she know where Davies went?"

"She saw him stagger out about an hour later, loading a suitcase and stereo in his car. Hasn't seen him since and don't know where he be goin'. Hopes he never shows up here again. Says he be a bad man—too much meanness in him."

"What about the girlfriend?"

"Went home to her parents."

"You know where?"

"Sure."

"Nice work, Snyder. How about you go talk to the girl and I'll head over to the Watering Hole to try to connect with Ursala Downing?"

"You think you be okay without me along?" he asked.

"I think I can manage."

The Watering Hole was a typical island structure, open on three sides with the breeze blowing through and a 180-degree view of the bay. Several boats were anchored in Cane Garden Bay: the *Wind Runner*, the *Dallas*, the *Calypso*, the Manettis' boat among them.

Except for a group of people lingering over lunch, the restaurant was empty. I pulled up a stool at the bar and waited. Eventually I figured a bartender would appear. In the meantime I was enjoying the view and the breeze. Two small boys were running along the water's edge, the waves chasing them to shore. Another was intrigued by the ghost crabs that scurried on the beach. He kept trying to sneak up close enough to capture one, but once he got about two feet away, the little crabs would scamper into their holes.

"Afternoon, ma'am. Sorry to keep you waiting. I didn't know you came in. What can I be gettin' you?" the bartender said, placing a napkin in front of me.

"Something cold and nonalcoholic would be great," I said.

"I be havin' just da thing. Dis here be fresh-made juice." He poured something pink into a glass.

"Do you know a woman named Ursala Downing?" I asked.

"Sure. Mos' everyone here knows Ursala. Fact is, she in here jus' about every day 'round three. Almos' set your watch by her," he said.

"Was she ever in here with this man?" I asked, showing him the photo of Allen that I'd gotten from Trish.

"Yeah. Maybe a week or so ago. He was already here. Seemed kinda angry and workin' to get hisself inebriated. Ursala came in, sat next to him, bought him a drink, and went to work. Dat's what she does. Kind of a game, I thinks. Tryin' to get any man she sees to like her. Doesn't take no for an answer. Just keeps flirtin' and flirtin' till a fellow gives in. For some it don't take much. That guy was pretty drunk. They staggered out together."

"You ever see him in here again?"

"Just one other time with another woman. Kinda thought it was his wife. They be just finishing lunch when Ursala came in, went over to their table, and damned if she didn't sit right in his lap. He be blushing, not knowin' what to do. His wife got up, pulled Ursala off of dat guy, and marched him right outta there. Ursala just laughed. Came over and sat at the bar. Sayin' some guys just be pussy-whipped."

"What do you know about Ursala?" I asked.

"Like I said, she's here most every day. Flirts with anything in pants. I think she be having some kind of complex or something. You know, have to prove she be attractive. Thing is, she be a good-looking woman. Lives just up the hill there in dat big house," he said, pointing to a veritable mansion built into the side of the hill. "Guess she be having money. Lives down here for about six months every year with her husband."

"She's married?" I asked, knowing she was but fishing for a reaction.

"Yeah, don't that just beat all? I've seen him around a couple times. Seems to let Ursala do what she pleases. Don't seem to care much. You be waitin' about ten or fifteen minutes, she be wanderin' in here."

I wasn't disappointed. At just about three, a woman walked in dressed to kill. The bartender was right. She was good-looking. In fact, she was gorgeous. I'd put her at around my age, thirty-seven, thirty-eight, and about five-seven. That was where the similarity ended, though. Her breasts were spilling over the top of a red swimsuit. Around her waist she'd tied one of those sarong things. She looked like she'd just stepped out of *South Pacific*. All she needed was an orchid behind her ear. Her hair was long and blond, I figured out of a bottle, but I was probably just jealous. She wore a lot of makeup but managed to look like she wore little. I walked over and introduced myself.

"Ursala Downing? I'm Hannah Sampson. I'm a

detective with the Tortola PD," I said, showing her my ID. "Can we talk for a few minutes?" I asked.

"Sure, darlin'. Let me just grab myself a Bloody Mary. Can I get you one?"

"No, thanks."

She strolled up to the bar, well aware that the two guys at the table couldn't take their eyes off her. The wives were glaring at the husbands. She smiled at them as she swayed back by, drink in hand.

When she sat across from me in the light reflecting from the beach, I realized that Ursala was older than I'd thought, probably more like forty-five. Her eyes were sad, real sad.

"So John has finally broken the gender barrier. About time, I say. And an American at that. How long have you been with the department?"

"Just a few days. I'd like to talk with you about Allen Robsen."

"Allen . . . Ah, yes, nice man, but a prisoner in his marriage."

"What do you mean?"

"Too afraid to take the leap, though he clearly wants to. I've been trying to redeem him. Sooner or later he'll come to his senses. They all do."

"I'm afraid Robsen won't be one of them. He's dead."

"Dead?" She didn't seem that surprised. "What a shame. And now he will never know the virtue of infidelity. His wife kill him?"

"That's a funny thing to say. Why do you think it was murder?"

"Because you are across the table asking about him. Accidental deaths don't usually bring out the police."

She had me there. "What makes you think his wife would kill him?"

"Oh, I wasn't being serious. But come to think of it, I suppose it's possible. Probably rather have him dead than in bed with another woman, and I think that ol' Allen was weakening."

"When did you see him last?" I asked.

"Let's see. Guess it was Sunday night. Frank—that's my husband—and I were over on the *Calypso*. Allen was there, the Pembrooks, couple of other fellows from Texas. Wives had all gone home. Stupid, leaving their husbands like that. The two Texans decided to go back in to shore, probably looking for action at the Reef Bar, since their wives weren't around. Frank and I left too. He went to join the Texans."

"Why didn't you go?" I asked.

"Well, to tell you the truth, I asked Allen to meet me. I was guessing he was about ready. Told him I'd be on the beach down there." She indicated some tables on the beach with umbrellas over them. "I sat out there long enough to finish off an entire bottle of champagne by myself. He never showed up. I figured his wife caught up with him and dragged him home. I gave up and went home myself." Ursala kept looking around the restaurant and glancing at the door, nervous about who might come in. Maybe she didn't like being seen with a cop. Or maybe she was rendezvousing with another prospective lover.

"What time was that?"

"Must have been around two-thirty or three. I shouldn't have waited that long, but I guess I'm just a foolish romantic at heart." She grinned after the last comment. I chose to ignore it.

"Did you see or hear anything unusual?" I asked.

"What's to see but a few boats in the harbor?" She was defensive, maybe even afraid.

"Was your husband home when you returned?"

"I guess not, although I didn't check. Frank and I don't keep close track of each other."

"Did you see anyone else? Talk to anyone after you left the *Calypso*?" I asked.

"Trying to establish my alibi, huh? You don't really think I had anything to do with Allen's death, do you? Because I didn't. He wasn't that important to me."

"Well, he never made it home that night. Some snorkelers found him in the water near Sandy Cay."

"Huh, he should have taken me up on my offer. Probably still be alive, and he certainly would be well."

"You sure he never made it here?" I asked. I could tell she was holding something back. "Maybe things got rough? Perhaps Frank showed up?"

"Don't be silly. Frank could care less. And you think I would kill him? No way. He was just a diversion. A challenge."

"Maybe you can't stand the rejection."

This pissed her off. "He had not rejected me! If he wasn't dead, he'd be yearning for my bed as we speak. This interview is over, Detective. You have any other questions, you can call my lawyer."

She was storming out when she ran smack into Guy Pembrook coming in.

"Watch yourself," Guy said, smiling and grasping Ursala's arm.

"Don't worry about it!" she said, pulling from his grasp and rushing out.

The guys at the table were giving me dirty looks for chasing Ursala away. The wives, on the other hand, looked somehow triumphant. Like they'd had a part in it. As if they had struck a blow against male chauvinism or something.

Pembrook picked up a beer at the bar before he walked over to my table and pulled up a chair. There was a hint of white around his left nostril, and I didn't think it was baby powder. He'd done a hit of cocaine right before he'd come in the door.

"Wow, what's up with Ursala?" he asked, sniffing and pinching his nose between his fingers.

"Upset about Allen Robsen, I guess."

"Yeah, I heard," he said. "Damn shame. How's his wife holding up?"

"About as you'd expect."

"Any idea who did it?" he asked.

"No, just beginning the investigation," I said, wanting to get back to the matter at hand. "How well do you know Ursala?"

"Met her and Frank the first night we anchored in the bay. Right here at the Watering Hole. Ursala's not one you miss, and she certainly likes to socialize."

"You ever do anything more than socialize with her?" After the encounter at the door, I wanted to know what Pembrook's relationship with Ursala was.

"Hell, no. She flirted. I flirted back. You know, part of the game, but she's not my type."

"What is your type?"

"Christ, not that it's any of your business, but you've seen Elizabeth."

"What was all that about at the door just now? You grabbed Ursala kind of hard."

"Hell, she almost knocked me down in her rush to get out of here. Guess she didn't like talking to you. What were you discussing with her, anyway?"

"I'm asking the questions here, Mr. Pembrook. What else can you tell me about the night of the party on the *Calypso*?"

"Nothing I haven't already told you," he said, then looked at his watch. "Damn, I'm late. I've got to go pick up Elizabeth at the market." He guzzled the rest of his beer and stood.

I stood as well. "Now that this is a murder investigation, I'll be talking again with everyone who saw Allen that night. Will you be around tomorrow?

"Guess I can stop by the police department."

"Oh, no, I wouldn't want to inconvenience you," I said. "I'll come to your boat." I liked meeting people on their turf. You find out all kinds of things when you sit in someone's space.

"Yeah, okay," he said, reluctant. "The guy from the *Dallas*, Rodriguez, is interested in buying our boat, so he's coming over in the morning to look her over. Maybe you can come by later, say around two o'clock."

"I'll be there." It was pretty obvious Pembrook wasn't the kind of guy who liked to talk with cops. He'd have to adjust.

Chapter 14

I headed over to Pickerings Landing to meet Snyder, so I could pick up the Rambler and he could take the *Wahoo* to Road Town. He was in the sand playing with Sadie and Rebecca when I pulled up. Just another kid, for chrissake. I tied the boat to the end of the dock and walked down to the beach.

"Sweet Sadie," I said as she ran to greet me. It always amazed me that Sadie remained my friend in spite of my neglect.

"Hannah, can I take Sadie over to the marina with me till you get back? Mama said it was okay," Rebecca asked, hopeful.

"Sure you can, Rebecca. Be a good girl, Sadie." She whined a bit, enough to make me feel guilty, then jumped up, gave me a slurpy lick, and went off with Rebecca.

I walked with Snyder down to the end of the dock. "So did you find the girlfriend?"

"I did. Dat girl's father is mighty angry. Ready to kill Davies. Daughter's got a black eye, cut on her forehead, arms all purple. She was happy to tell me where to find Davies. Says he's probably in Road Town. Hangs out with a Stuart Vine. Vine lives on Main right next to the post office."

"Okay. Let's go check it out. Why don't you bring the boat back? I'll drive over and meet you at the office." I couldn't believe I was including Snyder. But I had to admit, the kid had been good to have around.

Snyder jumped into the *Wahoo* and gunned the engine.

"Snyder!" I yelled as he sent spray over the dock and trailed a three-foot wake all the way out of the harbor. He couldn't hear me, but I'm sure he knew I was hollering. Once out of the harbor, he pushed it full-throttle and vanished around the point. Damned kid.

Snyder was standing in the department parking lot waiting for me when I pulled in. "Hey, Hannah, 'bout time you be gettin' here." He smiled that wide, disarming smile.

"Come on, Snyder, get in," I grumbled. This kid could drive me to straight shots of pure alcohol.

Stuart Vine's apartment was on the second floor of a crumbling concrete structure in desperate need of paint. Heavy bass blared through the open windows. I knocked several times, wondering if he could hear anything over the music. Finally a man in a dirty, once-white undershirt, shorts, and flip-flops opened the door.

"You Stuart Vine?"

"Who's asking?"

"I'm Detective Sampson, Tortola PD. This is Deputy Snyder."

Vine just chuckled.

"Something funny?" I asked.

"Well, come on, you two are a pair. White woman and a damned skinny black kid. You got ID?"

The smile faded when I pulled out a badge. "We're looking for Clement Davies. His girlfriend said he might be staying here."

"Why you looking for Clem?"

"That's police business. You seen him?"

"He's been around. Been crashing on my couch when he can't find some nice lady to stay with. Haven't seen him since yesterday."

"Any idea where we might find him?"

"Hell, I'm not his babysitter. Could be anywhere on the island, all I know. Last time I talked to him he was trying to find work on one of the fishing boats. He in trouble?"

"We just want to talk with him. Appreciate a call if you see him." I gave him a card, but I wouldn't hold my breath. Vine would probably tell Davies to get the hell off the island.

According to Celia, Robsen's complaint to Blue Water Charters had been the last of a long series of problems that Davies had had on the job. Was it enough to kill Robsen over? Could be. People killed for a lot less.

Davies had probably been trashed all weekend and looking for someone to take his anger out on, his girlfriend having run for cover. He could have been waiting for Robsen that night after he'd left the *Calypso*. Even more likely, it would have been a random encounter on the beach or outside a bar, Davies drunk and wielding a gun. Nine times out of ten it happened that way. So far, besides Trish, the jealous wife, and Ursala, the spurned lover, Davies was the only one with a motive.

I dropped Snyder off down at the docks. He'd make the rounds of the local fishermen and see if any of them knew Davies. I headed back to the office to call Mack. Maybe he'd discovered something.

I was on my way past the open market when I saw Elyse. I pulled over and parked at the curb. Elyse was pointing her finger in the face of one of the vendors, a burly guy wearing an apron covered in blood and guts. He didn't look like the kind of guy who should be threatened, but that was just what Elyse was doing when I walked over.

"Elyse, what's going on?" But I knew without asking. The gore on his apron was the result of all the fish he'd gutted—parrot fish, snapper, mahi mahi. But that wasn't the problem. The problem was the shark fins. He had about twenty-five of them arranged in a neat row. I didn't see any shark meat.

"I want to know where you got the fins." Elyse was actually poking the guy in the chest now.

"Elyse, cool it."

"Cool it?" She spun around and glared at me. "These fins translate to five or six dead sharks, maybe even the same ones we found yesterday. I want to know who's taking these sharks!" She returned her attention to the vendor, her body tense with anger.

"Well, it ain't me," the vendor yelled. "I'm just buying and selling."

"Yeah, well, if you didn't buy and sell, no one would bother to kill 'em," Elyse said before she quickly moved behind the counter, opened the display case, and began sweeping the fins out onto the floor.

I was about to intercept her when the vendor grabbed her and pushed her into the case. He was moving in, fist raised, when I slammed into him from the side. He ended up sprawled on top of fish guts and shark fins. He scrambled to get up but slipped in the slime. I could see he was furious.

"You got no right! I be calling the police," he yelled as he struggled to stand.

"I am the police," I said, showing him my badge. "If you want to file a complaint, you'll need to come down to the station."

"She shouldn't be meddling in my business," he said as I offered my hand and helped him up. "I just be making a livin' and feeding my family. I ain't doing nothin' against the law. Ain't nothing illegal about selling fins. You got no call to take her side."

"I'm not taking anyone's side here. Just breaking up a disturbance."

"Hell you ain't. She be a damned crusader, protecting the damned fish at the expense of island folk. And you, just an outsider thinking she got a right. Well, I got rights, too." He continued to yell as I ushered Elyse back to her car.

"Jeez, Elyse, what were you thinking?"

"I don't know," she said, and groaned. "That was plain stupid. But I saw those fins in that neat little row and all I could think about was that shark dying out near the *Rhone*. I know that guy is like a lot of folks on the island, just trying to survive whatever way they can."

I left Elyse at her car after making her promise she'd be more tactful next time, and then went back to the office. The only one around was Jean, trying to scrape burned, crusted coffee off the bottom of the pot.

"I guess I should have turned the burner off," she said apologetically.

"Jeez, Jean, seems like whoever emptied the pot should have turned the burner off. Why should you have to monitor it?"

"'Cause I be the secretary."

"That part of your job description?"

"Well, seems like most people think so."

"Forget it, Jean. Just because some people think so, doesn't make it true."

I went into my cubicle and called Mack.

"Mack, it's Hannah."

"Hey, Sampson, good timing. I just got back in."

"How did it go with the research?"

"Pretty well. Just a second, let me get my notes." I could hear him at the other end of the line rattling papers around. I could picture it. Mack's desk was always a disaster, yet he somehow knew exactly where everything was.

"Got it," he said. "Okay, let's see. Jack Rodriguez, no record, just a couple DUIs that went away."

"Yeah, I found that. Anything else?"

"The guy's got millions, most of it from oil. Owns a couple-of-hundred-acre horse ranch outside of Dallas, a penthouse in the city, a home in Aspen, the yacht in the Caribbean. Didn't find anything that smells of criminal activity."

"What about Pembrook?"

"An author, just like you said. Writes travel guides on the natural history of a region. First one was on the coast of California, next was on Hawaii. They do okay, but I'd say that unless he's got some rich uncle that I haven't turned up yet, Pembrook is living way beyond his means. He has a house worth a couple of million north of San Francisco, and the boat down there. He can write off all his travel expenses, but still, he's definitely in the hole. He's behind in payments on a big loan and the house is mortgaged to the hilt. He's done some wise investing over the years, had a pretty strong portfolio, but it's worth about half of what it was a couple of years ago."

"You come across anything about drug use?" I was thinking about the white powder around Pembrook's nostril.

"No, nothing like that."

"What about Robsen?"

"He was squeaky-clean as far as I can tell. Talked to his business associate. The guy was really upset to hear about Robsen's death. Describes him as the best partner he'd ever had—honest, smart, worked hard. His employees respected him. Guess he treated people well."

"What happens to the business with him gone?"

"Robsen's son will step in. He's been with the company for five years."

"Doesn't seem like a motive to kill his father," I said.

"There is one other thing, though."

"What?"

"Robsen's partner said that Robsen had an affair ten, twelve years ago. He doesn't think that Trish ever knew. Robsen broke it off after about six months."

"So not that squeaky-clean. Anything else?"

"Not on Robsen."

"What about Don Manetti?"

I could hear Mack chewing on something, probably a stale doughnut, and rustling through papers.

"Hardly anything. Usually means there's either nothing to find or lots to hide. Owns a real estate company, but nothing else comes up on him in the computer. I've got a call in to a guy I know in Miami PD. I'll let you know if anything else comes up."

"Thanks, Mack. Hey, how's the new partner?"

"Green. I'm breaking him in gently."

"Yeah, I bet."

I hung up and pulled out the yellow legal pad. I ripped the doodle-filled page out and tossed it in the trash. I could still hear Jean trying to clean the pot in the other room. I started on a list: Who would have wanted Robsen dead?

Ursala Downing was a likely candidate. She hadn't been that surprised when I'd told her that Robsen was dead, but I had the feeling that little surprised Ursala, and she had motive. Just the suggestion of rejection had sent her storming out of the bar this afternoon. Maybe Allen had gone to shore that night to tell her to lay off and she'd lost it, pulled a gun, in a moment of sheer fury squeezed the trigger.

Of course, it was also possible her husband, Frank, did it in a jealous rage. Maybe he had intercepted Allen on his way to meet Ursala and stopped him with a .22. That would explain why Robsen never rendezvoused with Ursala. Or maybe he'd found Ursala and Allen together and shot him. Ursala could be protecting him, or perhaps she was afraid of him.

Then there was the charter captain looking for revenge. From the neighbor's description, the guy was violent. He'd been really angry about being fired. Hadn't been around since Friday. I needed to talk to him and find out where he was Sunday night.

Trish could also have shot Allen, pissed and jealous that he was fooling around. Maybe she had known about the previous affair and had made it clear at the time that it had better be the last. Allen could have come back to the *Wind Runner* late after fooling around with Ursala. Hell, he may not have ever stepped out of the dinghy before Trish nailed him and hauled him out to deep water. But what had happened to their dinghy?

There were others with the opportunity, like Pembrook, but no obvious motive. The Manettis? Christ, they'd never be able to maneuver a dinghy out into open water at night—or would they? The Texans?

At this point everyone was suspect. All the motives pointed to jealousy and revenge. Enough. I threw the pad in the drawer and headed to the computer, hoping to stumble across some piece of information that Mack may have missed. No such luck. Besides Mack rarely missed anything. It was nine o'clock by the time I switched the computer off.

The Rambler was in front parked under a casuarina tree. Its feathery branches draped over the passenger side, obscuring the entire right side of the car. This had been the only space left when I'd driven it in that afternoon. Now the lot was deserted. I'd learned to be wary in places that were this quiet and empty. I scanned the lot, looking for shadows that moved, listening for sound.

That was when I heard rustling coming from the other side of the car under the tree. I found myself pulling the .38 from the holster I'd draped over my shoulder on the way out. I crept silently around the Rambler and stopped. More sound. I ducked under the branches. Christ, it was pitch-black in there. I couldn't see a thing, but didn't want to use a flashlight. It was like giving some nasty guy a target.

The sound came from under a stand of bushes, practically at my feet. When my eyes adjusted to the dark, I crouched and pulled back the branches. A cat lay there, nursing three tiny kittens, only a few hours old. I groaned—it had been a long day. I needed food, a hot shower, and a soft bed. I was relieved that someone hadn't been lurking in the bushes, but I really wanted to leave the tangle of cats where they were. I tried to tell myself they belonged to someone in the neighborhood, but I knew they didn't. The mother was all bones and had that scared, hungry look in her eyes. I doubted she'd even be able to provide sufficient milk for the kittens. Shit. I grabbed an old towel from the trunk, wrapped the whole bundle of cats up, and put them in the backseat.

By the time I got home, the Pickerings' apartment was dark, but a dim light glowed in the marina office. I found Sadie inside curled up on a blanket. She jumped up to greet me, sniffed the bundle of kittens in my arms, and whined.

"It's only temporary," I assured her.

Sadie followed me down the dock to the *Sea Bird*. The ocean was smooth, the night still. I could hear the distant rumble of a car up on the road. Otherwise it was quiet, almost too quiet. Something seemed wrong, out of synch. Nothing apparent, just a feeling. Jeez, I was way too nervous. I needed to get some sleep. But then Sadie growled. I placed the cats on the dock and, for the second time that night, I drew the .38.

"Stay, girl," I whispered and stepped onto the *Sea Bird*, careful to keep it from rocking.

The moon, just past full, lighted the boat in a dusky glow. I could see that no one was on deck. It was empty. I waited in the cockpit, listening for sounds below deck. A breeze came up, causing the boat to rock and the halyard to slap against the mast. Then more silence. I crouched at the top of the stairs and tried to see into the darkness below. No visible movement. I waited, eyes staring into the black, listening for any presence. Nothing. Maybe both Sadie and I had been mistaken. Still, I crouched, hesitant to go below.

Finally, my knees about to give out, I placed a foot on the first step and quietly started down into the dark, gun in hand. At the bottom I again waited. Still nothing. I was going to have to flip the switch on the instrument panel for lights. I moved a pace to my left, felt for the panel. I was pretty sure that the light switch was fourth down. I hesitated an instant, then flipped the switch.

Light blasted the interior. Relief quickly gave way to quick, hot anger. No one stood beside me ready to plunge a butcher knife into my chest, but the salon looked like a hurricane had been through it. Seat cushions were thrown on the floor, their insides spilling cotton and feathers. Clearly they had been sliced. Every cupboard had been emptied, the contents strewn on the floor. Broken glass mixed with cornflakes, flour, and tortilla chips crunched under my feet as I walked back to the cabin. I paused at the door, then stepped in, ready to shoot the bastard who had wrecked my boat. No one in the bedroom, no one in the head. Like the salon, the bedroom had been trashed—mattress slit, sheets torn. In the head there was a note—written in toothpaste on the mirror.

GO HOME! Simple and to the point.

Avoiding any surfaces that could hold a print, I piled the cushions on the wooden seats and swept the glass and debris into a corner. Then I retrieved the cats from the dock.

I found a cozy nook in a corner for them, filled one of the only unbroken bowls with water, and opened a can of tuna. The mother cat was too hungry to be shy. She lunged for the food, the three kittens hanging on her teats.

I grabbed some clean underwear, shorts, and a tank, and this time locked the cockpit—the old lock-the-gate-after-the-horse-escapes theory.

"Come on, Sadie. I'm sure O'Brien needs company."

Chapter 15

O'Brien's villa was an imposing peach stucco with white trim. All it lacked were porticos and columns. It sat up on the hillside, overlooking the bay and the SeaSail marina. O'Brien answered the door in a pair of boxer shorts.

"Hannah, what are you doing here? It must be midnight."

I just shook my head and remained stoic. I mean, I'm a cop, for chrissake, although right now I felt like a waif standing on his doorstep.

"Are you all right?" he asked, letting Sadie and me in and closing the door.

"I will be after some food and some sleep."

"Come to the kitchen. I'll fix you something."

The kitchen was in the back of the house. It was all tile and wood, surrounded on two sides by windows. I sat at the table, nestled in a glass alcove. O'Brien pulled several containers out of the fridge, filled pans, and stirred while we talked.

"What happened?" he asked.

I took a deep breath and told him about the *Sea Bird*, the message on the mirror.

"Hannah. Thank God you weren't on board. Are you okay?" O'Brien was really upset and angry. It was nice to have someone around who cared that much.

"Sure, but the boat's a mess."

"Who would do this?"

"Good question. I suppose it could have been a couple of the local fishermen. I got involved in a disagreement between Elyse and one of the vendors in the market today. I'm sure the word's gotten around. Maybe they're angry that an American is in their islands sticking her nose in their livelihoods."

"But why not threaten Elyse? She's the one causing the trouble."

"Yes, but she is an islander."

"You're right about that, I'm afraid. It takes time to be accepted by the people of these islands, and they don't like outsiders meddling."

"Yeah, I noticed. A couple of the guys on the police force wouldn't mind seeing me go home."

Indescribable smells were wafting through the kitchen. O'Brien placed a bowl of chowder in front of me at the table, along with a sandwich.

"What about the case? How many people have you angered so far?" he asked.

"A few, I guess. I've spoken to everyone who was on the *Calypso* the night Robsen died. Maybe I've scared someone. It's possible that Clement Davies heard I'm looking for him and came looking for me first."

"Clement Davies. He's a bad one. Hot-tempered and intolerant."

"You know him?"

"Yeah, he worked for SeaSail for about a month before Louis let him go. Davies couldn't handle the people he was accompanying out on the boats. Instead of treating them like guests, he'd treat them like intruders. But enough of this. Finish your food. We'll talk tomorrow. Right now let's get you and Sadie to bed. Guest bedroom or mine?"

"Yours, but I need sleep. It's been a rough day."

"Of course, Hannah," he said, smiling.

I woke only once, O'Brien's arm around me. I hated how good it felt.

The next morning I found him out on the veranda. He poured coffee. It was a gorgeous morning, residues of the cool evening still tucked in bushes and stored in tile. Sailboats were already making their way out of the harbor. Several were in the channel, tipped on their sides in the wind.

"You're right on time. Marta's making breakfast. How did you sleep?"

"Great. I think I can face the day."

"Good morning, Hannah," Marta said as she walked in. "So nice to see you this fine mornin'." She placed a colorful plate filled with food before me: eggs Benedict surrounded by fresh fruit—watermelon, cantaloupe, papaya, pineapple.

"Thank you, Marta. This is beautiful."

O'Brien and I ate in silence, enjoying the view. Christ, there was nothing like it.

"O'Brien," I said, giving Sadie the last few morsels from my plate, "what do you know about Ursala Downing?"

"Ursala? She is a piece of work."

"What do you mean?"

"I believe she's flirted with every man on Tortola between eighteen and eighty."

"Really, do you talk from experience?" I asked.

"Actually, yes," he said with that damn twinkle in his eye. "I met Ursala about a year ago at an opening for her husband's work over in a gallery on St. Thomas. He's a sculptor. I'd been somewhat interested in buying one of his pieces. Ursala had had quite a bit to drink. At one point she actually put her hand on my ass. Her husband was standing right there. I figured she'd just had too much to drink, would be embarrassed about it."

"Let me guess, embarrassment was the last thing she felt," I said.

"Right. She came by the marina the next day. Asked if I was involved with anyone. I wasn't. She wanted to have lunch. I decided I needed to be very honest with her. I told her I didn't date married women. She just laughed. 'How silly of you,' she said. 'What's in a marriage license anyway? Piece of flimsy paper is all.' She was very bitter."

"What about her husband? What's he like?" I asked.

"Frank? Self-absorbed, an egomaniac. Could care less about Ursala. All he cares about is building his reputation as a sculptor. Really plays the role too. Affected, aloof."

"Is he any good?" I asked.

"Actually, he's not bad, but some of his stuff is kind of warped, violent. He has sold a couple of pieces to some New York dealers. He's placed some of his work in a gallery in Soho."

"Have you seen Ursala lately?" I asked, hoping for a no.

"Sure. She kept after me for a month or so after Frank's show, coming by the marina, calling the house. Somewhere along the line we became friends."

"Friends?" I said, skeptical.

"I know, with Ursala it seems unlikely. To her, all

men are conquests, but that's just it. She's terribly inse-
cure. Hard as it may be to believe, I don't think she
sleeps around. She's a flirt, but it doesn't go further.
Every victory is confirmation that she is worth something, if not to her husband, then to every other man on
the planet. Her real goal is to make Frank jealous, to
make him notice. She's crazy about him, although only
God knows why. He's with her for her money, so he can
dabble in his art. And she knows it."

"What about Robsen? It sounded like she was ready
to jump in bed with him."

"Possible. Maybe Ursala was ready to cross the line.
Try to get Frank to react."

"Perhaps he did. Caught Robsen leaving the house
that night and killed him."

"With Frank, anything is possible. Ursala's actually
sleeping with someone else would have been a blow to
his huge ego.

"It's too bad. Ursala's a nice woman. During all her
calls and visits, we'd started talking, arguing really,
about marriage, relationships, trust, honesty. She quit
pulling all the bullshit she engaged in with other men. I
don't know, I think she just needed someone to talk to."

I could see it being O'Brien. He was just the sort to
confide in. Understanding, sympathetic, clear in his
ideas. But did it have to be with Ursala?

"Maybe she's just developing another strategy," I
said. I mean, how could Ursala resist someone like
O'Brien, for chrissake?

"Possible, but I don't think so," he said, "and I think
I'm a pretty good judge of character. After all, I've got
you figured out."

"You think so?" I said.

"Sure," he said. "An absolutely stunning woman

who returns men's stares with a 'get real' gaze. Doesn't like to let anyone get too close or take care of her. Someday, though, I hope you'll let me take care of you just a little," he said.

"I believe you took care of me last night, " I said, suddenly regretting the fact that I'd been so vulnerable and let my defenses down.

"Yes, and I bet you're sorry about it this morning."

"Maybe." Jeez, I couldn't believe O'Brien could read me that accurately.

"When do you have to be back at the office?" he asked. I knew where this was leading.

"Not till ten. I've got a meeting with Dunn."

"Perfect," he said, pulling me toward him. We headed back to his bedroom. This time we didn't sleep.

By nine-thirty I was driving back to Pickerings Landing to drop Sadie off.

Tilda and Calvin were dumbfounded about the destruction on the *Sea Bird*. "Nothing like this has ever happened here before," Calvin said. "I am so sorry. I have never thought we needed security here, but I suppose times are changing."

"Something I've done must have brought it on. It's not your fault."

I dreaded seeing the *Sea Bird* in the light of day, but, hell, it wasn't going to get any easier. It was as I'd remembered: a mess. O'Brien would notify the owners of the *Sea Bird* about the damage. I'd called Dunn. He hadn't wasted any time getting a lab tech over. The guy was in the bathroom, meticulously plucking hairs out of the bathroom sink with a tweezers.

"Gilbert Dickson. Won't shake your hand," he said, indicating the gloves. Dickson was small and pasty. I found myself wondering how anyone could be that pale in this climate. The guy probably spent all his time looking under a microscope. He wore wire-rimmed glasses, an earring in one ear, and his hair cropped in a crew cut. He'd already covered the place in fingerprint dust.

"I'm finished here," he said, sealing his evidence bag. "Should have results in about forty-eight hours."

He packed up his case, headed down the dock, and climbed onto a huge Harley. The sight was so absurd I almost laughed.

The kittens were sound asleep, buried in their mother's fur. Unlike the boat, she was looking better, not as desperate. When I bent and stroked her head, she actually started purring. Probably the only kindness she'd ever had from a human. I fed her and left for work. I had neither the time nor the inclination to start putting the boat back in order.

I put the top down on the Rambler. I intended to enjoy the drive, let the spiderwebs clear, my mind drift. Instead of turning on Blackburn Highway and driving along the waterfront, I headed up Paraquita Bay Road. It would take me to Ridge. As the name implies it runs along the ridge on the top of the island; the highest point is Mount Sage at about 1,780 feet. I'd get off Ridge at Belle Vue, which dropped down into Road Town. It was the long way, maybe four miles instead of three, but without the speed bumps that had been installed on Blackburn to prevent fast-moving vehicles from slaughtering chickens, goats, and small children that meandered across the road.

Paraquita Bay Road was just the way I'd hoped— deserted. I was the only car on the road. I drove slowly, but my mind refused to drift—too much disquiet. I was

uncomfortable with the fact that I had headed straight to
O'Brien's in the middle of the night the minute things
got a little rough. Why had I let this one get to me? I'd
been threatened before, plenty of times. Never, though,
had my home been invaded.

Whom had I threatened enough to warrant the utter
destruction of the *Sea Bird*? I actually hoped it was about
my investigation. But damn, the more I thought about it,
the more convinced I became that the message scrawled
across my mirror was composed by one of the guys in
the department. I couldn't think of anyone else who had
displayed such outright hatred of me. There was the fish
vendor, of course, but he hadn't struck me as the type
of person who would take the time to plan out such an
attack.

I sighed, not liking where my thoughts kept going. If
I couldn't trust the people I worked with, the people
who might be watching my back someday—well, that
was a big problem.

Chapter 16

Dunn was at his desk, deep in a pile of papers, when I knocked.

"Hannah, come in." He pulled out a chair and listened quietly while I spent the next half hour venting. The more I talked, the more upset I got.

"I'm beginning to think it was a big mistake coming here. Maybe this is all about my being an outsider. I've been foolish to think I could fit in here."

"Who have you angered so much?"

"You don't even need to look beyond your door for the answer to that. Stark and Worthington can't stand to see me walk into the office. Hell, they could have enlisted someone to trash my boat, or enjoyed the hell out of doing it themselves."

"Hannah, calm down. I've worked with Stark and Worthington for years. They would never be involved in that kind of activity. They're good men. Just give them time."

"I don't know, John. Maybe we both should have thought things through before we decided I should take the position down here."

"This surprises me, Detective Sampson." Dunn

straightened in his chair and folded his hands in front of him. I knew the posture. I was about to get a lecture.

"I thought I knew you," he said. "You mean to say you're quitting because you've been threatened? I would have guessed you'd be doing just the opposite. Did you think things would be any different here than in Denver? You ever heard the saying 'shit happens'? Well, it happens here too. You need to get past that damned idea that you can find some kind of nirvana on this earth. Everywhere you go, you're going to find evil. These islands are no exception."

Jeez, if I didn't know better I'd think Dunn had been philosophizing with Mack over a couple of beers. But he was right. I needed to quit feeling sorry for myself and get back on track. I hated watching people wallowing in self-pity, and I'd just been buried in it up to my eyebrows.

"Okay, Chief. You're right."

"Good. Dickson's already working on the stuff he collected from your boat. One thing you'll discover about this island is that it's too small to hide on for long.

"Now, tell me what you've turned up on the Robsen murder."

I filled Dunn in on what I'd learned so far, which didn't seem like much.

"More than likely you have put pressure on someone. The vandalism probably related to the case."

"Yeah, maybe. I just can't figure out who I could have pushed hard enough to warrant the effort." I still wasn't convinced it wasn't Stark or Worthington, but I kept it to myself.

"Knowing you, Detective, you've been pushing plenty, and it would take a blind man not to recognize that stubborn streak. The first time the killer met you, he would have understood that you aren't the type to stop until you've got him. Whom have you been talking to?"

"Everyone who was on the *Calypso* the night Robsen was murdered. Right now no one sticks out, unless this whole thing is about jealousy and infidelity—that could mean Trish Robsen, Ursala Downing, Frank Downing. I'm also trying to track down a guy named Davies. Had a run-in with Robsen."

I was interrupted by Dunn's phone. He spoke for a minute or two, then hung up.

"Okay, tell me the rest later," Dunn said. "Seems a dinghy washed up over at Great Harbour last night. Looks like it could be the Robsens'. Get Snyder and head over there."

I hesitated at the door. "Chief, thanks for the lecture."

"My pleasure." He smiled. "But Hannah, I want you to watch yourself out there."

"Yeah, I will."

Snyder steered our boat through the break in the reef at Jost Van Dyke and directly into the dock, narrowly but expertly avoiding the coral heads on either side. I had to admit the kid was skilled—I just wished he'd slow it down. Along the shore, a few small shops and restaurants dotted the beach in pink, purple, and yellow. We tied up to the dock and headed through the sand to the Government and Administration Building, a whitewashed two-story structure with blue doors. Around the side was the Jost Van Dyke Police.

A police officer greeted us at the door. "Hello, dar, Jimmy," he said, shaking Snyder's hand. "And you must be Miss Sampson. Chief Dunn be mentioning you.

"Dinghy's on da beach, washed up in front of Foxy's."

We walked down the stretch of white sand, past an ice-cream stand and a burger joint. The dinghy had been pulled up onto the beach and sat baking in the afternoon sun. It was fiberglass, painted white, with the SeaSail logo on the side. Nothing out of the ordinary in it—a couple of oars, the gas tank hooked up to the engine, a greasy rag, the top half a plastic milk carton, perfect for bailing. A bottle of suntan lotion floated in the water that had accumulated on the floor. I lifted the locker latch with a pen and pulled the locker open. It was empty. No anchor.

There were no obvious signs of blood or any indications of violence. It looked like the boat had simply let loose and drifted in to shore. We would haul it back to Road Town and have it checked out.

Snyder and I went up to talk with the bartender at Foxy's. I'd heard all about the place and its owner, Foxy, who played guitar. It is legendary among boaters for its wild parties and for the raucous New Year's celebration that takes place there.

Inside was a big open room filled with heavy wooden tables, the roof held up by bulky timber posts. The sand floor was being raked by one of the employees. A couple of people, clearly sailors, were sitting at the bar, barefoot, drinking beer. But otherwise the place was empty.

"'Bout eleven o'clock tonight this place be packed," Snyder said. "Folks be doing the limbo in da sand. One of the local fellas, he always around competin' 'cause he thinks he's the best. Kinda entertains da rest. He puts a full bottle of Heineken in his mouth, tips back till his head about a foot from the ground, and then he goes under the limbo stick drinking that damned beer."

"Probably a good way to get the customers to buy him more Heinekens," I said.

"Yeah, dat's for sure."

We found the bartender in back wiping down tables. He told us that the boat was washed up on the beach when he opened up that morning. He figured that one of the yachties, leaving with plenty of rum punch in his belly, had failed to secure it to his boat, and it had drifted back to shore. Evidently it was a common occurrence in this harbor. When no one was up claiming it by lunchtime, he walked over to the police office and told them about it.

Snyder and I went back down to the beach. He retrieved the *Wahoo* and brought it around to the end of the beach. I waded out to meet him, pulling the dinghy by its painter. We tied it to a cleat on the back of the motorboat and I climbed in next to Snyder.

I could guess what had happened. Someone had taken Robsen and the dinghy out a couple of miles from Cane Garden Bay and dumped him in the water, leaving the dinghy to drift. The current and wind had carried Robsen's body north, northwest to Sandy Cay. The boat would have floated farther, right into Great Harbour. Whoever dumped him probably thought that the body would have sunk and the boat would end up going straight out to sea. The murderer either didn't know the waters and wind in the area or was too panicked to take them out farther. Maybe it looked far enough in the middle of the night.

We pulled the dinghy back across the passage to

Cane Garden Bay and stopped at the *Calypso*. It was almost two o'clock, and I was due to have a talk with Pembrook. When we came alongside, Rodriguez was standing on deck with Pembrook.

"Ahoy," Pembrook shouted, "come on aboard."

"Hello, Guy, Mr. Rodriguez," I said. "You about to become the proud owner?"

"I'm very interested in her," he said. "She's the kind of boat I've always dreamed of owning."

"She's beautiful," I said.

"Yeah, she's an Alden schooner," Rodriguez said, excited at the prospect of calling the boat his, "built in 1929 in Maine. A husky boat in a strong breeze with good sea running. Can't wait to get her out under sail."

Another boat fanatic, I thought as Rodriguez turned to leave.

"I'll be in touch, Pembrook," Rodriguez said, stepping into his boat. "Nice to see you again, Detective Sampson, Snyder. Good luck with your investigation."

"Come on. I'll show you around," Pembrook said after Rodriguez left. He was being Mr. Hospitality. I guess he'd forgiven me for my questions yesterday. Or he was just happy that he was about to close a deal with Rodriguez.

We went down below. It was a gorgeous boat. The original character had been preserved. The portholes were cast bronze; a brass kerosene lamp hung from the ceiling over the table; others were fitted on the walls. The doors were four-panel teak with brass hardware, and wooden beams spanned the ceiling. An old brass foghorn dangled from a hook above the chart table.

Alongside the antiques were all the modern technological advances, a GPS, radar, a computer that hooked up to the Internet via a radio, a fax machine. Though built in the 1920s, the boat was definitely geared for the twenty-first century.

"This had to cost a fortune."

"Man, you don't beat around the bush, do you?"

"Nope, can't imagine how someone can pay for a boat like this on a writer's salary. Unless you're Stephen King or something." I was thinking about what Mack had said about Pembrook's finances.

"Well, she was a good investment. The plan was to sail her down here while I wrote the book, then sell her for a profit. I make plenty on my books and my other investments. Not that it's any of your business."

"Really, even with the stock market going the way it's going?"

"Yeah. Even then." Pembrook was lying, but I guess a lot of people didn't admit it when they were about to go under the thumb of the mortgage company. According to Mack, if he didn't sell the boat, that was just what Pembrook was facing.

"Why don't you keep her, then?"

"Too much work."

That I did believe. Pembrook was not the type to be sweating over polished brass and shining teak. And he probably couldn't afford to hire anyone else to do it.

We settled down below at the table in the salon. I could see the expectant look on Snyder's face turn to disappointment when Elizabeth emerged from the forward cabin in an oversize T-shirt and baggy shorts. Poor kid.

"Would you like a beer?" Elizabeth asked, popping one open and handing it to Guy.

"No, thanks. Just want to ask a few questions about Allen Robsen. Then we'll get out of your hair."

"I don't know what else we can tell you," Guy said. "We hardly knew him. Had seen him around the dock once or twice; then had him over that night. That's the only time we really talked to him."

"Can you think of anything at all that was unusual about that night? An argument or just something that didn't seem quite right?"

"No. It was a friendly get-together. Oh, sure, there were the usual dynamics that happen when men and women are together drinking, but nothing out of the ordinary."

"What kind of dynamic is that?"

"Oh, you know, bullshitting, some flirting. Like I said, I wouldn't have been surprised if Robsen was planning to see Ursala. But then he could have just planned to have drinks with the Texans. They're a rowdy group and really wanted to keep the party going on shore. All Robsen said was that he was going into shore, got in his dinghy and motored in. We went to bed."

"Did you talk much with Robsen?"

"Sure, he was a nice guy. Really interested in the *Calypso*. I showed him the entire boat.

"We even came below so I could show him the chart that maps out where we'd been sailing. That kind of thing. Robsen really had the bug. Had this idea about taking a year and sailing all through the Caribbean. We talked about the various islands, my work."

Pembrook was opening another beer when I heard a boat engine, then shouting. Elizabeth excused herself, saying that she and the two women from the *Dallas* were headed into Road Town to shop. Guy followed her upstairs.

While they were up top, I snooped. What can I say? It's what I do. The shelf behind the table was lined with books—mostly natural histories. One was *The Nature Lover's Guide to the Hawaiian Islands* by Guy Pembrook. I pulled it down. Just then Guy came back down. He looked perturbed. I felt guilty.

"Sorry, couldn't help but take a look at your book. You must be quite an authority."

When I replaced the book I noticed a tiny round hole just above the row of books.

"This looks like a bullet hole," I said.

"Cleaning my gun," he said. "Damned if it didn't still have a bullet in the chamber."

"Glad I not be standin' in front of dat pistol," Snyder said. "That be kind of careless."

"Yeah, well, that's the only time I've ever shot anything I didn't mean to hit," Guy said, obviously insulted.

"What does that mean? Have you shot at someone?" I was puzzled by Guy's remark.

"No! Just do some target practice, that kind of thing."

"Why do you have a gun?"

"Got to watch out in some of the remote places in these islands, especially around the southern Caribbean. You never know what you might run into. Someone wanting to rob you, maybe take the boat. I wouldn't want to be without some kind of protection. Matter of fact, I have a couple, all nice and legal—registered, permits, the works," he said.

"Mind if I take a look?" I asked.

Pembrook went to a locked cabinet that was attached

to the bulkhead and unlocked it. Inside were a couple of rifles and two handguns.

"A lot of weaponry to have on a boat," I said, picking up one of the handguns—a new Springfield Sub-Compact XD. It was a solid, chunky little 9mm—not loaded.

"Hell, no way I'm letting anyone aboard my boat uninvited," he said, taking the gun from me and replacing it in the rack. "I'd shoot in a minute. These outlaws see that and they take off."

He showed us the paperwork. It was all legal, just like he'd said.

Snyder and I spent a few more minutes talking with Pembrook. He had little else to tell us about the night on the *Calypso*.

"What do you think, Snyder?" I asked as we pulled away.

"I don't like that man's all I know. Seems to me he be having money he don't deserve. In da islands folks work hard for what dey got."

"Yeah, Pembrook seems to have come by it the easy way," I agreed.

I could see Trish and her son sitting in the cockpit of the *Wind Runner*, so we pulled alongside. I held on to the rail, keeping the *Wahoo* from bumping Trish's boat while we talked.

She recognized the dinghy right away.

I told her we'd found it washed up over at Great Harbour. We would take it into town and have it checked out more closely.

"I'll ask the people at SeaSail to bring you a replacement."

"That would be great," she said. "One that has a working engine."

"What?" I asked.

"Well, the engine had quit," she said.

Just then Snyder jammed the boat into gear and hit the gas in order to avoid the huge wake from a power-boat that was entering the harbor and threatened to crash us against the *Wind Runner*.

Chapter 17

A half hour later we'd dropped the dinghy off at a protected slip near the SeaSail docks. Dunn would send someone down to dust for prints and check for bloodstains or anything else that might provide a hint to what had happened to Robsen.

Then Snyder eased the *Wahoo* into its slip in Road Town. As we walked down the dock, I noticed a guy in a dirty red shirt standing up ahead on a nearby fishing boat, arms crossed, glaring our way. Before he even moved, I knew he was trouble.

"You know that guy?" I asked.

Snyder stared straight at the guy.

"Snyder! Can you be less obvious?"

Snyder dropped his gaze and we kept walking. "Don't know who he is, but dat boat's the one I heard Davies hired out on, da *Dolphin*. Musta just come back into the harbor."

"Okay, let's talk to the guy."

He saw us coming. I could tell he was trying to decide whether to jump us or run. I knew what he was thinking—a woman and a skinny kid. Maybe he could take us both. I hoped he'd try.

"You Clement Davies?" I asked.

"Who the hell wants to know?"

"I'm Detective Sampson, Tortola PD."

Davies continued to lean casually against the side of the boat. The hold was filled with fish. Stacked on deck were several bundles of what looked like fins, maybe shark fins. Davies was still trying to decide whether to fight or flee. He was big, but out of shape, a cigarette dangling from his mouth. He tossed it in the water and took off running.

Snyder shot off after him. I was right behind. Nothing like eighteen-year-old reflexes, but Davies was motivated. He was halfway up Pasea Road by the time we reached the end of the dock. I caught a glimpse of him just as he dropped off a chain-link-fence into the boatyard. When we got up there, he had disappeared somewhere in the maze of boats that were scattered inside. Damned if Snyder didn't climb effortlessly to the top of the fence and jump. I never even considered it. By the time I'd have made it to the top, Davies would have been on the other side of the island. Besides that, the stupid kid was going to end up breaking a leg or worse. I motioned to him that I'd head around to the other side. Hopefully I'd intercept Davies coming out.

A couple of minutes later, Snyder staggered out of the boats, breathing hard and holding his side.

"What happened?"

"Never saw him. He didn't come past you?"

"No. He's got to be still inside."

We headed back into the boatyard. Snyder rushed off one way; I went the other. There were fifty or sixty boats in various stages of repair in the enclosure. And plenty of places to hide. I stopped and listened for any sound, watched for movement. I could hear Snyder over on the other side of the yard clattering into one boat after another. Someday Snyder would learn to channel that damned energy. Hell, I admit it, I was jealous.

A sound drew me from the noise Snyder was making. It came from a small rowboat lying on its side in the grass. I was just a couple of yards from the boat when Davies darted from behind it and took off out the gate.

I yelled at Snyder and reached the gate in time to see Davies duck into Seaside Marine Supplies. When I dashed into the shop flashing my badge, the only one inside was a clerk who pointed toward the back of the store. I moved past the cash register to a shelf laden with boat gadgets and peered down the aisle. Nothing. I crept to the back of the store and listened for sound. Then I heard it, the scraping of a boot on tile the next aisle over. I slipped around the corner and found him. He was holding a can of WD-40, which he was about to fling at me when he saw the .38 in my hand.

Snyder rushed in behind me, knocking over a display of engine oil that had been stacked in a pyramid, sending the cans all over the store. He pulled out his cuffs and clicked them around Davies's wrists. I could tell he was disappointed that he hadn't caught up with Davies first.

"Thanks, Snyder," I said. "We make a good team."

"No problem," he said, smiling.

Back at the office we took Davies into what Dunn called the interrogation room. It was just a spare room in the back with a couple of chairs and a table. No two-way glass or closed-circuit cameras here, but I did have a tape running. Dunn was standing at the door, leaning against the jamb.

"Why the hell did you run?" I asked Davies.

"Shit, think I want to go to jail? Hell, I was drunk. I didn't mean to hurt anyone."

"You want to tell me about it?" Jesus, was it really going to be this easy? I tried to go slow. Keep him talking.

"Hell, I lost my damned job. I was pissed. I went and bought myself a couple bottles of rum and got drunk."

"When was this?"

"Friday, boss called me in. Told me he'd gotten his last complaint. Damned tourists. None of 'em know how to handle da boats like I do. Hell, I been sailing for years."

"What about that anchor letting loose over at Cooper?" I asked.

"Well, hell, how anyone supposed to get six, seven boats anchored at once? So I made one little mistake."

"Sound like the mistake was taking a swing at one of the tourists."

"Yeah, well, he deserved it."

"Is that why you killed him?" Dunn asked.

"Killed? Killed who?" Davies sounded bewildered.

"Allen Robsen."

"I didn't kill nobody! Shit, don't know no Robsen!"

"He's the guy you took the swing at. The one who got you fired."

"Christ, is that what dis is about? Shoulda known it was 'bout some damned tourist."

"Why did you think we were after you?"

"'Cause I got drunk and punched my girlfriend. Figured her father be down here throwing one big fit, demanding you come get me."

"No one has lodged an assault complaint," Dunn said.

"Well, shit, then let me outta here," he said, standing and heading for the door.

"Don't think so, Mr. Davies," Dunn said, his mass blocking the doorway.

"Where were you Sunday night, early Monday morning?" I asked.

"Hey, no way you going to pin no murder on me," he said, pulling a cigarette from his pocket and lighting it.

"No smoking in here," Dunn said, snatching it out of his mouth and pulverizing it under his shoe. It was a warning.

"Christ, I was drinking with Stuart Vine and another guy owns the *Dolphin*," Davies said. "We was down at the Doubloon till they closed. Had to be about two o'clock. Then I went out fishing early Monday morning and just got back this afternoon. Vine come by and told me you be looking for me. Figured it was about me roughin' up my girl. Hell, I didn't even know that guy was dead."

So much for easy. We'd check out his story, but I was pretty sure he was telling the truth. So was Dunn. He just looked at me and shook his head.

"Okay, Davies, you can go," Dunn said, "but don't be goin' too far."

Davies was almost out the door when I stopped him.

"One other thing. What were those fins stacked on the *Dolphin*?"

"Shark fins. Why?"

"What do you do with them?"

"Boss lets any of the guys on the boat lucky enough to wrestle in a shark take the fins for themselves. Kind of a little extra incentive to sign on for a week or more at sea. The guys get a small percentage of the profits from the fish dat are caught. If the fishing is bad, it might mean a week's work and no money. But a few shark fins can make up for it. Some people pay real good for dose fins."

"Like who?"

"Every once in a while a fishing boat comes through dese waters looking for fins, drifts out in deep water. Guess dey probably sell dem to shippers who can get the product to markets in Asia. Local fishermen find out real quick when there's someone out there buying."

"Do you know of any in the area now?"

"If I did, don't think I'd want to say and don't think I'd have to. It's not against the law to fish for sharks, you know?"

"Yeah, so I've heard."

According to Elyse, it's the United States that outlaws shark finning. There are no laws in the Caribbean. The UN has developed a global plan for the conservation of sharks, but enforcement is often impossible. It appeared no one on the *Dolphin* was breaking any laws.

"If there's nothin' else, I'll be going," Davies said. He couldn't get out of there fast enough.

I followed Dunn back to his office. "What was all that about shark fins?" he asked as he sank heavily into the chair behind his desk. Dunn was tired and disappointed that Davies wasn't our man. He wanted to put this thing to rest. It would have taken a lot of pressure off.

"Elyse Henry has found some dead sharks out at the *Rhone*, fins amputated. She's very concerned."

"Christ, Detective Sampson, let's keep the focus on the case."

"Yeah, the thing is that Trish Robsen mentioned coming across a boat like the one Davies described when they were on their way into Tortola from St. Croix. She said the guy on the radio warned them off, didn't want them coming near the boat. Maybe the Robsens saw something they shouldn't have."

"You know how many fishing boats are out on the water like that? Besides, if the Robsens had seen something on that boat, Trish Robsen would be dead too, and like Davies said, it's not against the law to kill sharks."

Not unless a U.S. boat is involved, I thought to myself. Trish had said the *Emerald Queen* was out of St. Thomas, part of the United States. If they were loaded down with shark fins, were discovered by U.S. authorities, they stood to lose millions in cargo. I didn't push it with Dunn, though. He was probably right. I was getting off track.

"Anything on that dinghy?" he asked.

"It's Robsen's. Dickson will be going over it."

"What else do you have on the murder?"

"I'm guessing that Robsen's body was dumped two, maybe three miles out along with the dinghy. He washed into the coral at Sandy Cay. The boat drifted into Great Harbour. He was killed sometime after the party on the *Calypso*. Whoever did it loaded the body in a boat, took it and the dinghy out to where they hoped both would just disappear, wrapped the anchor around the body, and threw it overboard. One of the sailors at Cane Garden Bay saw a boat motoring out late. Thought it was pulling something. Had to be Robsen's dinghy."

"You must have some suspicions about who did this."

"Well, Davies was at the top of the list."

"Let's not rule him out then till we check his alibi. Why don't you talk to the captain of the *Dolphin*?" Dunn stood and yelled out the door. "Snyder!"

"Yeah, Chief?" Snyder had been hovering right outside at the coffee machine.

"I want you to go down to the Doubloon. See if Clement Davies was down there drinking Sunday night. What time he left."

"No problem, Chief!" Snyder practically ran out the door.

"Okay, who else should we be checking out?"

"Trish Robsen has a motive—jealous wife, no alibi, went home to bed after she left the *Calypso*. She could have shot him when he came home that night and dumped him out there, but why leave the dinghy, and how would she have gotten back to the *Wind Runner*?"

"Maybe she had help."

"But who? The Manettis? I seriously doubt they would get involved."

"Who else?" Dunn demanded.

"Could be Ursala Downing. She's got motive—spurned lover. No alibi, and she'd asked Robsen to meet her. Sat on the beach waiting for him. Says he never showed, so she went home. Maybe Robsen showed up to call the whole thing off and she got pissed. But she also would have had to load him in a boat, dump him and the dinghy. All without being seen."

"Maybe Frank helped her."

"Yeah, or for that matter, maybe Frank killed Robsen himself. He could have been jealous that Ursala was actually following though with Robsen. I hear he's got a huge ego problem."

"What about the other folks on the *Calypso* that night?"

"That would be the two couples on the *Dallas*, the Manettis and the Pembrooks. I'm checking them all out. So far I haven't come up with anything. The Manettis and Robsens did some socializing in the last week. No one else knew Robsen well, and as far as I can tell none of them had any reason to want him dead."

"Well, keep after it."

"Don't worry, Chief. Something will turn up."

Jean intercepted me in the hall.

"Hannah, there's a phone call for you. Lady says it's urgent."

Chapter 18

Damned if it wasn't Ursala Downing. I could barely hear her. She was whispering into the phone. In the background people were laughing, ice rattling and glasses clinking. Drinks were being made.

"Detective Sampson, I need to talk with you." I could hear the fear, even in her whisper.

"Where are you?"

"The Watering Hole."

"What's going on?" I asked.

"Not on the phone. Can you meet me at my house? Right away?"

"I can be there in twenty, thirty minutes."

"Do you know where it is?"

"Yes, I know, the big place above Cane Garden Bay."

"That's it; take a left off of Luck Hill. It's almost at the end. You'll see our name at the entrance."

Suddenly she stopped talking. At first I thought we had been disconnected, but then I heard women chattering in the background. Then the voices faded.

"You still there?" I asked.

"Yes. Please come right away," she said. Then the line went dead.

I pulled out of the parking lot and headed up Joes Hill Road to Cane Garden Bay Road. The sun lay just on top of the water, shooting orange and pink up into the clouds. The road was shadowed in dusk. Dark had already eaten its way into the trees. Twenty minutes later I turned off at Luck Hill and followed it to Ursala's driveway. It was well marked, "Downing" etched in big letters on a bronze sign.

The house perched on the side of the hill, with a spectacular view of the bay. I could see the horseshoe of lights that twinkled below, marking the restaurants and homes on the shore. A few lights from boats reflected into the water in the harbor—the *Calypso* and the *Dallas* distinct enough to pick out among the others.

The driveway was one of those circular things with trees and shrubs growing in the center. No other cars were parked outside. I left the Rambler right in front and stepped out. The house was palatial. Expanses of manicured lawn filled with flowering bushes had been thrashed out of the wild vegetation that still surrounded the perimeter of the yard and continued all the way down to the bay. Crickets and tree frogs were beginning their night songs.

A muted light glowed from an upper window; otherwise the house was dark. The place looked deserted, but Ursala had said a half hour. It would have taken her all of ten minutes to get home from the Watering Hole. Maybe she'd decided to stay for a nightcap, but I didn't believe it. There had been too much fear in her voice.

I rang the bell and waited. Nothing but silence. I rang

again. No one. I didn't like it. Something was wrong. I
pulled out my weapon. Then I turned the knob and
stepped into a towering foyer, in the middle of which a
crystal chandelier reflected shards of light from the
room above.

Once inside I waited for my body to adjust to the
space. The foyer felt hollow, cold. Green marble tile
ended at a white-carpeted staircase that curved up to the
second floor.

"Ursala?" I called, my voice echoing into the house.
Christ, this was not good. I was about to turn on my
flashlight when I felt movement in the shadows, under
the stairway. It was slight, maybe just imagination or
my taut nerves sending false messages to my brain. I
waited, heart rate doubling. Senses on alert. Straining to
see into the blackness.

"Step out," I said drawing my gun. "Police."

I felt the sting in my hair about the same time I heard
a blast reverberate through the foyer. The last thing I
saw was green and felt hard against my cheek.

When consciousness once again took shape, I
thought I was in bed nursing a hangover. The thing was,
I didn't remember the party. It sure felt like a hangover,
though. My heart was pumping a rhythmic drumbeat
into my head—expand and thump, expand and
thump—each thump produced a searing pain in my
temples. I didn't want to open my eyes.

Maybe if I went back to sleep, I'd feel better next
time I awoke. Not likely. I opened my eyes and tried to
clear the mottled green that floated in my vision. Then I
realized I was staring at the hard marble in the foyer of
Ursala's house. I tried to think in spite of the stabbing in
my head and finally realized that something besides al-

cohol was responsible for the pain. I'd been shot. I felt
around my head trying to determine the extent of my
wound. I could feel wet slime sliding down the right
side of my head. When I touched fingers to my temple,
they came away red and sticky. If the bullet had been
just a tad to the left, I would be lying on the floor dead.
Christ, just a matter of a damn inch. As it was, the bullet had put a groove just above my ear.

Now the question was where the hell was the shooter.
Still there, standing above me ready to put another well-
placed bullet in the back of my skull? I lay quietly, playing dead, and listened, trying to bring all my senses into
the space.

A warm breeze drifted through my hair. The front
door was still open. An unimportant observation except
for the fact that I could hear the periodic croaking of a
frog on the doorstep. The frog didn't detect any danger
as he perched singing on the porch. Either nothing else
was moving or it was one brazen frog. I could still feel
my finger wrapped around the gun in my hand. I pushed
myself up to a crouch, ready to shoot the first thing that
moved. Nothing did, except the frog. It took a flying
leap into the bushes.

I sat up, waiting for my head to adjust to an upright
perspective. Finally the pounding and nausea dropped
down a notch or two. I managed to get a foot under me
and stood, leaning against the wall. The foyer was still
dark. I wondered how long I'd been unconscious. Minutes? An hour? Not long enough, I realized, hearing
shuffling in the back somewhere.

I was in no shape to go after anyone, but damned if
I'd let the guy just walk away. I pushed myself off the
wall and started down the hallway. The adjoining room
was lit only by moonlight. One wall was entirely glass,

with French doors out to the patio beyond. Moon glow
illuminated a lush garden. In the dimness I saw two
people locked in an embrace that seemed distorted
somehow. It took a second before I realized it was a
bronze sculpture.

I stood in the shadows, quiet, waiting for a sound or
a shape to emerge from the dark. Seconds passed, nothing. Had I really heard something or had it been the hal-
lucinations of a damaged brain? Then the damned statue
moved. Things were definitely getting surreal. A man
stepped from behind it and off the patio, a form, headed
across the lawn.

I moved to the door as fast as I could and eased it
open. The darned thing squeaked. In the still night it
was like the shriek of a banshee. Until that moment the
guy probably thought I was lying dead in the house
and that he was alone, escaping unnoticed into the
night. He turned, surprised. I couldn't see his face. A
hat, one of those full-brimmed canvas things, kept any
light from reaching his face. He was maybe five-ten,
wearing shorts, tennis shoes, and the damned hat. In
this light he looked like half the tourists on the island.
Definitely a white man, and maybe someone I'd met.
All I had time for was a quick snapshot impression before he lifted his gun my way and fired. He wasn't
even close.

"Police! Stop where you are!" I yelled. Right. He
was already headed for the thick brush that bordered the
lawn. I took off after him, trying to ignore the fact that
my head felt like it was being pounded with a jackham-
mer. He disappeared in the thick tangle of green. I stum-
bled in after him. The place was swarming with
mosquitoes, just waiting for flesh; they descended en
masse. I kept going. I could hear the guy ahead of me

crashing through the bushes, cutting a path that I easily followed. I yelled again.

"Stop or I'll shoot." I didn't have a clear shot but I fired, hoping it would scare him into stopping. No such luck—he only went faster, and he was pulling ahead of me. I knew I wasn't going to be able to outrun him. I was dizzy, and the wet, gooey, red stuff was dripping off my chin. I stopped.

"Goddammit," I muttered. My head was on fire. I heard him ahead, thrashing through the bush, the sound receding, then nothing. "Goddammit!"

I sat, pulled my knees to my chest, rested my head on them, and waited for the world to stop spinning. After a while I realized a stick was poking me in the butt and I was being consumed by mosquitoes that were especially gratified by the blood that covered my face and matted my hair. I swiped at them furiously, arms flailing, taking my anger and frustration out on the damned bugs. I got up and retraced my steps to the house. Where the hell was Ursala?

I went back in through the patio doors and flipped on a light. The room was plush, thick mint carpeting, more sculptures, all abstract shapes of what looked like men in the process of rape, the women's faces grotesque—misshapen, pained. I'd say whoever did these had a warped view of sexuality. Why would any woman, Ursala included, have such crap in her house? There was only one reason: Her husband had done them. I looked closely and saw *F.D.* engraved in the base—Frank Downing.

I continued through the first floor—no one, and nothing out of place. I went back to the foyer. The front door was still open, the tile splotched with blood, my blood. I touched my head lightly, thankful that my brains weren't splattered all over the floor. I shuddered and headed up the steps to the room that was lit.

It was the master bedroom. A king-size bed filled the space. Ursala lay in the center of a purple brocade bedspread, arms out, legs draped over the side. Her skirt was hiked up around her waist, underwear thrown in the corner. A tiny black circle marked her forehead, just like Robsen's. Her lip was bloodied, face bruised. I wondered where Frank Downing might be.

I sat down on the bed next to Ursala's still form and called Dunn. Then I went outside to wait, away from the dead. When he got there, I was sitting on the front stoop, chin propped in my hands.

It had been a bad day. The morning in O'Brien's bed seemed an unfamiliar and unlikely event in someone else's past. Right now, reality was a dead woman in the bed upstairs. My body carried the evidence, a slash on my temple where the blood still seeped.

I was lost in the sounds of the night when the police cruisers pulled up. Dunn took one look at me and insisted that Snyder take me to the hospital. There was nothing I could do to convince him that I was fine.

It took over an hour at the hospital—all for a piece of gauze taped on the side of my head and a few aspirin. Snyder dropped me off at Pickerings Landing. I dreaded facing the ruined boat and the night alone, but I just wanted to collapse into oblivion for a few hours. I'd thought briefly about having Snyder drop me at O'Brien's but dismissed it. It bothered me that I'd even considered it.

When I got to the end of the dock, I could see lights on below the deck of the *Sea Bird*, and Sadie didn't rush up to greet me. Somehow, for the third or fourth time

today, my body tapped some final store of adrenaline
and sent it coursing to my brain. Panic set in.

I knew I had turned the lights off this morning when
I'd left. What more could anyone possibly hope to do to
the already ruined boat? Sink her, I supposed. Or maybe
someone was waiting for me this time. I drew my gun.
This was getting old.

I heard talking below and a bunch of clanging and
clattering. Then Sadie came bounding up on deck, followed by a dark figure.

"Hannah. Please don't shoot." It was O'Brien.

"Jeez, you're lucky I've been trained to look first,
shoot later. What are you doing here? Who's below?"

"Come on down," he said, smiling.

Tilda and Calvin were in the galley, working over the
stove. Rebecca and Daisy sat cross-legged on the floor,
petting the kittens. Elyse was poised at the table with a
needle and thread, just putting the finishing touches on
one of the torn cushions.

"Hannah, come join the party," she said.

The four of them had obviously been working for
several hours to restore the boat. It looked better than
before it had been destroyed.

When I stepped into the light, they all noticed the
bandage.

"What happened?" O'Brien moved to my side, taking in my ragtag condition.

"I'm fine, just a little run-in at the Downings'." I
nodded toward the two little girls and left it at that.

"Sure hope there's someone who wants to have a little kitten in a few weeks," I said, changing the subject.

"We do! Oh, Mama, can we?"

"We'll see, children."

"What did you name them, Hannah?" Rebecca asked.

"I haven't really thought about names." I knew what happened when you named something. It became yours.

"Well, then, we'll call this yellow one Butterfly, the white-and-black one is Drum, like one of those drum fish, and the littlest one is Tiny." Rebecca had it all figured out.

"What about the mother?" Tilda asked.

"Hannah has to name her."

"Why me?"

"'Cause you've got to keep her, Hannah. You saved her," Rebecca reasoned.

"I don't think Sadie would like it," I said. At the moment Sadie was busy cleaning one of the kitten's paws.

"Hannah!" Rebecca stood, hands on her hips.

"Okay, okay," I relented. "Let's call her Nomad." Christ, I had just inherited a scrawny yellow-and-white cat that still looked half-dead.

"Yea!"

After the Pickerings left, I told Elyse and O'Brien what had happened to Ursala and that Dunn was looking for Frank Downing. I could see that O'Brien was upset.

"That woman deserved more," he said. "She was so alone. What a shame."

"Yeah, I think Dunn believes Downing is responsible for Allen Robsen's death too. It's not making much sense to me, but we've pretty much ruled out Clement Davies. First thing in the morning I'm going to talk to the captain of the fishing boat to make sure Davies was where he says he was when Robsen was killed."

Then I made the mistake of telling Elyse and O'Brien about the fins I'd seen on the *Dolphin* and what Davies had told me about the local fishermen selling them to a fishing boat that was out in the deep water.

Elyse was furious. "Don't you see, without that middleman, the locals have no reason to kill sharks. They can't make anything selling fins locally. You saw those fins in the market the other day. No one was buying. They were rotting in the sun. I want to find that boat."

"Jeez, Elyse," O'Brien said. "It's probably long gone by now."

"Well, then why are the locals still collecting fins? I'm going over to the *Dolphin*. I'll get them to tell me where they're unloading them."

"Elyse, it's almost midnight," I said as she stood. Damned if she wasn't going to go down to the docks right now. "There won't be anyone down there. Wait until morning. We'll go together. Besides, you know they aren't breaking any laws with those fins. Neither you nor I can do anything at all if they don't want to cooperate."

"Okay, Hannah. First thing in the morning. But legal or not, I will find a way to stop this." She stomped off the *Sea Bird*, and a few minutes later we could hear her banging around in the galley of the *Caribbe*.

"You'd better be careful," O'Brien said. "When it comes to the maiming of innocent sea creatures, Elyse can spit fire."

"I know. I'm hoping that by tomorrow morning she'll have calmed below the burning point."

God, I was tired. Just a couple of hours ago I'd been chasing Ursala's killer through thick brambles. The wound was minor, but I was bruised, scraped, and bug bitten. What didn't ache or burn itched.

I ran my tongue around the rim of my glass, gathering the last drops of red wine that O'Brien had poured me.

Somehow I'd managed to get smashed on one glass of wine. Now I wanted to dance—the slow, hip-crunching kind of dance. I stood and hung my arms around O'Brien's neck and swayed. All the shit of the day melted to insignificance.

The next thing I knew O'Brien was tucking me into bed. I could hear him rumbling around in the galley, cleaning and doing dishes, as I fell asleep. At some point he slipped into bed next to me. God, it felt good, body wrapped around mine, safe. I was glad he was staying.

Chapter 19

When I opened my eyes the next morning, O'Brien was gone and Elyse was standing over me with a coffee cup in hand.

"Come on, Hannah; let's get going before the *Dolphin* heads out to prey on more sharks."

"Jeez, Elyse, let me wake up first." My brain felt like it was embedded in wet cotton; my head pounded. I wasn't sure whether it was from bullet or Beaujolais. My limbs did not want to unfold.

"You can wake up on the way. I filled a thermos with coffee and already fed Nomad and Sadie."

Two aspirin later, a cup of coffee balanced in one hand, I steered the Rambler toward Road Town with the other. Once we were away from the water, the temperature jumped about twenty degrees. Only six in the morning, and damn, it was hot. Already I could feel the perspiration in my hair, the salt burning the cut on the side of my head.

Somehow Elyse managed to look like she was standing in a cool breeze. She wore an aqua knit shirt with a matching skirt that looked like ice against her mahogany skin. She was an attractive woman, though I doubt she ever gave it much thought.

"Saw Peter leaving the *Sea Bird* this morning," she said, eyes twinkling.

"Yeah, it's getting to be a habit." I didn't like the idea that I liked the idea. Things were moving too fast with O'Brien. I got scared thinking about it. I needed to slow them down.

"Don't you be hurting that man," Elyse said. "There aren't many around like Peter. You'd be crazy to let him go."

"Yeah, maybe."

"No maybe about it."

By the time we got to the marina most of the fishing boats had already gone out; others were starting engines, loading coolers, throwing nets on board.

"Damn, I hope the *Dolphin* hasn't pulled out yet." Elyse marched quickly down the dock, taking two steps to every one of mine. Every man on the dock knew she was trouble the moment she passed by.

"There she is," Elyse said.

The *Dolphin* was right where she'd been when Snyder and I had spotted Davies yesterday.

"Okay, Elyse. Let's go slow here. You won't accomplish anything by pissing these guys off."

"Don't worry, Hannah. I'm an islander. I know how to manage these guys.

"Good day to ya," she hollered to a man who was standing on the bow coiling a line. "You be goin' out today?" Damned if she wasn't flirting. Whatever works, I thought.

"Sure," the man said, giving Elyse a look that went way past admiration, something like lust. "You want to be comin' along, miss?"

"Actually, we'd like to speak with the captain," I said. "Is he around?"

"Now, what do two beautiful women like you want to talk to that ol' salt for? Be glad to help you out."

"I'm the captain." A big man of at least sixty-five, face wrinkled from the sun, stepped out of the hold, wiping greasy hands on a stained rag. "Name's Theodore, Theodore Bentley. Folks call me Teddy."

"I'm a police officer, Hannah Sampson. This is Elyse Henry."

"Come on aboard," he said, holding out a hand. His grip was like iron. "Got to get this damned engine running. Mind if I work while we talk?" He picked up a huge wrench and bent over a heap of metal covered in oil. Pieces were scattered over the deck.

"What can I be doing for you ladies?" Not a trace of concern that I was a police officer. It was obvious that Bentley had nothing to hide.

"Actually, I was hoping to talk with you about Clement Davies. He work with you?"

"Davies? Sure. He's a no-account but I was short-handed. Hired him on."

"When was he out with you?"

"Let me think." He ran an oily hand through his hair. "We went out early Saturday morning, came back yesterday. Haven't seen him since. Probably spending all his pay in town."

I had no reason to doubt Teddy. Davies had been out at sea when Robsen was killed. One loose end tied up.

"What about those shark fins?" Elyse said, nodding toward a stack of freshly cut fins piled in blood-tinged ice.

"What about them?"

"We've heard someone is buying those fins. Like to know who it is."

"What's your interest in that?"

"Elyse works with the Society of Conservation," I said. "She's concerned about the killing of sharks."

"What's a few sharks? My guys make a little extra, put food on the table, maybe buy their missus a new dress. Don't see no harm."

I could see that Elyse was about to lose it and launch into an angry diatribe about the slaughter of innocent sharks. I didn't think that Teddy was going to care a whole lot.

"We just want to talk to the guys, make sure that they are following guidelines for shipping the fins. Don't want anyone getting sick on fish coming from the BVI, right? Something like that gets around, say over in the U.S. Virgins, folks will think twice before buying from our local fishermen," I said quickly, hoping Elyse would get hold of herself in the meantime.

Teddy could see the logic in this. "Well, the fellows collecting them fins be on the *Emerald Queen*. Guess they've been around for a week, maybe more. Can't imagine they be around much longer. Soon's I get this engine fixed, I promised the guys who got these fins we'd head out there to offload them. You can come along if you want."

"Yes, we would like to go along," Elyse said. "Okay, Hannah?"

I didn't object. The *Emerald Queen* was the boat that Trish said they had encountered on their way to Tortola. It might be a good idea to check it out. Besides, I didn't want Elyse going out there alone. No telling what kind of trouble she could get into.

"How long before you head out?" I asked.

"Just about got it," Teddy said, tightening the last bolt down on the engine. "I hold my mouth just right, I believe the old girl will fire up."

He flipped the switch on the console and turned the key. The engine sputtered, then came to life.

"Okay, let's go," he said, closing the engine compartment.

One of the guys untied the lines and jumped on board as Teddy put the *Dolphin* in gear and pointed her out to sea.

This was not the way I'd intended to spend the morning, but I stood on the bow, enjoying the breeze and the salt spray that misted the air. Elyse stood at the helm with Teddy. They were engaged in an animated conversation about one of Teddy's sisters, who it seemed lived next door to Elyse's parents near Spanish Town on Virgin Gorda. That was the way it went in the islands. Everyone was connected.

I smelled the *Emerald Queen* before I spotted her. A mile downwind the stench of rotting flesh was unmistakable. She was floating low in the water, just as Trish had described it. There was no fishing gear in sight. Instead, on deck was a huge container, like some I'd seen ferried on barges. As we got closer, the air began smelling like the back of a butcher shop—dead and rotten.

"What the hell," Teddy said, pulling alongside as his crew threw out bumpers and tossed lines to the men on the *Emerald Queen*.

The boat was loaded with shark fins; bundles three feet wide were stacked up to five feet in every available space. Each bale contained hundreds of fins, many of them rotting. Each two or three fins represented one shark. The number was staggering. This was a massacre.

Elyse stood beside me, her dismay overpowering her anger. We couldn't believe what we were seeing. Even

Teddy was speechless. I saw Elyse whisper something in his ear, and he picked up the radio and made a call.

"What the hell is this?" I asked, showing one of the crew my badge as I stepped on board. God knows what I thought I was doing. I had no jurisdiction with these guys, and as far as I knew there was nothing illegal about carrying a bunch of rotten fish. The smell on the ship was unbelievable. It took every ounce of my willpower to keep from heading to the rail. Not cool for the official on duty to be emptying the contents of her stomach in the sea.

"This is a U.S.-registered boat," Elyse said, stepping on board behind me.

"So what?" The captain had finally appeared from the forward section of the boat, upwind, the only place to get away from the stench. "We are simply transporting fish products from commercial fishermen to exporters in Guatemala. Nothing illegal about that."

"I'm afraid you're wrong," Elyse said. "It is illegal for any U.S. fishing boat, even in foreign waters, to possess shark fins unless the rest of the carcass is on board."

"What the hell business is it of yours?" the captain asked.

"I'm not going to let you get away with this kind of slaughter," Elyse said, shaking a finger at him. The captain followed her as she walked around checking the cargo and cursing at him.

He was saved by the U.S. Coast Guard cutter that was just coming up alongside. They had been patrolling a few miles away over on St. John when Teddy made the call.

The men on the coast guard cutter were as shocked by what they saw as we had been. The commander,

Johnson according to the name under the insignia on his uniform, ordered a search of the ship. They found the hold stuffed with fins. When they opened the container up on top, huge bales of tightly wrapped fins tumbled out onto the deck.

"There's got to be at least twenty tons of fins on this thing," said Johnson. "At a hundred dollars a pound, that's four or five million dollars' worth of fins."

The captain of the *Emerald Queen* agreed that the rotting fish was a problem. He was very upset because the refrigeration unit in the aft storage area had burned out, but he didn't seem to have any idea that they were breaking any laws. Though what they expected to do with rotten fins was anyone's guess.

Commander Johnson ordered that the crew be taken into custody. They didn't resist. They clearly didn't understand the law and figured this was one big mistake.

"We'll be escorting the ship back to St. Thomas," Johnson said. "I'll be in touch if we have questions. But feel free to call the office. I'll be glad to let you know how this turns out," he said, handing me his card.

"I'll be anxious to hear," Elyse said. "If you can eliminate the people who are transporting the fins to distributors, you will eliminate any reason to take shark fins."

"By the way," Johnson said, turning to Teddy, "I'm afraid I'm going to have to confiscate those." He indicated the fins stacked on the *Dolphin*.

"There's no law about finning in the BVI," protested one of Teddy's crew, who had expected to earn some money in this transaction.

"It's coast guard policy. We're making every effort to stop the transportation of wildlife plunder. If we have to, we'll work with your local government. We could make a case against you. But of course, we don't want to prosecute local fishermen. We would just like the activity to stop."

"No problem," Teddy said. "Take them." Teddy would have been worried that his captain's license might be at risk, but I could tell that it was more than that. He had been upset by the carnage he'd seen on the *Emerald Queen*.

In spite of the horror, Elyse was also clearly feeling a huge sense of relief. At least for a while, the killing of sharks for their fins had slowed a bit. We'd put the *Emerald Queen* out of business.

It was not even nine o'clock when I got to the office. Dunn was gloating over the fact that he had Frank Downing in custody. As far as he was concerned, Allen Robsen's and Ursala Downing's murderer was behind bars.

Chapter 20

"Not long after you went to the hospital last night, Downing just came waltzing into his house like a drunken sailor," Dunn said. "He took one look at Ursala, smirked, and passed out right next to her on the bed."

Frank was stretched out on the cot in his cell, arm across his face. He stood, unsteady, when Snyder opened the cell door.

"Mornin', Frank," Dunn said. "You be ready to answer a few questions?"

I had never met Frank Downing before, but he could be the man I had chased through the woods last night. Same general build, though heavier than I remembered the man who had stood on the lawn. He certainly looked like he could have been running through thick brambles. His clothes were dirty, shirt torn. He was a mess. Given the nature of his art, I'd expected to find cruelty etched in his face. I wasn't disappointed. Along with it was a smugness, an above-it-all attitude.

Of course, he had a motive. If Ursala had taken her flirting to the next level and actually slept with Robsen,

Frank may have been pushed enough to kill. It could be all about ego for him. Nothing to do with caring what Ursala did.

Dunn and I sat across from him in the sparsely furnished interrogation room. He fingered an unlit cigarette and glared.

"Can you tell us where you were last night?" Dunn asked.

"Out drinking," he said. "Went over to Road Town."

"Were you with anyone?" Dunn asked. "Anyone who can vouch for you, say, between six and seven, eight o'clock?"

"Come on, John. Do you really think I'd kill Ursala? Why? I had a good thing going."

"How much do you stand to inherit?" I asked, realizing that perhaps greed rather than jealousy motivated Frank Downing.

Downing shrugged, matter-of-fact. "Everything," he said. "Ursala didn't have any other family."

"When did you last see Ursala?" Dunn asked.

"Down at the Watering Hole," he said.

"What time was that?" I asked.

"Must of been around four-thirty, five. We went down there together. Had a few drinks. She started in about me not loving her. It was always the same crap. Me telling her to get a divorce, she saying she just might."

"Maybe you killed her before she could divorce you," I suggested. "Good way to protect your investment."

"No way. Ursala would never divorce me. She threatened it all the time. Ask anyone. Once, things had been good between us, and every once in a while they still were. Ursala hung on to that."

"How did you tear your shirt?" I asked.

He smirked. "Found me a cute little whore over at Road Town. When I flashed a hundred-dollar bill at her, gal got real enthusiastic. Damned if she didn't pull me into the bushes right there behind the bar, tore my shirt open, didn't even bother with buttons. We rolled around under that bush for a half hour. As soon as I gave her that hundred, she took off."

"Can she verify your story?' "

"Christ, I don't know who the hell she was, just one of the hookers. Can't say I've ever seen her before."

"Sounds like a romantic encounter," I said. The story seemed a weak cover to explain the state of his clothing. Pretty coincidental with the fact that whoever I chased into the woods would look just like Frank Downing looked now.

I thought about those statues I'd seen at the Downing house. "You know, it looks like Ursala was roughed up before she was killed. May have been raped," I said.

His look was incredulous. "Rape? Christ, why would I do a thing like that? I didn't need to rape my own wife."

"I saw your work at the house," I said. "Seems like rape was on your mind a lot."

"Those statues are statements about existence, about relationships; they are not meant to reflect approval but just the opposite."

Right, I thought. I'd bet it was a way for Frank to get off. "Where did you go after the party on the *Calypso* last Sunday?" Dunn asked.

"Hey, don't try to pin Robsen on me too, for chrissake. I had a drink with the Texans and went home."

"Was Ursala home when you got there?"

"No, she was still out. I went to bed."

"Any way to prove that?"

"There was no one else at the house, if that's what you mean."

Stark interrupted, asking Dunn to step outside. When he came back in, he looked both smug and relieved. He gave me a satisfied glance and said, "Found a gun, a twenty-two-caliber. Won't know for sure till it's tested but it looks like the murder weapon. Know where it was?"

Downing looked scared, confused.

"Under the seat of your car," Dunn said.

"No way," he shouted, rising from his chair. "It's not mine. Someone must have put it there. I didn't kill Ursala."

He fell back into his chair, looking numb.

I could see where this was going. Frank had killed Robsen. Hell, maybe he didn't care about Ursala, but he didn't like being made a fool of. Ursala somehow had found out that Frank had done it. Maybe she'd threatened to expose him.

She'd called me from the bar after Frank left, then headed up to the house to wait for me. He could have followed, in a rage that only rape could relieve, taking the upper hand, gaining power, control first. Then killed her to protect his financial interests, and to keep her from talking to me about Robsen. Frank Downing had plenty of motivation. Why the hell didn't I think he'd done it?

I drove over to the Watering Hole. I needed to find out what had gone on there last night when Ursala had called. When I'd left the office, Dunn was booking Frank Downing for the murder of both Ursala and Allen Robsen. Case closed. Something just didn't fit, but hell if I could figure out what it was. Nothing felt right.

The Watering Hole was empty except for the bartender washing glasses. He pretty much confirmed Downing's story. He and Ursala had been in about five. Had a few drinks, fought.

"They were always fightin'," he said. "One or the other of 'em storming out. Last night it was Frank left. Ursala hung around, talking with that guy from the *Calypso*."

"Guy Pembrook?"

"Yeah, that's his name."

"Where was his wife?"

"She came in later, looked like some harsh words.

"Ursala made a call. I remember 'cause she seemed kinda upset, scared maybe."

That must have been the call she made to me. The phone was down the hall just outside the bathrooms.

"Could anyone have overheard her phone conversation?" I asked.

"Don't know 'bout dat," he said. "S'pose someone comin' out of the rest room coulda heard her."

"Did you see anyone coming out?"

He thought about it for a while. "Jeez, I don' know, lotsa people in here las' night, comin' and goin'. I saw her talkin' real quiet into the phone. Let me think," he said, closing his eyes.

I could tell he was trying to visualize the scene. I did it all the time, like rerunning a movie.

"I do remember a couple of dem women from that sailboat from Texas come out of the bathroom, with that Miz Pembrook."

"Frank Downing wasn't around then?"

"Naw, like I said, he'd already left."

"Did you see Ursala talk to anyone besides her husband and Guy Pembrook?"

"Didn't notice anyone else, but the place was kind of crowded. She rushed right out of here after she hung up the phone. Didn't pay me for her drinks."

"Would you call the department if you think of anything else?"

"Sure will," he said.

The Manettis were just getting into their dinghy when I came out of the Watering Hole. I flagged them down and hitched a ride with them over to Trish Robsen's boat. I figured she deserved to know that an arrest had been made. And I still couldn't help feeling that I was missing something. Maybe talking to her again would help.

I settled into the middle of the dinghy next to Melissa Manetti. Don was in the rear, pulling on the engine cord and swearing.

"Damn things never work right." He squeezed the rubber bulb that pumps gas into the engine and tried again. The engine caught. Manetti put it in gear and maneuvered the boat away from the dock, managing to clip the corner as he headed out. No wonder these boats didn't work, I thought. They clearly took a lot of abuse from careless or inexperienced handlers, Manetti among them.

That was when it dawned on me: Trish had mentioned the dinghy the other day. Snyder had pulled away so quickly, I hadn't had the chance to ask her about it. Then the call from Ursala, my trip to her house, Downing's arrest. In all the activity, I'd forgotten. Trish had said the engine on the dinghy was not functioning. So how had they gotten to the *Calypso* that night? And how had Robsen motored it to shore? Pembrook had said the last time he'd seen Robsen he was driving it in to shore. I was sure of it. How the hell did it end up on the beach in front of Foxy's?

A new dinghy was tied to the back of the *Wind Runner*. Thanks to O'Brien, Trish and her son had immediate transport back and forth to shore. Trish was standing in the cockpit of the *Wind Runner* when we pulled up. In the few days since Robsen's death, she'd lost weight, her shorts hanging loose around her waist. And in spite of all the sun, she looked pale, gaunt. Dark circles marred her eyes. I thanked the Manettis and climbed onto the *Wind Runner*. Her son, she explained, had gone into Road Town for supplies.

I told her about Ursala's murder, Frank's arrest. That the gun had been found, probably the same one that had killed Allen. She sank onto the cushioned cockpit bench. Finally she spoke.

"This seems so unreal," she said. "Like something out of a B movie. And so senseless. Do you think that Allen actually met that woman?" she asked, tearing. "God, was Allen killed by a jealous husband?" she asked, her face collapsing in hurt. "How can I ever tell the children this?"

I wish I could say it wasn't so, but more than likely it was. When she calmed, regained some composure, I asked her about the dinghy.

"The dinghy?" she asked, confused.

"The other day you mentioned that it wasn't running."

"Yes, that's right. Allen had trouble getting it started when we left the restaurant that night. It turned over a couple times but wouldn't catch. Allen spent a few minutes checking it out. Then he yanked on the cord till the thing started smoking. We were going to leave it at the dock and ride over with the Manettis, but Allen was a little uneasy about leaving it there all night. He decided to row it over to the *Calypso*, not a big deal, really. All of a sudden it turned into a rowing competition with Don Manetti. We won." She smiled, remembering. "Allen was sometimes such a kid at heart. Raising an oar above his head and laughing. 'You never had a chance,' he'd kidded Don."

"Did Guy Pembrook know the engine wasn't working?" I asked.

"Well, he might not have. We climbed aboard the *Calypso*, everyone laughing. I can't remember anyone mentioning the engine. I'd forgotten about it myself until the Manettis dropped me back here that night, but I knew Allen would simply row back to the boat. He enjoyed being on the water without the engine noise. Used to kayak whenever he had the chance. Loved gliding silently through the water."

Her son was just pulling up in a taxi when Trish pulled their dinghy up to the dock and dropped me off on shore. I helped them load groceries into their dinghy, pushed them away from the dock, and watched as they motored back to the *Wind Runner*. Now that the investigation was closed, I expected that they would return to the States. Maybe Trish could begin to heal, to put it all behind her. I wondered if she'd ever again come to these islands to sail. I doubted it. I wish that I'd had better news for her. That I'd been able to tell her that her husband had been faithful.

As I headed to my car, I spotted Guy Pembrook walking down the beach toward the dock. What the hell, a few more questions wouldn't hurt.

"Mr. Pembrook," I yelled, intercepting him under a nearby palm tree.

He turned, irritated. "Detective Sampson, how's your investigation?" he asked, covering the irritation with a smile.

"Looks like we got our killer. Chief arrested Frank Downing this morning," I said, though I figured Pembrook and half the island already knew this by now.

"Really?" He actually smiled for real this time.

"I've been wondering about something, though," I said. "You said Robsen motored his dinghy to shore that night after the party?"

"Well, as I said before, he was heading that way."

"Did he have any trouble with the engine?" I asked.

Pembrook hesitated. "Not that I recall. Why do you ask?"

"Trish said the engine quit at the dock that night. That they were planning to get someone from SeaSail out to look at it in the morning."

"Well, now that you mention it, I guess Robsen did have some trouble getting it started. You know, swore a bit, kept trying. The thing finally turned over. Why is this important?" he asked, irritation rising again.

"Just dotting the Is and crossing Ts" I said. Christ, I hated that expression. It's what the bureaucrats always used as an excuse for their damned red tape.

"Well, I'm getting tired of the questions, Detective," he said. He climbed into his dinghy, fired it up, and sped away from the dock before I could get another word in. But I had what I needed.

I stopped at the SeaSail dock on my way home. The *Wind Runner*'s old dinghy was nestled among a bunch of others. The engine had been removed. I found Louis in the office and asked him if anyone had had a chance to check out the engine.

"Yeah. Got to replace the thing."

"Could you get it started?"

"Naw, the engine's shot."

So why had Pembrook lied? I could think of only one reason: Robsen had never left the *Calypso* at all. Or at least he'd never left alive.

Chapter 21

It was all pretty flimsy. One little lie about the dinghy engine. Dunn wasn't buying it.

"Maybe Pembrook had passed out below, too embarrassed to admit it, never saw Robsen leave," Dunn said.

"Well, why not admit it when I asked him?" I said. "Pembrook's hiding something. And how the hell does someone like him end up with a boat like the *Calypso* to begin with? He looks and acts more like a con man than a writer."

"Jeez, Hannah, can't you just be grateful that this crime has been solved? Accept that it was Downing? He had motive for both murders and no alibi during the time of either of the killings. But most important, the murder weapon was in his car. What else do you want? Blood on his hands?" Dunn said.

That would be nice, I thought. Right now everything was too circumstantial, and why on earth would Downing have left that weapon under the seat of his car, for chrissake?

I knew that the pressure Dunn had been getting from the commissioner had eased some with Downing's arrest. I guess I couldn't blame Dunn. I mean, really, everything pointed to Downing, and Dunn still had the damned burglaries to contend with. There had been another last night.

"Anyone hurt?" I asked.

"No, folks were locked in the basement all night. Finally got the neighbors' attention early this morning. Burglars took an expensive diamond-and-ruby ring, necklace, and matching earrings, several other valuable pieces—worth maybe two hundred and fifty thousand. There will be hell to pay. These victims are well connected, know the commissioner personally."

"Is there anything I can do to help?"

"No. Stark and Worthington are on it. I want you to take the rest of the afternoon off," Dunn said. "You deserve it, and I've been hearing you haven't even taken the time to settle in, go to the market."

How the hell would Dunn know that?

"You been talking to O'Brien?" I asked, uncomfortable with these two exchanging stories about me.

"Don't worry about it," he said, noting my discomfort. "Ran into O'Brien buying food for that cat you rescued. He said all you've managed to stock were some basics from Tilda's little market."

What the hell. I could use the time. I left Dunn's office just as the phone rang.

"Yes, Commissioner," he was saying as I closed the door.

I drove into town and stopped at Bobbies, the big market in the middle of town, and managed to fill a cart: cleaning supplies, canned goods, boxes of pasta and rice. Kitty litter, for chrissake. I had never planned to be a cat owner. Right now I had four.

All the while, though, Pembrook's lie gnawed at me.

There was just no way I could let it go. I went home, unloaded the groceries, and continued to obsess.

"I'll bet Pembrook is up to his ass in this," I said aloud. Sadie's ears perked up and she cocked her head, trying to understand. Then she came over and licked my toes in sympathy.

What the heck. I was on my own time. I grabbed my swimsuit, a beach towel, filled a cooler with ice and a couple of beers, filled a jug of water, and loaded it all plus Sadie into the Rambler. I put the top down and headed over to Cane Garden Bay, Sadie beside me, ears flapping in the wind. An afternoon on the beach would do me good, and hell, you just never knew what kinds of things you'd see going on.

I spent a half hour throwing the Frisbee into the water for Sadie to retrieve, two young French children laughing and clapping on the beach every time she crashed into the surf and came back, Frisbee in her mouth. She was really showing off. The kids' mother lay topless on a blanket down the way; the father was perched on his elbow reading. Pointedly ignoring me and Sadie, he called the children back when they came to sit with me and play with Sadie.

There were several others on the beach, mostly parents, many British, vacationing with their children, a few sailors, spending the afternoon off their boats on solid ground. I had just opened a Carib, the local brew, when I saw Guy and Elizabeth Pembrook climb from the *Calypso* into their dinghy. He cranked it up and they headed into shore. I pulled on my hat, a full-brimmed straw affair that covered my face. I looked like all the other tourists on the beach. They got into a taxi, never even glancing my way.

I left Sadie sleeping under a palm tree and went for a

swim. I did the stingray shuffle through the sandy shallow water. O'Brien had warned me about the stingrays, burrowing themselves in the sand, invisible till you stepped on one and their barbed tail shot up in reflexive self-defense to inflict a severe wound on foot or calf. Obviously dogs and small children were immune as evidenced by Sadie and the two French children, all of whom had been frolicking unconcerned in the water just moments ago. But I wasn't taking any chances.

Finally I plunged beneath the surface, the warm, tropical salt water washing sand and sweat from my body. I swam out until I was treading water among the sailboats. I could see the *Wind Runner* still anchored nearby and the Texans' yacht over off the point. I intended a short look around the *Calypso*. Might as well.

I swam over to her and glanced around the harbor. No one was visible on any of the boats. Everyone was either napping below deck, off somewhere snorkeling, or exploring on shore. I took one more quick look around then, hoisted myself quickly out of the water and onto the *Calypso*.

I sat for a moment, trying not to look guilty—difficult for a Catholic girl who was always guilty of one thing or another. I hoped that no one had noticed me. Hell, I looked like just another sailor sitting on the boat in my suit, drying in the sun. I thought again about the Pembrooks and this boat. How the hell could a couple like them be on a boat like this? It just didn't fit. People with boats like this had an appreciation for character, charm, beauty. Guy Pembrook was more the live-fast type, functional boats with all the gadgets. Once again I admired this classic.

An antique compass covered by eight-sided domed leaded glass, its brass pedestal reflecting light, was bolted into the floor in front of the wooden eight-spoked steering wheel. The boat had been carefully tended, every detail considered, brass and wood lovingly polished to rich chocolates and golden oak sheens. The empty beer can washed into the corner along with a couple of cigarette butts was incongruous. How could Pembrook take such care of the boat and then leave trash about?

I went down the steps into the salon. Unlike the day I'd sat here with Guy, it was a mess: dirty dishes, pots and pans in the sink, food stuck to the teak table, wet towel in a heap on the floor. I supposed they'd cleaned it the other day to show it to Rodriguez. It hadn't taken long for Guy and Elizabeth to achieve that lived-in look.

Where to start in this mess? I didn't really know what I was looking for or what I expected to find. I went over to the bookshelf and pulled several of the books down to expose the bullet hole I'd seen the last time I was down here. It was a tiny round spot in the teak. Could be a .22. I was sorely tempted to dig the thing out. But I had no warrant. I wasn't even supposed to be on the boat. Any evidence I found would be useless without having the proper authorization.

I scanned the books on the shelf, an esoteric mix of technical books on sailing: one called *Adlard Coles's Heavy-weather Sailing*, another a manual called *Practical Celestial Navigation, Longitude* by Dava Sobel, and novels, Hemingway, Steinbeck, of course Melville. I pulled out Pembrook's guidebook and examined the jacket, a smooth beige heavyweight paper with a photo of a Hawaiian harbor on the cover and Guy Pembrook's name below.

The inside flap described the work as an extensive natural history of the islands. The bottom half of the back flap had been torn out. I took the dust jacket off the book and placed it inside a plastic bag I found in the kitchen, tied it closed, and stuffed it into the top of my suit.

I continued my search, opening cupboards and drawers and peering into cubbyholes. A roach scurried out of one. In the forward cabin the bed was unmade, sheets tangled in the center, a coffee cup with a cigarette butt in it sitting on the ledge that ran the length of the bed. Nothing unexpected in the closet or drawers—an assortment of socks, skimpy underwear, shorts, and T-shirts.

I pulled the mattress up, hoping that the cockroaches would scatter quickly in the light. They did. Only one remained, smashed flat under a beautifully bound leather journal hidden way down at the foot of the bed. Elizabeth Pembrook's name was embossed in gold letters. I turned to the first entry.

April 2: *Today we launched the* Calypso, *after eight months repairing her. She is beautiful and absolutely sound and seaworthy. Tomorrow we leave for the long haul from Miami to the Caribbean. Sam will come with us as far as Cuba, spelling us on the long open-water trip. Guy and I are treating this as a working honeymoon. Can't believe we've been married almost a year.*

I suddenly realized a boat was approaching. I stuffed the journal back under the mattress and took a quick glance around the cabin to make sure I hadn't left any sign of my invasion. Hell, the state the place was in, they'd never be able to tell. I climbed up the ladder to the deck, then hunched down and scurried to the front of the boat, climbed over the edge, and slipped quietly into the water. I stayed alongside, treading water and listening.

Pembrook was handing stuff from the dinghy to Elizabeth, who was standing on the back of the boat. I heard Pembrook step aboard and tie the dinghy up. Then Elizabeth went below and Pembrook followed. It sounded like they were arguing, voices raised. I swam along to the side nearest the galley. Lots of clattering and banging of cupboard doors. They were putting groceries away.

"Let's just sail over to St. Thomas," Elizabeth was saying. "I bet we could sell the boat there in no time."

"Look, it will only be a day or two. Rodriguez is ready to buy. As soon as his funds are transferred, we make the deal and leave. I mean cash, for chrissake. It's not that many people can get their hands on that kind of cash that fast. We've got to wait."

"I don't like it." she said.

"Aw, darlin', don't you worry. We'll be leaving by tomorrow, next day latest. Come here, baby."

That was the end of any discernible conversation. It didn't take much imagination to figure out what happened next. A good time to head to shore. They wouldn't be noticing any cop swimming away from their boat.

When I got to the beach, the only people around were the French family. The two young kids were sitting in the sand next to Sadie, showering her with attention. She was sprawled on her back, paws in the air, daring them to scratch her belly.

When I approached, the father again called to his children. He glanced out toward the *Calypso* and gave me an accusing look. Surely he hadn't seen me on the boat. Then I noticed the binoculars lying on the blanket. He'd probably been watching me from shore as I swam out. He might have caught a glimpse of me on the *Calypso*. Damned binoculars were a hazard.

I sat next to Sadie and picked up where the kids had
left off, absently scratching behind her ears and gazing
out at the *Calypso*. Nothing about the Pembrooks fit.
Elizabeth Pembrook was just not the type to have a
gold-embossed journal hidden under her mattress, much
less write in it. And she'd sounded scared. Why was she
in such a hurry to leave Cane Garden Bay?

Dunn was still at his desk when I walked back into
the department. It was well past six. Just about everyone
else had left for the day.

"Detective Sampson," Dunn said, looking up from a
pile of paperwork, "I thought I told you to take the rest
of the day off. What are you doing back here?"

"Just wanted to check something out," I said. "Why
are you still here, Chief? Marie's probably got dinner
waiting." I hoped to avoid giving Dunn any details. Fortunately he didn't ask. Dunn looked tired; dark
splotches were beginning to appear under eyes marred
by overwork. I could tell he didn't need the grief, and
he'd be really pissed if he knew I had just searched the
Calypso uninvited while the Pembrooks were ashore.

"Nothing else on the burglaries?" I asked.

"Nothing, and another one reported this afternoon in
broad daylight," he said. "Something's got to give on
these break-ins. These fellows can't just disappear into
the woodwork, though that's what seems is occurring.
Folks are getting real nervous. At least the Robsen affair
has been cleared up. Course, Frank Downing's yelling
foul; hired some big lawyer from the States. Be here tomorrow. I hope you're not stirring up trouble about that
case."

"No way, Chief, just tying up some loose ends," I
lied.

"Just make sure they're tied up good and tight," he warned.

I left him at his desk and went downstairs to the evidence room, a cinder-block, windowless room with fluorescent lights, dusty and damp, filled with gray metal shelves. I found the row marked "P–S" and made my way down the narrow aisle to the Rs. The box marked "Robsen" was near the top.

I narrowly avoided pulling the whole damned shelf over on top of me trying to finger the box off the shelf. Christ, I'd have been trying to resort evidence all night if I had. I always did things the hard way. A damned stool was right at the end of the row.

I sat on the floor and opened the box. Inside was the wallet I'd retrieved at the scene. It was still damp and covered with salt. I was looking for the piece of paper I'd taken from Robsen's shirt pocket. The lab tech had actually sealed it, still damp, inside a plastic bag. When I'd found it in Robsen's shirt pocket and left it at the coroner's, it had been soggy, the text indistinguishable. Now it was also mildewed and soft.

I removed it carefully from the bag, trying to unfold it without completely destroying it. I flattened it out on the floor and then I pulled out the book jacket I'd taken from the *Calypso* and lay the torn piece in the place where a piece of the book jacket had been torn away. It pretty much matched. Same type of paper, and the right size.

So Robsen had torn it out and stuffed it in his shirt pocket the night he'd been on the *Calypso* sometime before he died. Had it gotten him killed? Surely not. Would Pembrook or anyone else murder Robsen over that piece of paper?

It was pretty obvious that I needed to find out what was on that piece of paper.

Dunn was still buried in paperwork when I came back upstairs. "Get that loose end taken care of?" he asked.

"Yeah, no problem, Chief." I didn't have the heart to tell him that I thought the whole ball of yarn was about to unravel.

Chapter 22

Blue Island Books was a turquoise-and-yellow structure nestled between a plumbing store and a lawyer's office. The place was shut down tight, its wooden doors closed and padlocked. I wondered when it had been opened last. It looked like maybe 1984. The sign was one of those "Will return at . . ." with a clock below it. Both hands were pointed down to the six, a result of age and gravity. My sister complained about it all the time—the sagging that came with time.

It was almost nine-thirty A.M. and I was pretty sure that the proprietor would not return at the indicated six-thirty. I was rattling the door in a futile gesture of hope and frustration when a woman in a tan suit, briefcase in hand, came scurrying down the sidewalk.

"I'm comin' along now," she said. "So sorry, my children be makin' me late dis mornin'."

She spent several minutes digging through an enormous purse and complaining about her son, who I learned was an unruly seven-year-old determined to spend the day sailing with his uncle instead of in school. Finally she found the keys and opened up the shop.

The store was a long and narrow affair, with bookshelves lining every available wall. The place was reputed to be the best bookstore in the islands. At least according to their ad: *If we don't have it, no one does.* They didn't have it. Nothing at all by Guy Pembrook. It had been a long shot. "Why we be carrying a book about Hawaii here?" the proprietress asked, confused. When I suggested that someone might want to travel to the Hawaiian islands, she was incredulous.

"Why would anyone want to go there, when they be here?"

I guess she had a point. I ended up buying a book about fish behavior and walked around the corner to the Internet Café. Inside, strains of Bob Marley's "Buffalo Soldier" seeped through the wall from the bar on the other side. I sang along as I booted up one of the computers. While the shops in the BVI display styles of an era when gold brocade dresses and patent-leather shoes were in vogue, the islands are well along on the information highway.

I logged in and did a search for Guy Pembrook. His book about the natural history on Maui came up with a review that said, *a must-have for all nature lovers who will visit these Pacific islands. Pembrook provides detailed accounts of hiking trails, nature preserves, and underwater parks for snorkelers.*

There was a short biography about Pembrook. He'd written scores of articles about traveling and sailing, most focused on the natural history of the places he visited. He was quoted as saying it allowed him to do what he loved, traveling to glorious locations and sharing his discoveries with his readers. His new wife had become his companion and adviser in these endeavors. "We are living the dream," he'd said, "sailing the *Calypso*, a completely restored wooden sailboat, into the most beautiful ports in the tropics."

Nice work if you can get it, I thought. The Guy and Elizabeth Pembrook I knew just didn't fit the picture. Elizabeth acting as an adviser for the books? Right! The only photo on the Web site was a cover of the book—a palm-lined trail leading down to the shore.

I walked back to the office. One block off the water's edge, the temperature had to be 105, and no breeze. I could not understand how the islanders managed to maintain the dress code that they did: suits, ties, long-sleeved dresses with panty hose. It made me feel smothered just looking at them. And then there was me—clearly a foreigner.

Dunn and I had reached a compromise about the dress code. He'd suggested that because I was new and clearly not a native islander I begin my duties in a damned uniform: a long, dark pair of pants with a shiny strip along the side of each leg, a gray shirt with epaulet, one of those awful billed hats. I'd agreed to wear long pants and a buttoned shirt instead of my standard tank top. I would not give up the Birkenstocks, and I donned a pair of shorts whenever I figured I wasn't going to be running into Dunn. Now I was wearing tan khakis and a sleeveless white shirt, which was already sticking to my belly, and cursing Dunn.

Back at the office, Jean was buried under a stack of papers that she was trying to organize and file.

"Good day to you, Hannah."

"Hi, Jean. Is the chief around?"

"They made an arrest in the burglaries. Chief actually went home for lunch." I hoped that Dunn would be taking a long afternoon with his wife. He deserved a break.

And it would be best if he didn't know I was still snooping around about the Robsen case.

When I went down to the jail cells, Stark was just locking three boys into the cell next to Frank Downing's.

"Hey, congratulations," I said. "Jean said you made an arrest."

"Yeah. We'd sent descriptions of the stuff that'd been stolen to every pawnshop on the island. Stupid kids trying to sell the stuff in the middle of town. Owner called us right away."

"You don't seem that happy about it," I said.

"Not very."

"Yeah, they're young, huh?"

"Two are twelve; the other one is thirteen. Live up by Green Ghut. Couple are brothers. Big families. Fathers are out of work. Not like they aren't lookin', but things just haven't gone their way. Kids tryin' to help out. Damn, they deserve more."

"Did you recover everything?"

"Not much. These kids aren't saying what they've done with any of it. All we've found are a couple of TVs and a bunch of CDs. No jewelry. They deny knowing anything about it."

I could see that Stark hated his job at this moment. He didn't want to leave the kids down in that cell.

"Don't worry, Stark. They'll be okay."

"Yeah, right."

Downing was stretched out on a cot, hands behind his head, staring at the ceiling. He didn't move when he saw me come in.

"Don't bother," he said. "I'm not talking to you or anyone else without my lawyer here. To think, you've arrested me—me. I'm an artist, an intellectual, not a murderer."

Like one rules out the other. Frank Downing was a snob. And that damn pompous attitude.

"Look, Frank, I'm not here to interrogate you. In spite of the fact that I don't like you, I'm afraid that I have difficulty believing you're a killer." I didn't say that I thought he was a weak, sniveling coward without the balls to kill and that he was not the God's gift to art and all that was aesthetic that he thought. I figured that was the wrong tack to take if I wanted him to talk to me at all.

"Well," he huffed, "at least one of you with some intelligence."

"Do you have any idea at all about who would want Ursala dead?" I asked.

"No one, everyone," he said. "Ursala was just a dumb blonde who slept around. She could have gotten in bed with the wrong guy at some point, one with a wife that didn't put up with it. Maybe a lover who didn't like seeing her with other men. That sure wouldn't have been me, though. Ursala and I had an understanding. She could fool around all she wanted as long as she supported my art."

"Hum, seems like a good deal for you. What was in it for her?"

"Me," he said in that damned egotistical tone. What an ass.

"Did Ursala say anything to you? Was she in any kind of trouble?"

"Ursala and I didn't communicate much. But lately she seemed jumpy. Damned if she didn't lock me out of the house a couple of nights ago. When she came down to let me in, she made sure it was me before she opened up. She'd never locked the house up before. When I asked her about it, she said something about all the burglaries on the islands." He glanced at the kids in the nearby cell.

"How well did Ursala know the Pembrooks?" I asked.

"Not well. They'd only been around a week or so, but Ursala meets everyone who anchors in the bay and comes into the Watering Hole. Course, we went to that party on their boat."

"Ursala said she was down on the beach after the party, waiting for Robsen. Did you know that?"

"Sure, I saw her. Went down there and told her I was headed into Road Town, probably wouldn't be home that night.

"She was sitting at one of those beach tables sipping champagne. She'd managed to finish off half the bottle, another empty glass on the table. I figured that by the time Robsen arrived, there would be nothing left to share. She had those damned little rhinestone-studded binoculars around her neck."

"Really? How come?" Ursala had not mentioned watching anyone when I'd talked to her about waiting for Robsen on the beach.

"She was always trying to see what was happening down the beach or on other people's boats. Nosy. A voyeur. I told her someday she'd see someone looking straight back at her. 'Well, I hope so,' she'd said in that suggestive tone of hers. You think she actually saw something? The moon was full that night, enough light to see out into the harbor. Maybe that's what had her so scared. Maybe got her killed."

"Yeah, maybe."

I went back up to my desk and called Mack. He picked up the phone on the first ring.

"Sampson, good to hear your voice. How's the investigation going?" he asked, chewing on something I was sure was cold and greasy.

I told him we'd made an arrest, but I didn't think we had the right guy.

"Typical Sampson, just can't leave it alone. So what do you need?"

I asked him if he would get a copy of Pembrook's book about Hawaii and fax me the back jacket.

"No problem, Sampson. I'll get on it this afternoon. Hey, let me know when you're ready to come back. I'll plan a coming-home party. We can drink a whole bunch of tequila and take oaths about some kind of shit or other."

"Mack, just fax the stuff, okay?" I said, and hung up. I wondered when Mack would finally accept the idea that I was not coming back. Maybe when I did.

I found the *Wahoo* in its slip, tank full. I figured I'd spend a few hours over at Cane Garden Bay. I was hoping that Trish Robsen had not yet left the islands. I was in luck. The *Wind Runner* was still anchored where it had always been, and Trish was still there, sitting in the cockpit. A paperback book on her lap, she gazed blankly out to sea. She didn't see me coming until I was about to tie up to her boat. She leaped up, and hardly noticed when she spilled iced tea all over the cockpit. As she grabbed my line, the novel she'd been holding fell into the water. I tried to grab it but it sank too fast. I watched it drift down to rest on the sandy bottom.

"Damn," I said.

"Yeah," she agreed, but I didn't think she was referring to the lost book.

"How are you, Trish?" I asked as I went below to grab some paper towels.

"Fine," she said, watching me soak up the tea. She was hardly aware of what I was doing. Ever notice how people say they're fine when they're not?

"I thought you might have returned to the States by now."

"Oh, it's not that easy arranging to transport a body. My son has been working on it, talking to the airlines. I don't seem to be able to concentrate long enough to accomplish anything. Maybe tomorrow."

"I'm glad you're still here." I had the feeling that Trish didn't care if she ever went home to deal with the loss and the implications of what had gotten her husband killed. It would be hard to face her family and friends. I'd like to tell her that her husband really hadn't been killed by a jealous husband, but damn, I just didn't have enough. It would be cruel to raise her hopes and then bring them crashing down.

"I know you've told the story again and again, but is there anything else you can think of that happened at the *Calypso* or in the restaurant before Allen disappeared?"

"There's nothing else," she said, voice flat. "Why are you asking? I thought the case was closed."

"Just trying to finalize a couple of things for the file," I lied. "I found a torn piece of paper in one of your husband's pockets. I'm pretty sure it came from Guy Pembrook's book cover."

"That seems strange," she said.

"Can you think of any reason he would have torn it out and put it in his pocket? Would he have been a fan of Pembrook's or wanted the information on the jacket? It was from Pembrook's guide to Hawaii."

"No, couldn't be. We'd never heard of the Pembrooks before we met them that night, and we certainly had no plans to go to Hawaii. Why would he do that?"

"Probably not important, just one of those unanswerable questions."

I left her sitting on the deck, empty-handed, no book, no tea. She didn't seem to care.

Chapter 23

Before heading into shore, I took a cruise around the anchorage. The *Dallas* had pulled out, but the Manettis were still in the bay. They had moved their boat farther from shore and were anchored just off the starboard side of the *Calypso*. With all the room in the harbor, I wondered why anyone would want to anchor right next to another boat. Don Manetti had probably dropped his anchor well in front of the *Calypso*. When he'd let out enough scope to ensure good holding, he'd drifted back almost even with the *Calypso*, but figured he still had enough room to swing. It was pretty obvious that Don Manetti was a novice. An experienced sailor would have known where he would end up after he dropped his anchor.

I'd bet the Pembrooks weren't too happy having the Manettis practically on top of them. Especially Guy, given Elizabeth's form of sunbathing. Maybe that was really what had motivated Don to move next door. Not a mistake at all.

It seemed odd that the Manettis hadn't moved on to one of the other islands by now. Surely they intended to tour the Baths, sail up to Virgin Gorda, maybe to Anegada. That trip took some skill, though, maneuvering through shallow water. Don probably realized he was not up to it and remained content in the idyllic Cane Garden Bay.

There were a dozen other boats scattered around the bay. I spotted the Pembrooks maneuvering their dinghy up to the docks and headed into shore. I wasn't averse to harassing him a bit. See if I could shake anything loose. What else did I have to do?

I followed them into the little dive shop on the beach and wandered to a remote corner where I could listen and observe. Elizabeth was examining the latest in swimwear. She'd hold a top up to her chest and look in the mirror, turning one way and then the next, evaluating just how much she could get away with showing. The more the better, it seemed, but clearly there was some undefined limit in her mind, because she'd reject one, pick up another.

She finally decided on the tiny angelfish-over-each-breast design and headed to the cash register. Guy had been in the back, where his tanks were being filled, and was now in the process of purchasing a couple of underwater lights and a large spool of yellow-and-blue-flecked line.

"Christ, you really need another suit," he was complaining as I walked up to the register with batteries that I didn't really need or want.

"Planning on some night diving?" I asked.

"Nope, maybe a couple of deep dives, a little wreck diving. Out at the *Rhone*, maybe the *Chikuzen*," he replied.

"What's the line for?" I asked.

"Is this police business?"

"Not at all. I'm always curious about diving techniques. I've learned all sorts of esoteric stuff from the divers I've met over the years."

"I sometimes use it for long penetrations inside wrecks. Reel it out as I swim. That way I can follow it back out if I get lost. Doubt if I'll need it for the wrecks down here, but I like to be prepared. Lost my last one. Got completely tangled in it trying to gather artifacts off a wreck down in South America. Had to cut myself loose.

"What are you doing back in Cane Garden Bay?" he asked. "Thought you were finished here. How is ol' Frank holding up in jail, anyway?"

"He'll probably be out by this afternoon, as soon as his lawyer arranges bail."

"Too bad about Ursala. She was one nosy bitch, but I liked her."

"What do you mean nosy?" I asked. Pembrook realized his mistake immediately. He knew very well about Ursala's binoculars.

"Those tanks ready?" he asked, squirming out of further discussion.

He loaded his tanks into a cart and wheeled it down to the docks. I followed.

"Have you had any luck selling the *Calypso*?" I asked. I tried to be casual, but I wanted to know what the Pembrooks were up to and how long they planned to be around.

"Looks like Rodriguez is set to buy," he said. "Hoping to finalize it in the next day or two."

"Bet you hate to give her up," I said as he loaded the tanks into his dinghy.

"Naw, it's time."

"What are you going to do next?" I asked, hoping to tangle him in his story.

"Head back to the States, of course. Get that book done."

"Oh, yeah, the book. Have a lot of work to do on it?"

"Enough."

I was sitting at the end of the dock, dangling my feet in the water, and thinking about heading back to Road Town, when I heard an anchor rattling its way off the bottom and onto the deck. Elizabeth was at the bow in her new bikini, operating the windlass. By the time I got the *Wahoo* started and the lines untied, the *Calypso* was just outside the bay. Pembrook turned her into the wind and hauled up the mainsail, then fell off the wind, pulled out the jib, and headed upwind into the Narrows. He'd be tacking all the way up the channel. I'd have no trouble keeping just far enough behind him in the *Wahoo*. I headed out into the channel, put the engine in idle, and waited. The Manettis motored by and waved. They obviously had no intention of putting up sails.

I watched Pembrook expertly tack the *Calypso* up the narrow channel. He waited until the very last instant— till it looked like he'd run her aground—then turned her through the wind. Sails flapped momentary; then he quickly pulled them across to the other side of the boat and winched them tight, never losing speed. Pembrook was good and he wanted everyone sailing up the channel to know it as he passed them by.

At the western end of Tortola, Pembrook made his way into the Sir Francis Drake Channel. Then he pulled in the jib, started his engine, and changed course, away from Tortola and across the channel. Where the hell was he going?

I kept behind him, just far enough so that he would not see me following. God knows, if they headed out of the channel and into open sea, I'd have to let them go. He sailed past the Indians, a popular snorkeling and diving site, every mooring taken with sailboats and dive boats.

Just when I thought he was going to head straight out to open water, he turned in and headed around the southwest side of Norman Island. I could see him heading into shore. Odd. There were no good anchorages on this side of the island. The seas were rough, open to weather. Damned if he didn't drop his anchor in about sixty feet of water. This was definitely a place off limits to any charterer, and deserted. The shore was steep, rocky, and uninviting.

I stayed around the other side of the point that jutted out into the bay. The seas were calmer here, but not by much. Christ, Dunn would be really pissed if I smashed the boat on the rocks. I headed her over toward the only sandy spot, a twenty-foot-wide patch of sandy shore that stretched out into the water. When it started to shallow to about ten feet, I tossed the anchor in and waited. It seemed to be holding. I let out a few feet of extra line and hoped it would be enough to keep her from letting loose and blowing into shore.

I grabbed a face mask, snorkel, fins, and booties from the locker. As I did, I quietly swore at Dunn for insisting I wear the damned long pants. I attached the swim ladder to the side and pulled my foot gear on. I spit in the face mask to keep it from fogging and snugged it in place, then dove down to check the anchor. It was not dug in at all, but just lay on the bottom. Not good. But there was a huge boulder close by. I grabbed the anchor line, wrapped it around the rock a couple of times, and swam to shore. I stood on the beach for a moment in god-awful wet pants that clung to my body. What the hell did I think I was doing, anyway? Anchoring on this treacherous shore and standing soaked on this isolated beach?

I climbed up to the top of the rocky point and, well hidden from view, I gazed down at the *Calypso*. Pembrook was just getting ready to dive. He had the flashlights he'd bought at the dive shop attached to his dive vest and was carrying a huge wrench, of all things. He put his regulator into his mouth and rolled into the water. Elizabeth stayed on deck watching him as he went under. Why would he be diving out here? This site was not marked on any of the dive maps.

I could see his air bubbles skitter up along the side of the *Calypso*, then remain stationary about midway down the hull. He was right under the boat, the bubbles silvery globs bursting along the side. He remained there for almost a half hour. What the hell was he doing under there? Strange place to anchor to decide to do repairs on the hull.

Finally he surfaced and swam back to the *Calypso*. He was pulling a line behind him, with something bulky attached and floating under the water. He tied the line to the boat, climbed aboard, and grabbed a fresh tank. Then he went back in, untied the rope, swam with it toward shore, and went under. I could see his bubbles breaking along a flat rock that towered out of the water. It looked like Pembrook was swimming back and forth along the rock wall. Then his bubbles disappeared. Where the hell had he gone?

I waited, baking in the rocks, no shade, sweat burning my eyes and forming pools in my armpits and under my breasts. My pants would have already dried if they hadn't been saturated with salt. As it was, they were radiating hot moisture into my thighs.

Almost an hour passed before the bubbles reappeared at the same place they had vanished and moved back toward the *Calypso*. Pembrook surfaced beside the boat and yelled at Elizabeth, who had been sunbathing on deck. She stood, naked and unconcerned, and stepped onto the back transom. Pembrook handed her his weight belt, then his tank and his fins, and climbed up the ladder.

As she leaned over to stow his equipment, he came up behind and grabbed one ample breast in each hand. She stood as he ran his hand down her belly and between her legs. Christ. No wonder Ursala had carried those binoculars with her. Pembrook was stepping out of his wet suit and buck naked when I headed back down to my boat. No point in sitting in the rocks for another hour while they rolled around on the deck.

It would be dark in two hours. The Pembrooks wouldn't be going far if Guy hoped to sell the *Calypso* to Rodriguez, and he couldn't stay where he was at night. It was too rolling and too close to the rocky shore. He'd be heading into a secure harbor or bay. Maybe just around to the other side of Norman, in the Bight or Benures Bay, or over at Peter Island. More than likely, though, he'd be heading back to Cane Garden Bay or into Road Town. He wouldn't be hard to find if I needed to find him.

I fired up the *Wahoo* and went back around to the north side of Norman into the quieter water of Drake Channel. The Bight was filling up with boats, at least fifty already and more coming in for the night.

The old-timers complain about all the mooring balls that have been installed in the once-pristine anchorage—not to preserve the bottom, which is sand, but to make a killing in fees for mooring rentals. Once, they say, only five or six boats would be anchored in the Bight, and the place was alive with pelicans fishing and goats crying on shore. Now there is no place to anchor and the only cry emanates from a Madonna album blast-ing from the new restaurant on the beach. Rumor is that the entire island has been bought and a resort will be built on the shore. It's called progress; that is, destroy the natural environment so people can pay to be more comfortable in a modified version.

As I passed a popular snorkeling spot called the In-dians, I could see a couple of boats moored out there; one was the *Celebration*, the Manettis' boat. When I got closer, I waved. The two of them were sitting out on the bow with binoculars, gazing out past Norman Island.

When I pulled up to the *Wahoo*'s slip, James Carmichael was just locking up his dive shop.

"Good evening to ya, Hannah," he called, and hur-ried over to grab my bowline and tie it down.

"Thanks, James," I said, throwing him the stern line.

"Look like you been swimming in dem clothes," he said, a smile filling his face.

"Yeah, well, you know, I forgot my suit," I said, avoiding the real question. I tied the boat bumpers in place to keep the boat from rubbing up against the slip and stepped ashore.

"James," I asked as we walked down the dock, "do you know of any dive site out on the south side of Nor-man Island?" James had been diving in the islands since he was ten years old. He'd started his business with an air compressor, a few tanks, dive gear, and an old boat. Now Underwater Adventures had facilities on three of the islands and a team of guide divers among the most qualified around. James made sure of it. Still, in diffi-cult conditions, James was the one to have by your side. He'd been right there shoving his regulator in my mouth when I'd run out of air inside a wreck a while back.

"The south side of Norman?" he asked, a mixture of surprise and anxiety replacing his smile.

"Yeah, down at the far end past Money Bay."

"Jeez, Hannah, that Satan's Cellar. A death dive. Divers go in dar, they never come out."

Chapter 24

"**O**kay, James, let's hear the rest," I said. We'd run into O'Brien and just finished dinner at one of the dockside restaurants in Road Town Harbor. I'd ignored O'Brien's sarcasm when he'd said it was nice to see me. Christ, how long had it been? A couple days maybe. I guess I was a little embarrassed. The last time I'd seen him, I'd been putting the moves on him, then fallen asleep while he cleaned the galley.

The *Calypso* was tied up across the way at the Inner Harbor Marina. I'd watched her come in, followed closely by the Manettis' boat. I was relieved to see they'd made it into the harbor.

All through dinner, James had avoided any further discussion about Satan's Cellar.

"Why you be wantin' to know about dat place? Need to be stayin' clear of it."

I told O'Brien and James about following Pembrook out there and watching him dive the site.

"He'd have had to know where it is," O'Brien said. "No one's been out there in six years. About the only people who know it exists are the dive shop operators and a few locals. All agreed that the place was strictly off-limits. Dive shops won't even acknowledge that the place exists. People kept dying out there. We never found the last three divers who went in.

"James and I were part of the recovery effort. Would have died myself down there searching if James hadn't come looking for me. I'd gotten turned around and was heading down a side tunnel instead of out to the entrance. That's when the local dive shops, Dunn, and Island Search and Rescue lobbied to have the place made off-limits. No more diving at the Cellar. Too many divers were risking their lives trying to find others who got lost. We put a warning sign out there at the entrance and covered the opening with mesh netting to keep people out. Neither one of us ever want to go into the place again."

"How could a dive be that deadly?"

"It's not just a dive; it's a cave dive. The place where you saw Pembrook's bubbles disappear is the entrance to a maze of tunnels that wind around under the seafloor for miles. No telling how far. It's a no-man's-land, never penetrated farther than about a mile. The dive shops used to take experienced divers in as far as Purgatory Cavern, a place about a thousand feet back where the tunnel opens up to a cavern above water."

"How would Pembrook know about it?" I asked.

"Christ, there are always the stories. Divers bragging about diving the Cellar and living to tell. At least one book talks about the site and includes a map, shows the route to Purgatory and some of the side tunnels. Or he could have heard some bar talk. One of the retired divers bragging about his exploits. A fifty-dollar bill would buy the information."

"Why would Pembrook or anyone else want to dive out there?" I was thinking aloud.

"Stupidity, especially alone and unprepared," James said. "A lot of divers are hooked on diving caves, though. Some want the thrill and the notoriety. There's this mentality among cave divers. Machismo. Call to adventure. The search for the undiscovered, the unknown. Others look for artifacts.

"Some of these guys are determined to set new records—the longest penetration, the deepest cave dive. Records keep expanding—eleven thousand feet into a cave system at depths of three hundred and sixty feet. Crazy. You know about the martini effect?"

I did. It's a pretty loosely defined rule of thumb about nitrogen narcosis. Some say that every thirty-five feet of depth is like drinking a martini; some put it at every fifty feet. Some say the effects don't kick in until you are at a hundred feet. And it varies with every diver and even for an individual diver, depending on his or her physical or mental state that day.

Underwater the body does not expel all the nitrogen when the diver exhales. As the pressure increases, nitrogen is forced from the lungs into the tissue, including brain tissue. The deeper the dive, the worse it gets. Some divers feel euphoric or drunk; others get paranoid or disoriented; some feel sad. Coordination deteriorates.

I knew my own body's reaction at depth. Without even checking my depth gauge, I could always tell when I had reached ninety feet. I start to feel the pressure and breathing becomes difficult. Then the paranoia sets in and I can't breathe. It feels like a standard panic attack. I've learned to work my way through it.

"Well, diving to three hundred and sixty feet is like drinking seven martinis," James continued. "And depending on how long the diver is at that depth and how many previous dives he's done, decompression could be a complicated process involving several stops at various depths that could take hours."

I knew the process. Without these decompression stops along the way, the nitrogen that had built up would not have time to escape. Everyone knew the result. Some divers never recovered fully from a serious case of the bends. Some died.

"This is diving at the extreme," James continued. A huge number of these cave divers never make it back up to the surface. The stories are always circulating in the dive community. Just a month or two ago a couple of guys were diving at a site in Florida. Only one had experience with cave and deep diving. The other had never been deeper than a hundred feet and never dived in a cave. They headed into the cave system, planning on a dive of two hundred and seventy. They never came out. It looked like both divers lost consciousness breathing compressed air at depth. Then they just breathed down there unconscious until their tanks were empty and they drowned."

"What about Satan's Cellar? How deep does it get?"

"God knows. The farthest it was penetrated before we closed it down was about thirty-five hundred feet. The deepest section was one-sixty. The entrance is thirty feet down the rock face. Once inside it gradually slopes down. Lots of side tunnels that dead-end. The main tunnel bottoms out at about seventy-five feet, then starts back up to Purgatory Cavern, a big cave that is partly above sea level. Used to take divers in there on short dives that didn't require decompression on the way out. We'd take them in and let them explore the grotto."

Pembrook had probably had some experience diving in these conditions. He'd seemed to know what he needed before he went down. That's why all the line and the extra lights and tanks.

After James left, O'Brien and I took a walk around the harbor. The water was like glass, lights reflecting from shore and the few inhabited boats in the harbor. Tiny balloon fish gathered in the lights. There were millions of the newly hatched young bobbing in the water.

"They cause all kinds of havoc when they get caught in a boat's engine-cooling system, causing overheating," O'Brien explained.

I had no sympathy for the complaining boat owners.

O'Brien bent over and scooped one out of the water. We watched as the little guy inflated in defense, its spines sticking straight out. A good system for keeping predators at bay. Few would want to gulp this round pincushion. O'Brien placed his cupped hand back in the water and the pincushion swam away, deflating to its normal size, spines lying flat against its body.

We walked back toward the marina. O'Brien knew I was put out by his comment earlier. "Look, Hannah, I'm sorry. But is it so bad to want to spend time with you? I enjoy your company. I thought you felt the same."

"I do," I said. "But I need my space. Besides, these murders have taken up a lot of my time."

"I thought the murders were solved," he said.

"Well, we'll see."

"You sure this isn't just your way of keeping your distance?" he asked.

"Come on, O'Brien. Let's go close the distance," I said.

"Not tonight, Hannah. I've got an early morning." He walked me to my car and gave me a quick peck on the cheek. I have to admit I was hurt, but I guess I couldn't blame him. Since Jake died, I had not been in a serious relationship. I kept things casual and dropped anyone who tried to take it further. Damned O'Brien. I was having trouble keeping him away—mostly 'cause I didn't want to.

But I liked my freedom. I liked being alone. I liked not answering to someone else, and I hated the damn guilt trips that seemed to develop with a relationship. That's why O'Brien's comment had pissed me off so much. But I liked O'Brien, maybe even loved him. Christ, he was one of the most desirable men around, good-looking, rich, for chrissake. But it was the eyes that got to me.

I went to bed wishing that O'Brien were next to me. As it was, Sadie would have to do.

"Sweet Sadie," I said as she curled up on the floor beside the bed.

I lay awake for a long time thinking about the murders and about Pembrook. What the hell had he been doing out at that cave? I suppose it was possible that he was simply one of those thrill seekers, someone who needed to push the limits to explore caves that had never been explored before. Perhaps it was material for his next book. I doubted any of it. I was sure it was all connected to Robsen's death and Ursala's murder. God knows how. What could be in those caves that would lead to murder, and how was Pembrook involved? I needed to dive Satan's Cellar to find out.

Chapter 25

I grabbed a quick cup of coffee and headed over to the office. As I drove past the harbor, I could see the *Calypso* still in a slip over at Village Cay, as was the Manettis' boat.

The fax had come from Mack, the back of the book jacket from Pembrook's book. It talked about Pembrook's background. He was a former journalist, and his love of the outdoors had led to the nature writing. When his publisher had perceived a niche for the nature guide to the islands, Pembrook had taken it on with enthusiasm. The fact that he was already an expert sailor and knew how to dive made it a natural fit.

The important part was at the bottom—the author photo. This was not the Guy Pembrook that I knew. I can't say I was that surprised.

So who was the man on the *Calypso*? What was he doing with the yacht? And where the hell was the real Guy Pembrook?

Before charging over to the *Calypso* and accusing Pembrook of piracy, I thought it wise to do some checking with people in the States who might know the Pembrooks. I started with the publisher, no easy task on a Saturday. I was finally connected with an overworked editor and managed to convince her that I was a police officer. She gave me Pembrook's editor's home number. He picked up on about the tenth ring, and I spent fifteen minutes explaining who I was and that I was calling from the islands. The connection was static filled, making graceful communication impossible. I found myself yelling.

"Have you heard from the Pembrooks?"

"No, why are you asking? Is there a problem?"

"Just doing some checking about their boat papers," I lied. "When did you talk to them last?"

"Guy was due to check in about a week ago, but he hasn't called or e-mailed. I didn't think much about it, though. He often gets so involved that he loses track of the days. Sometimes he is too remote to check in on time."

"When were they due back to the States?"

"Anytime from last week to next month. His schedule was pretty flexible. But I was to get a draft of his manuscript by the first of next month."

"I'd like to talk to the family. Do you have a number?"

"We don't normally give that information out," he said.

"Look, I'm a police officer, and I need to talk to someone who may have been in touch with the Pembrooks."

Finally, after I'd done a lot of whining and cajoling, he gave me a phone number for the daughter, an Ellen Musiak in Des Moines, Iowa. When I called, a harried voice answered.

"Ellen Musiak? This is Detective Hannah Sampson."

I could hear kids screaming and a dog barking in the background.

"Just a minute," she said. "Susan, you and Danny take the dog and go outside! I'm sorry," she said. "Who's calling?"

"Hannah Sampson. I'm with the British Virgin Islands Police Department."

"Oh, God, it's my mother." Fear filled the phone line.

"Look, there's nothing to be alarmed about. I'm just doing some checking on the boat. Looks like they want to sell her. I was asked to make sure everything was on the up and up for the buyer," I lied.

"Sell the *Calypso*? Well, I suppose they could decide to do that."

"When did you talk with them last?"

"Well, my mother e-mails me a couple of times a week, tells me everything they've been doing, all about the ports they've been to, the people they've met."

"She didn't mention selling the boat?"

"No. But it's been strange. She hasn't been her newsy self. I thought that maybe they had just been too busy. In fact, she'd been out of touch for almost a week a while back. I had e-mailed and e-mailed without a response. I was really getting worried. Finally she wrote back. She said the radio that provides the connection for the Internet had been out. I couldn't understand why she hadn't telephoned. She knew I'd worry. I finally got an e-mail last week saying they were in Tortola."

"What did she say?"

"Well, it was weird, hardly anything. It didn't seem like her. She didn't ask about the kids or anything."

"When are they due to return?"

"They were supposed to have been back by now. I asked them about it in my last e-mail, but haven't heard back. Funny, a guy from the publisher called looking for them too. Said he was supposed to meet them in Miami over a week ago. I told him they were still down in the BVI. Why all these questions? What's going on?"

"As I said, I'm just checking about the boat sale."

"I don't believe that. Have you seen my mother?"

"Not recently." More like not at all. I knew that the woman on the *Calypso* was not Ellen Musiak's mother. The Elizabeth Pembrook I knew was not the mother of a woman with two children, and definitely not a grandmother.

"I've never liked Guy," she said. "He's nothing like my father, and I don't think my mother's been happy with him at all."

"How long have they been married?"

"Only a year. My father died six years ago. If you see my mother, please tell her that I am worried and that she needs to call me."

I tried to reassure her and hung up before she could query me further. Then I called the editor back. He said he was sure that no one from the publishing house was meeting Guy in Miami.

Who was it on the *Calypso* if not Guy and Elizabeth Pembrook? What had happened to the real Pembrooks? Who were they supposed to meet in Miami? Had whoever was posing as the Pembrooks stolen the boat from them? They'd certainly taken their identity.

And they'd lied about Robsen motoring away from the *Calypso* that night. Robsen had found out that Pembrook was not who he said he was. He'd probably seen the book when he was looking around the *Calypso* that night, torn out the photo on the book jacket, and stuffed it in his pocket without Guy ever knowing it. Then Robsen had been stupid enough to confront him about it and Guy had killed him to prevent exposure.

But what about Ursala? Was Pembrook involved in her murder? How could she have been involved? Had Robsen said something to her that night? Had she seen something when she'd been out on the beach waiting for Robsen? If so, why hadn't she gone to the police immediately instead of waiting and calling me? I remembered her encounter with Guy on her way out of the bar. Ursala had clearly been afraid. And he had been very interested in knowing what Ursala might have said to me. Had Pembrook threatened Ursala to keep her from talking until he could get to her and kill her?

If Guy had stolen the boat, and run up the charge cards while sailing the boat to the BVI to sell, what the hell was he doing diving out at the caves instead of getting the boat sold, taking the money, and getting out of the islands, especially after killing Robsen?

Dunn was not going to like it. I had been investigating behind his back. But damn. What else could I do? I was on my way out the door, headed for a visit to the *Calypso*, when Snyder caught me.

"We got the results back from the dinghy. Lab guy, Dickson, didn't find no trace of blood or nothing, but there were some fingerprints. Course Robsen's were there. Lots of the rest couldn't be matched—all dem folks working on the docks, maybe even some former charterers."

"Snyder, was there anything at all useful?" I wondered why the hell he was bothering to tell me all this.

"Well, yeah. Dat's what I was about to tell you. Dickson found a match. Set of prints on the bow of the dinghy, like someone pushing it off. Prints were in the database. Dis man has a record." He pulled out the report and handed it to me.

The prints belonged to a guy named Curt Wold, the son of a wealthy family on the East Coast. A spoiled rich kid, living off his parents, he had been in trouble since high school. He'd wrecked his parents' yacht when he took it out joyriding and ran it into a concrete pier when he was sixteen. Family was always bailing him out. Several drug charges. Time in a rehab hospital. More arrests for possession of heroin. By the time he was twenty-five, his parents had had enough. They threw him out and stopped supporting him.

The last time he'd been arrested was for stealing a boat, which he'd decided to throw a big party on, providing cocaine for all his friends. Somehow he'd made bail and skipped. That had been five years ago. The police suspected that he'd vanished in the islands.

The photo was a bad reproduction, passed along by fax.

"Hey, Snyder, who does this look like to you?"

"I know, dat's da fellow on the *Calypso*. Guess he found another way to live da life he be accustomed to."

"Yeah, nothing like having your own classic wooden sailboat with all the amenities for a month or two."

"How you think his prints got on dat dinghy?"

"Could have been when he helped the Robsens tie up to the *Calypso* that night."

"Yeah, then again, maybe he be lettin' it loose in da middle of da ocean after throwing Robsen's body in the sea."

"Let's head over to the *Calypso*."

As we pulled alongside, I realized that the guy standing on deck was Jack Rodriguez talking with another guy, who was examining the rigging.

"Ahoy," he called, grabbing the line Snyder threw him. We climbed aboard and Rodriguez informed me that the *Calypso* was now his boat.

"She's a beauty, isn't she? Always wanted a classic like this."

"Do you know where I can find Pembrook?" I asked.

"He was talking about renting a motorboat for a few days. Seemed like he was kind of in a hurry. They were all packed and ready to get off the boat when I got here. We loaded the dinghy and I took them over to the marina."

"Do you mind if I have a look around the *Calypso*?" I asked. I hoped that whoever had been posing as Pembrook, and I was sure it was Wold, had left some clue about where he was headed or what he was up to.

"Hey, be my guest. I'm just having the rigging and engine checked out before I take the boat up to the States. We plan to sail her up there next week." I didn't have the heart to tell Rodriguez that the guy who sold him the boat didn't own it and had no legal right to sign the boat over to him.

Snyder and I went below. I checked the bedroom. It was cleaned out. But when I pulled up the mattress, the journal was still there, right where the real Elizabeth Pembrook had kept it hidden. It told the entire story of the Pembrooks' travels. This time I thumbed to the last week of entries.

February 6: *Guy has invited another couple to accompany us from Venezuela up to Grenada, Suzie Tagan and Curt Wold. We met them on the docks in Port of Spain. They are experienced sailors looking for crew slots. They said they had just sold their boat and are working their way up through the islands to*

Puerto Rico, where they will catch a flight to the States. I don't like it, but Guy wants to let them sail with us as far as St. Vincent. Something about them makes me uncomfortable. Wold is too slick. And he must have money if he just sold a boat of his own. So why does he want to crew our boat? Why not just fly home from South America? Guy says I'm being foolish, and that having a couple of extra hands for the long sail up will take a lot of strain off. He reminded me of the trip down. It was hard, and I know we can use the help during the long overnight hauls.

February 8: We left Port of Spain in Trinidad this morning and are headed for Grenada. The day is typically Caribbean. By noon it is a clear and sunny eighty-five degrees with wind out of the southeast at fifteen knots.

I'm finding myself afraid. I don't know what's gotten into Guy. He didn't tell me what he'd done until we left port. All I knew was that while we were in Venezuela for that week, he was having the bottom worked on and the keel reinforced. I never thought a thing about it. Nothing I can say will change his mind. He's intent on what he says is a foolproof way to improve our finances.

This is the first I have heard of any financial difficulty. When I'd voiced concern about buying the Calypso, he'd just laughed and said we were fixed for life. Now it seems he lied. I thought I knew him when we married, but now . . . well, I wonder. He tells me this is the only possible way that we can continue to live the way we do, traveling and sailing the Calypso. His books don't even begin to make the payments.

I told him I'd be happy living in a little house in Iowa. He laughed. "No way I'm living in Des Moines with a bunch of your screaming grandkids." When he realized how hurt I was, he apologized, but he is determined to go through with this. He told me he'd been approached by a friend of a friend when we were in Miami picking up the Calypso. They assured him it was a safe way to make some easy money. Guy says it's worth twenty-five million dollars, pure Colombian cocaine. No one will ever find it in the keel, he tells me. As if getting caught is the only issue. I want no part of any drugs on this boat. But what can I do now? I'm determined to leave him as soon as we make it back to Miami.

Well, that was it. Cocaine being transported from Colombia into Venezuela and onto the Pembrooks' boat for smuggling to the United States.

That was Elizabeth's last entry. I presumed that the real Guy and Elizabeth Pembrook had been dumped at sea somewhere south of Grenada. Somehow Wold and Tagan had found out about the drugs.

Snyder and I headed over to the marina to track down Wold-alias-Pembrook. We were about fifteen minutes late. Wold and Tagan had rented a fast boat and left. They had a good twenty to thirty minutes' head start, but I knew he'd be heading back to the caves. Wold would never have sold the *Calypso* with those drugs still on board. That was what he'd been doing out at Norman Island yesterday—getting the drugs out of the keel and stashing them in one of the underwater caves, a good place to store them for a day or two, private, no prying eyes except mine.

I wondered how many drug smugglers had redesigned

keels to transport their contraband. The coast guard wouldn't consider going into the water to search for drugs without good cause. Even then, if it were done right, there would be no indication that anything on the bottom of the boat was out of order. The real Pembrook would have had some expert help in Venezuela fitting the boat for his trek up to Miami. He'd have had a buyer on that end all set to meet him. It had been the buyer who had called Ellen when Pembrook didn't show up as arranged.

Now Wold was back out there diving in the caves. Once Wold had those drugs, he'd be disappearing somewhere in the islands. Snyder and I would be there in time to intercept him when he surfaced.

Chapter 26

I let Snyder take the wheel. He'd have us over there in fifteen minutes. A few misplaced vertebrae would be worth it. We headed out of Road Town Harbor and into the channel, then straight toward the Indians. Snyder never backed off the throttle. He raced past Pelican Island, then took a hard turn around the point to the other side of Norman Island and headed into the bay.

There were two boats at anchor. Damned if one wasn't the Manettis'. Melissa Manetti stood up top, waving. There was no one on Wold's motorboat. He had to be diving. Where was Suzie? Diving with Wold? I didn't see Don Manetti either. Something was off. But by the time I yelled at Snyder to pull away, he was already alongside the Manettis' boat and throwing Melissa a line. Too late. Don Manetti appeared from below and pointed a 9mm Glock dead center at Snyder's head.

The last piece. Damn, I'd missed it. I should have known. They'd been so inept with the boat. It should have been my first question. Why rent a boat when you can't sail? Louis had said they get it all the time, and I'd left it at that. I'd been too involved looking elsewhere.

Mack had found nothing at all suspicious about the Manettis because they were good, professionals.

The Manettis had come down looking for the Pembrooks. They'd found Wold and hung back, watching them and waiting for the opportunity to get to Wold and the drugs.

"Down below," Manetti ordered, pointing the 9mm toward the hold.

Snyder started down. I followed. Manetti knew what he was doing. He never gave me an opening, standing back as we climbed down the stairs, Melissa following. Then she covered us as he stepped down. Suzie Tagan was sitting on the floor in the corner, hands tied.

"So you're the Miami connection," I said. "Came looking for Pembrook when he didn't make it to Florida."

"That's right. We were supposed to meet Pembrook in Miami two weeks ago to get the cocaine. When they didn't show, we figured they were planning on double-crossing us. No way we were letting twenty-five million worth of pure Colombian cocaine slip through our fingers. Should be five hundred pounds of it down there packed in watertight bags. Trouble is we don't dive. We had no way to get at them."

"We've been sitting in the harbor on this damned boat for days, keeping an eye on the *Calypso* and waiting for reinforcements to arrive from Miami before Wold could sell the boat and take off with the drugs. My guys are professionals—quiet and effective killers and expert divers. They'd have boarded the *Calypso*, taken care of Wold and little Suzie here, and pulled those drugs out of the keel. We'd have scuttled the *Calypso* out at sea and been out of here by now."

"What happened to your guys? They run out on you?" I asked.

"They're in a Puerto Rican jail. Damned hotheads got in a fight at the San Juan airport while they were waiting for their connection down here. Seems a couple of the patrons took offense at their drunken attempts to pick up their wives. Now it's up to Melissa and me to take care of things, huh, darlin'?" he said, smiling at his wife.

"You'll never get past the coast guard once you have those drugs on board."

"I was worried about that too. Now here you are with your police boat. Nobody gonna stop us in that. We'll have those drugs out on the streets in St. Thomas within a day and be on a plane back to Miami. No one will ever know the Manettis were involved. We stay clean."

"I told Curt we should just get out of here after he shot Robsen," Suzie whined from the floor. She was scared shitless and rambling. "But no, he's got to have it all, money from the *Calypso* and the drugs. And that damned Ursala saw him put Robsen's body in the dinghy. Curt said he scared her real good, but I knew he wouldn't just let Ursala be. He'd kill her as soon as he got her alone. When I heard her calling the cops from the bar, I pleaded with him. But he was starting to like the killing.

"Just let me go. Take the drugs. I won't tell anybody anything." I knew she was wasting her time with Manetti. He probably didn't like killing the way Wold did, but he was a businessman. He'd make a business decision when it came to Suzie—and to me and Snyder, for that matter.

"Sure, Suzie, just tell us where Wold and those drugs

are." Manetti managed to sound like a father soothing an upset child. I almost believed him myself.

"He hid them in the underwater cave. He's down there now. He'll be up any minute. Please let me go."

"First, there's one thing I'm kind of curious about, Suzie. How did you and Curt know about the cocaine?" Manetti would want to keep this kind of thing from happening the next time he smuggled millions in drugs out of South America.

"Curt was a pro at breaking into the boatyards after dark, scoping out the nicest boats. He just happened to be there that night. He hid on a nearby boat and watched the whole thing—all that cocaine being sealed in the keel of the *Calypso*. He couldn't believe his luck. He didn't have any trouble convincing Guy Pembrook to hire us on as crew when they sailed out of Trinidad."

"Untie her, Melissa."

"Oh, God, you won't regret it. I'll never say a word. You'll never see me again."

"That's right, Suzie." Manetti followed her up the ladder. Seconds later a gunshot echoed through the hold. Then a splash.

Just business.

After about fifteen minutes, it became pretty obvious that Wold wasn't coming back. I mean, why would he? If he'd come out of the cave and seen two more boats on the surface, he would have known something was wrong. He'd either made it out and around to the other side of the island or run into trouble. Manetti had scanned the shoreline and the water with binoculars. Melissa had been watching the dive area for signs of a diver—nothing.

"Okay, Detective Sampson. Get your gear on." I

knew there was a reason that Manetti hadn't already dumped Snyder and me in after Suzie. This was it.

"You don't come back with Wold or those drugs, Snyder here will be joining you in the water. Only he'll have a hole in him."

"Don't be worried about me, Hannah. You just get in dat water." I knew what Snyder was trying to tell me. So did Manetti.

"Detective Sampson won't run out on a colleague. I know her type. You can just relax. Get her gear out of your boat."

Snyder climbed into the *Wahoo* and handed me my wet suit, BC, and the tank. Manetti watched him carefully while Melissa stood on the bow still watching for Wold to surface.

"I be gettin' your weight belt," he said, returning to the locker and kneeling to reach the belt on the bottom. Christ, I knew the dive knife was down there too. And I knew Snyder was just reckless enough to try for it.

"Manetti," I said, "you really think Wold isn't already halfway back to Road Town by now?"

"Guess you'll be finding out for me, won't you?" He glanced at me just long enough. Damned if Snyder didn't manage to slip the knife under his shirt into the waist of his shorts. The kid was slick.

I took my time suiting up, hoping for an opportunity to catch the Manettis off guard. It didn't come. They stayed back, weapons zeroed in, one on me, one on Snyder. All I could do was get in the water and hope that Snyder didn't do anything stupid while I was gone.

I swam on the surface until I got to the rock face. Then I released the air from my BC and started down. I watched my depth gauge, and at thirty feet I stopped and swam along the rock wall. I found the entrance easily. It was just as O'Brien and Carmichael described. The sign was affixed in the rock with rebar: "Warning: Off-limits! Do Not Enter! Divers Have Died Here." Heavy wire mesh covered the entrance, but a hole had been cut into it. No doubt by Wold.

I switched on my light and started in, careful not to catch a hose or valve on the jagged wire. I shone my light ahead, the beam disappearing in the black. Inside, the tunnel was about four feet in diameter and seemed to go on forever, into the bowels of the earth. The blue-and-yellow line that Wold had purchased in the dive shop was tied onto a rock on the side of the tunnel wall. It disappeared into nothingness. It would be good insurance, a way to find the route back to the opening without getting lost forever in the maze of Satan's Cellar and swimming blind through tunnel after tunnel until every molecule of air was depleted from the tank. I followed the rope into the void. The tunnel angled down. When I next checked my gauge, I was at sixty-five feet.

Except for the beam of my light that I shone ahead, I could see nothing. I was surrounded in black—dense, absolute, consuming. This was about as claustrophobic and alone as I had ever felt, above or below the water. When I pointed my light up, it bounced off the solid dark mass above my head. Air bubbles, caught on the rock ceiling, glistened like glass marbles.

The floor of the tunnel was covered in sandy sediment. I tried to keep my fins off the bottom. If I stirred it up, even my light would be useless, bouncing back at me off a bank of silt.

At seventy feet the tunnel narrowed. My tank clanked and scraped against the rocks. It would be impossible to turn around at this point. The space was too constricted to do anything but move forward. I was about ten minutes into the dive and about eight hundred feet into the tunnel. I kept going, knowing that it had to widen out again, unless I had taken a wrong turn down one of the dead ends. I was still following Wold's line. He had tied it off on the rock wall at about twenty-foot intervals. About the time I was sure that Wold had made an error and headed down the wrong tunnel, it opened into a huge amphitheater. Ghostly shapes emerged in my light, sculptures in a watery gallery.

I could see why divers were attracted to such places. It was spectacular in an eerie and frightening way. Walls were covered with drab, colorless sponges, completely unlike the color found on the reef. I kept moving, swimming farther into the room, past several tunnels that led farther through the maze, God knows how far. To the core of the earth, maybe. I swam through a bizarre labyrinth of pure white. Stalactites, like giant icicles, plastered the ceiling fifty feet above my head, some extending all the way to the ground in misshapen layers where elves and trolls hid. Stalagmites jutted from the sand, shapes that could horrify and captivate—gravestones, contorted gnomes, mushrooms, toads, and Cheshire cats—they sparkled in my light. This cave had been above the water at some point, the limestone formations developed by water seeping though the earth.

I kept moving, swimming through sweeping arches and around boulders. Finally the cavern opened up to a vast room above the water, the ceiling like a cathedral dome, towering into blackness. This was Purgatory Cavern.

I broke the surface and swam to a nearby ledge. I hoisted myself out, pulled my face mask down, and dropped the regulator out of my mouth. The air was heavy and mildewed. Signs of other visitors were apparent, a rusted flashlight battery, a broken dive slate, marks on the rocks where tanks had brushed. The grotto had been formed by hundreds of years of water carving the rocks. Its walls were smooth and hollowed out, with nooks and crannies and a big back room.

This was obviously the place where Wold had chosen to hide the drugs for a day or two until he could get back to retrieve them. It was fairly dry. The blue-and-yellow line was tied off on a nearby rock. He would have left it tied there when he'd hidden the drugs. All he had to do was follow the line back in today to retrieve them. But the cavern was deserted. There wasn't any sign of Wold. How the hell had he gotten out and past Manetti? Maybe he really was halfway to Road Town by now. Or maybe he'd never made it in.

I unclipped my BC and tank, pulled my feet out of the water, and removed my fins. I made sure my tank was secure and turned off the valve to ensure that it didn't leak. The last thing I needed was to be stuck here without air.

I walked into the recesses of the cavern, the sharp limestone slicing into my booties. Red crabs scurried into crevices as I went. Water seeped down the walls and from the ceiling. No sign of Wold and no drugs. Where the hell had he gotten to?

I'd been gone for close to half an hour. I hoped Manetti hadn't gotten trigger-happy in my absence and that Snyder was okay. What the hell would happen when I returned empty-handed? Both Snyder and I would have outlived our usefulness. I'd have to find a way to deal with the Manettis when I surfaced.

I struggled back into my equipment, pulled on my fins, and checked my pressure gauge. I'd used about

1,200 psi coming in, a third of my tank, a safe margin for getting out. I slipped into the water and headed back the way I'd come, following Wold's line into the narrow tunnel.

About halfway into the tunnel I was pulled up short and yanked back like a bungee jumper reaching the end of the cord. I was caught. I was unable to move any farther, and in the tight confines I could not maneuver well enough to turn around to see what I was caught on. Goddammit! *Okay, Sampson, relax; take a breath. Wait.* It was that reliable inner voice that I'd learned to count on when danger threatened to push me over the edge. I did what I was told.

When reason again caught hold, I began to investigate the problem. I could move enough to tell that neither my tank nor any of the valves were caught above me in the rocky ceiling. Next I pulled on my regulator hose, then the depth and pressure-gauge hose. All moved freely. It was my alternate regulator. It had worked its way out of the restraining strap on my vest and dragged on the bottom until it had snagged on something.

I would have to back up. I grabbed a knobby protuberance on the ceiling and pushed, managing to maneuver back about a foot, working my fins at the same time in a kind of reverse motion that wasn't working at all. I kept at it, finding rocky knobs to push off of every couple of inches. Finally the regulator slacked and I worked it out from under a rocky shelf on the bottom of the tunnel. I snugged it back in place and moved on.

Another hundred feet and the tunnel opened back up to a roomy six or eight feet. I stopped and shone my light around the space, grateful to be out of that damned narrow tube. That was when I caught a glimpse of yellow just ahead on my left. I swam to it and found myself staring down a side tunnel. The yellow was Wold's BC. I'd swum right by him coming in because the tunnel was obscured from that side by an outcropping. It was visible only coming from the other direction.

Wold had swum right into it on his way out. God knows how he'd managed to lose track of his line. He'd probably been more intent on hanging on to the damned cocaine. At some point he'd realized his mistake and was headed back out. By then he would have been low on air and hadn't had the control required to work through it under duress. He had clearly panicked. He was hopelessly tangled in the ropes that were wrapped about the waterproof containers filled with cocaine. It was pretty obvious that the more he'd struggled, the more entangled he'd become. His dive knife was lying in the sand out of his reach. His eyes reflected his last moments of horror, his regulator dangling by his side, millions in cocaine floating in bundles beside him.

Chapter 27

I retrieved Wold's knife from the sand and cut the tangled ropes from his body. I wasn't about to exert the energy and a lot of extra air trying to haul him to the surface. But I did intend to swim out with the cocaine. This was a bunch of coke. There were two bundles of it, packed tightly in heavy-duty waterproof bags and wrapped with mesh netting, each bundle about the size of a human torso.

Though cumbersome, Wold would have been able to maneuver them back into the cavern and out again. Five hundred pounds of pure cocaine. Just a little air in the bags would keep them pretty much neutrally buoyant in the water.

This was my insurance policy. As long as I controlled the cocaine, Manetti had to let me live. I'd bring out one bundle and leave the other behind.

My air supply was nearing the red zone, and I'd stirred up so much sediment freeing Wold from his cocaine that I could barely see. I felt my way around the rocky outcropping, trying to locate Wold's safety line. I had to be able to feel my way out by sliding that line through my hands. There was no other way I'd get out of there in the silt fog that enveloped me. I'd end up turned around or headed down another tunnel that veered off the main one, and dying.

Again I relied on my inner voice. *Don't panic. Don't swim blind. Be smart. Take your time. Find the god-damned rope, for chrissake!* I felt around the rocky wall. The rope had been on my left side as I'd followed it down the tunnel and encountered Wold.

I shone my light, now almost useless, on the rocks and ran my fingers from the sandy bottom all the way up to the ceiling. Nothing. Again I resisted the urge to head out of there, start swimming the way I thought the entrance might be. Where the hell was that damned line? I looked again. Nothing.

I forced myself to think rather than simply act. Was it possible that I'd gotten completely turned around, that left was now right, what I thought was the way out was the way in? I moved to the other side of the tunnel and again searched, running my hand over the rock. No rope.

It took every ounce of will to swallow the panic. *Okay, Sampson, look again.* I repeated the procedure, starting in the sandy bottom and moving my hand up the wall, going slower this time, feeling every bump and indentation in the rock. I was about halfway up when I felt the cord. I'd almost missed it, part of it tucked into a crevice. Momentary relief till I thought about my air. My tank had to be close to empty now.

Still, I needed to take the time to think it through. The rope, which had been on my left side, was now on the right, which meant I was facing the wrong way— that is, into the maze of tunnels. I couldn't believe that I had gotten turned around that easily, but clearly that's just what had happened. My instincts would have led me back into the interior if I hadn't found the damned line.

I turned around, placed the rope in my left hand, and started out, dragging the bundle of cocaine along the sandy bottom, stirring up a swirl of sediment behind me. I knew I was fast using whatever air remained in my tank, the exertion and the adrenaline rush placing huge demands on my respiratory system. I kept moving down the tunnel, aware of every breath, legs working my fins. Finally I could see the opening ahead, the outline of blue light.

But what the hell was I going to do when I got there? I had Wold's knife. Little good it was going to be in the water with Manetti pointing a gun at me. I was making it up as I swam, a half-baked plan with about a 10 percent chance of working. Better than zero was the only consolation.

Once out of the tunnel I swam down the exterior wall to the ocean bottom. I could see the outline of all three boats—the *Wahoo*, Wold's cruiser, and the *Celebration*, Manetti's sailboat. I was betting that the Manettis were watching for my bubbles and tracking my progress, waiting for me to surface. I stayed down and swam slowly toward them.

When I was under the bow of the *Celebration*, I pulled the bundle to me and held it captive underneath my body. Then I sliced into the outer heavy plastic and into each of the watertight bags inside, positioned my alternate air supply inside, and pushed the purge button. Air rushed into the bag and sent the whole mess floating to the surface, leaking white powder as it went.

Quickly I unclipped my BC and slid one arm out, holding on to it with the other, the regulator still in my mouth. I released my weight belt, pulled the other arm out of the BC, and took one final breath of air. Then I positioned the regulator so that air flowed freely, sending bubbles to the surface along with the cocaine. Hopefully Manetti would see the bubbles breaking on the surface and believe I was still on the bottom. As my tank settled to the sandy bottom, I headed for the surface. A couple of hard kicks and I came up at the back of the Manettis' boat.

I slipped the fins off in the water and silently pulled myself aboard, keeping my head down. I could see Don and Melissa scrambling around the bow, trying to snag the cocaine with the boat hook before it all dissolved into the sea. In their haste they'd left Snyder standing in the cockpit. He was already moving up behind them along the starboard side. I scurried along the other, ducking under the boom and past the mast.

Just then Melissa turned toward me. Recognition shifted quickly to disbelief, followed quickly by sheer rage. I had just dissolved half their twenty-five million in cocaine into the sea. She raised her gun and squeezed the trigger in one swift action, pointing dead center on my sternum. I heard the gun fire as I dove for the deck, knowing that if the first bullet missed, the second wouldn't.

A second never came. Snyder had nailed her from the other side, stepping right in front of the bullet meant for me. Snyder crumpled as Melissa went over the side, the dive knife in her chest. Her gun skittered across the deck just out of my reach as Don turned. He went for the gun that he'd tucked in his belt as I lunged for Melissa's. I made it first. I didn't hesitate to fire. He tumbled over the side into a cocaine sea.

I rushed to Snyder. He was lying across the bow, his

shirt soaked in red. Blood was already pooling on the boat and dripping into the water.

"Jimmy, you're okay," I said, wrapping an arm under his neck and raising his head. I was holding my palm over his chest in an absolutely foolish attempt to keep the life inside him.

"Just keep breathing, Jimmy. Keep breathing, for chrissake."

"Hey, Hannah. Guess we got them, huh?" He smiled.

"Yeah, Jimmy. We did."

Chapter 28

I blamed myself for Snyder. Just a damned kid.

"Listen, Hannah, this is not your fault," Dunn said.

"I should never have taken him out there with me." I was hunched over on the hard wooden bench, head in hand, still in my wet suit. It was soaked in Jimmy's blood. Dunn sat beside me. A dozen empty cardboard cups were scattered on the table. Between the two of us we'd probably consumed half the coffee in the vending machine.

"You know Jimmy," Dunn said. "You think he was going to let you leave him behind? He was where he wanted to be."

"Yeah, well, it should be me lying in there now. That bullet should be lodged in my chest, not his. He dove right in front of it, for chrissake."

Jimmy had been in surgery for almost an hour. No one was telling us a damn thing.

I'd brought him in, sure I was causing all kinds of further damage as I struggled to get him into the *Wahoo*. I didn't think he'd make it to shore, but I wasn't about to sit by and watch him bleed to death out there on that sailboat. He'd managed to hold on, shallow breaths still rattling deep in his chest when I'd pulled the *Wahoo* into the dock at Road Town.

"Chief. Detective Sampson." It was Hall, one of the doctors on staff at the hospital. A tall, thin, and pasty man, I thought of him as Ichabod and just barely kept from calling him that now.

"Dr. Hall. How is he?" I asked.

"He's still in surgery. It's been touch and go. His heart stopped once but they got it going. He's lost a lot of blood and there's extensive internal damage. He'll be in there for at least another two hours, maybe three."

"Will he make it?" I demanded.

"I don't know," he said. "You should go home. It will be hours before we know anything."

"I'm not going anywhere." I wasn't about to abandon Jimmy. I had some idiotic notion that if I left, he'd die on me.

Dunn could see it was useless to argue. He bought me another cup of lukewarm coffee and headed to the crime scene. Stark and Worthington had gone out already to secure the area. I'd left Don and Melissa Manetti floating in an ocean of cocaine and blood. Dunn had called Edmund Carr to help retrieve the bodies. He'd also called O'Brien and James Carmichael, both familiar with Satan's Cellar, to recover Wold's body and the rest of the cocaine. I told them where to look.

Now I sat in the waiting room, replaying the sequence of events, trying to figure out where the hell I had gone wrong. I was staring at the floor, elbows on knees, chin in hand, thinking about Jimmy creeping up to the bow of Manettis' boat, when Elyse walked up.

"Hannah, you're a mess. Come on, I brought you

some clothes. Hall said you could use the doctor's lounge for a shower."

She kept up a steady stream of chatter as she led the way down a back hall to a door marked "Private." I knew what she was doing, but it wasn't working.

"Elyse, I'm fine," I said, interrupting her discourse midsentence.

"Okay," she said, wrapping an arm around me. "Get in the shower. I'll be back later."

"Elyse," I said as she walked away, "thanks."

The lounge was deserted when I stepped inside. I hoped it stayed that way. I relished the time alone. I went straight to the shower, peeled off the sticky wet suit, and stood under the hot water, washing away salt and Jimmy's blood. Watching the red swirl down the drain.

When I came out Jimmy's mother was in the waiting room, her small form enveloped in a chair in the corner. Her hair was bristled white cotton, skin wrinkled and ebony. She wore a dress scattered with yellow and purple flowers, with a pair of matching purple slippers on her tiny feet. I knew who it was right away. Even now I could see the same mischief behind her eyes. So Jimmy got it from her, I thought.

I didn't want to face her, but what could I do? I walked over, sank onto the red plastic sofa beside her, and introduced myself.

"I know who you are. Jimmy be always talkin' 'bout you," she said.

"I'm so sorry about what happened," I whispered.

"Don't you be blaming yourself," she said, taking my hand. "Jimmy be stepping into the middle of things since he be taking his first step. He's a strong boy. He be comin' through dis just fine."

I wished I had her confidence. We sat together a long time, quietly waiting, a noisy clock on the wall above our heads relentlessly clicking off the minutes. I found myself drifting in an old familiar nightmare. The one where Jake is sinking, hand reaching out. Me straining, trying to grasp him, my fingers just inches from his when he disappears into the black void.

"Sampson, Sampson, wake up!" When I opened my eyes, I realized it was Stark of all people, and that I'd had my head on his damned shoulder.

"Stark!"

"It's okay, Sampson. I didn't mind being your pillow. Been here for about a half hour listening to you mumble in your sleep. You started gettin' kinda noisy."

I sat up and finally remembered where I was.

"No, nothin' yet," he said, anticipating my question.

A crowd had gathered around Jimmy's mother—sisters, brothers, nieces, uncles, aunts, cousins, all talking quietly. Stark and I were sitting in the middle of it, mine the only white face. I seemed to be the only one who noticed. To the others I was simply Hannah, Jimmy's colleague.

"I came on ahead," Stark was saying. "Others will be here in a while. You're lookin' like a zombie, Sampson." Stark had never put this many words together and actually directed them at me since we'd met. And damned if he didn't have his arm around my shoulder.

"Brought you somethin' to eat." He pulled a sandwich and a soda out of a brown sack.

"Thanks, Stark." It seemed like days since I had swallowed anything other than caffeine.

"What did you find out there?" I asked him between bites.

"Everything you told Dunn. The Manettis were floating in the water. Carr pulled Suzie Tagan off the bottom, and O'Brien and Carmichael found Wold."

Suddenly the door from surgery banged open and Hall burst through, white coat flapping behind him. I jumped to my feet and felt myself close down, dread turning every cell icy. I knew what Hall was about to tell us—that Jimmy hadn't made it. That damned pasty Ichabod countenance said it all.

Then the guy actually smiled. "He's in recovery. Looks like he's going to pull through."

"Course he be makin' it," Jimmy's mother said.

Stark gave me a ride back to the *Sea Bird*. "You know, Sampson, I've been thinkin' maybe you stay around long enough, you'll be turning into a real islander. See you tomorrow."

"Thanks, Stark," I said, and smiled. "See you tomorrow."

O'Brien was below, a bottle of merlot and two glasses on the table.

"Jimmy's going to make it," I said as he stood and folded his arms around me. He still had marks on his face from his diving mask, and his hair was wet. He smelled like soap and the sea.

"Yeah, I called the hospital. They said you'd just left. You okay?"

"Fine. I'm glad you're here," I said, pulling him against me, feeling the warmth.

We never got around to opening the wine.

The next morning I dove under the *Calypso* to check the keel. The compartment was obvious once Wold had pried it open and removed the drugs. It was just big enough to hold what amounted to about seven cubic feet of cocaine. Once Wold had pulled it from the keel, he would have been able to handle it fairly easily. Under salt water the bundles would have weighed about fifty pounds total. And, of course, Wold was motivated. Rodriguez had been really upset to learn that the *Calypso* would not be his.

By noon we had the entire picture. Elizabeth's journal made it all pretty clear. Her husband had thought drug running would be an easy way to make enough money to keep the *Calypso* and their million-dollar home in California, and continue in his endeavors as a nature writer. If not for Wold, maybe it would have worked.

Pirating was a habit with Wold and Tagan. They would hire on as crew on expensive boats, kill the owners, take their identity for a while, run up their charge cards, sell the boats in some port, and then grab another. The life of luxury without the expense. For Wold the *Calypso* was a double bonus—a boat worth several million and drugs worth twenty-five million. Even that hadn't been enough, though. All the jewelry that had been taken in the robberies was found on Wold's rented motorboat, stashed in the head. The kids that Stark had arrested would be charged with theft but were off the hook for armed robbery.

Mahler and Worthington had arrested the guy who had trashed my boat. He was a local fisherman, out of work and broke when he met Wold. He'd been down at the Doubloon, bragging about the fun he'd had wrecking a boat over at Pickerings Landing. He identified Wold from a photo and confessed that Wold had told him to scare me out of the islands one way or another. Said that Wold had offered him a

bonus if I happened to be on the boat and have an un-
fortunate accident.

"Hell, wrecking a boat's one thing, but I ain't no
killer," the guy had said.

Still, Dunn was not pleased. Sure, Ursala Downing's
and Allen Robsen's murders had been solved once and
for all. But the BVI stakes its reputation on law and
order. That's what makes it so attractive to all the offshore bankers. This did not look good. The murders of
the Pembrooks, millions in drugs dissolved in territorial
waters, Don Manetti dead. It turned out that Melissa
would survive. She'd be charged as an accessory to
Tagan's murder and drug running.

At least Trish Robsen did not have to live with the
fact that her husband had died in a sordid manner—
tangled in another woman's sheets. Instead, he'd simply
made the mistake of looking at the dust jacket of a travel
guide to Hawaii.

I'd caught up with Trish at the airport. She and her
son were about to board a flight back to the States. Out
the window I could see the ground crew struggling to
load Allen's casket into the luggage compartment. She
managed a fleeting smile when I told her what had happened to Allen.

"We'd talked about taking a trip to Tahiti someday,"
she said.

I waited as they handed their tickets to the agent and
walked out the door. Trish turned briefly, mouthed,
"Thank you," and was gone.

That evening I went to see Jimmy.

He was asleep, his head propped up on pillows, his
bed surrounded by a maze of tubes and monitors. The
room was crowded with outlandish island bouquets,
boxes of candy, and magazines, none of which Jimmy

was yet able to enjoy. I made my way through the jungle of color to his bedside and stood watching him breathe. God, he was so young. He stirred and opened his eyes.

"Hey, dar, Hannah," he said.

"How you doing, Jimmy?"

"Doin' real good. I be ready to take you riding in da *Wahoo* 'fore ya know it," he said, managing his wide smile.

Same Jimmy. Damned kid.

AUTHOR'S NOTES

While many of the places in this book are real, events and people are entirely fictitious, and I am unaware of any underwater caves in the British Virgin Islands. In addition, to the best of my knowledge, shark fins are not taken in that region. However, shark fins are harvested in other parts of the world and shark populations have plummeted. Conservation efforts are underway. For more information about sharks, ocean ecology, and conservation, go to:

Reef Environmental Education Foundation:
http://www.reef.org/

Reef Base: http://www.reefbase.org/

National Oceanic and Atmospheric Adm.:
http://www.coralreef.noaa.gov/

The Guy Harvey Research Institute:
http://www.nova.edu/ocean/ghri/sharkresearch.html

The Shark Trust: http://www.sharktrust.org/

ACKNOWLEDGMENTS

Thank you to the folks at Dive Rescue International, especially Sue Watson; to Sgt. Steve Ward, Underwater Search and Recovery Unit, Colorado Springs; Allen Meador, Colorado Springs Fire Dept; and to a man I've never met, Cpl. Bob Teather of the Royal Canadian Mounted Police, whose *Encyclopedia of Underwater Investigations* is the definitive text in underwater crime scene investigation.

Thanks to my agent, Jacky Sach, for her guidance and support; my editor, Martha Bushko, for her perceptive comments on the manuscript; and those hard working people behind the scenes at New American Library.

And as always, deep gratitude and love to my family for their constant support and enthusiasm. As for my husband, Ron, well, thanks hardly does it.

The beginning of the thrilling series where
murder runs deep...

Swimming with the Dead

*An Underwater Investigation featuring
CSI diver Hannah Sampson*
by Kathy Brandt

Summoned to the sun-drenched beaches of the
British Virgin Islands, Hannah Sampson is fully
prepared to face unknowable dangers beneath the
crystal-clear waters of an idyllic paradise.
But the possibility of murder runs deeper and
darker than the sea itself.

"TAKES HOLD OF YOU AND DOESN'T LET GO."
—MARGARET COEL

"SURE TO PLEASE THE OUTDOOR ENTHUSIASTS."
—CHRISTINE GOFF

"A VERY EXCITING NEW SERIES."
—MIDWEST BOOK REVIEW

0-451-21020-4

Available wherever books are sold or
to ordercall 1-800-788-6262